THE URBANA FREE LIBRARY

W9-AYS-532

DISCARDED BY THE
URBANA FREE LIBRARY

this is how

it happened

(not a love story)

The Urbana Free Library

To renew materials call
217-367-4057

3-08

DATE DUE		
~~APR 0 1 2008~~		
~~APR 11 2008~~	~~JUL 05 2008~~	
~~APR 2 6 2008~~	~~JUL 1 7 2008~~	
~~MAY 0 1 2008~~	~~AUG 2 6 2008~~	
~~MAY 2 4 2008~~		
~~JUN 2 6 2008~~	~~SEP 0 6 2008~~	
	APR 1 6 2011	

By Jo Barrett

THIS IS HOW IT HAPPENED (NOT A LOVE STORY)
THE MEN'S GUIDE TO THE WOMEN'S BATHROOM

DISCARDED BY THE
URBANA FREE LIBRARY

3-08

Don't miss the next book by your favorite author.
Sign up now for AuthorTracker by visiting
www.AuthorTracker.com.

this is how
it happened

(not a love story)

JO BARRETT

URBANA FREE LIBRARY

A

AVON

An Imprint of HarperCollinsPublishers

3-08
14-

This book is a work of fiction. References to real people, events, establishments, organizations, or locales are intended only to provide a sense of authenticity, and are used fictitiously. All other characters, and all incidents and dialogue, are drawn from the author's imagination and are not to be construed as real.

THIS IS HOW IT HAPPENED (NOT A LOVE STORY). Copyright © 2007 by JoAnna Barrett. All rights reserved. Printed in the United States of America. No part of this book may be used or reproduced in any manner whatsoever without written permission except in the case of brief quotations embodied in critical articles and reviews. For information address HarperCollins Publishers, 10 East 53rd Street, New York, NY 10022.

HarperCollins books may be purchased for educational, business, or sales promotional use. For information please write: Special Markets Department, HarperCollins Publishers, 10 East 53rd Street, New York, NY 10022.

FIRST EDITION

Designed by Elizabeth M. Glover

Library of Congress Cataloging-in-Publication Data
Barret, Jo.
   This is how it happened : not a love story / Jo Barret.— 1st ed.
      p. cm.
   ISBN 978-0-06-124110-9
   1. Revenge—Fiction. I. Title
   PS3602.A77749T47 2008
   813'.6 .—dc22   2007043363

08 09 10 11 12 OV/RRD 10 9 8 7 6 5 4 3 2

For my mother, Mary Ann

An ounce of mother is worth a pound of clergy
—*from the Spanish proverb*

And the Oscar goes to...

Writing a novel is like the bobsled. You need a brakeman. Carrie Feron, my editor at HarperCollins, along with Tessa Woodward, kept this sled from zipping off the track. As did my literary agent, David Hale Smith, and his assistant, Shauyi.

In my previous novel, *The Men's Guide to the Women's Bathroom*, I was remiss in mentioning Regina Lee who was central in bringing the idea of a television show to actor Hugh Jackman and Seed Productions.

Karen Hamilton of Creative Convergence pushed the idea through to CBS Network.

My agent, Ryan Saul, is the living, breathing, finer version of Ari Gold from *Entourage*.

For three extraordinary men for whom the world of ideas is not dead: Brian Swier, John Zimmerman, and George Jones, CEO of Borders Books.

For Tim Ruch of Sanford Bernstein, Michelle Ruch, and Becki McClanahan of Sanford Bernstein.

For the superb Charlie Pigeon, CEO of Tige Boats.

And let's not forget the dazzling Cindi Rose, and Dr. Franklin Rose. You add a spark to Houston, Texas, that has been sorely missed.

For Linda Luna, P.R. Chic, Joanna Vorachek, Erin Powers, Ron Hogan in New York, and Cynthia Jenkins who runs the splendid sugar mama column in Orange County.

For my stylish and intriguing friends, Sharin and Scott Gaille, for whom the world itself is too small, and Angola, Dubai, and Russia just a plane ride away.

My lifelong companions: the brilliant and esteemed Lawrence Cunningham—who wields a pen like a blade; and for LL: Heather Phibbs.

For the hip chicks in Austin and Houston who serve as inspiration: Amy and Melissa, Georgia and Paige Ridenhauer, Lynn, Meredith, Laura, Lisa, Courtney, and Whitney Casey. (As far as I know, these women have never hired a hit man...yet.)

Doug Agarwal of Capital Commercial Investments in Austin, Texas, is an important friend, and one of the finest men I know.

For Congressman Peterson, and his Washington, D.C., staff: Mark, Cherie, Rob.

To Mike Shea at *Texas Monthly Magazine* for reviving the art of crisp writing.

For Gary Cogill because he gets it.

For the inspirational Ryan Brooks of Goldglove Productions in Los Angeles.

For Dr. Victor Levin and Laurel Westcarth of M.D. Anderson Cancer Center in Houston, Texas, for taking such extraordinary care of my father during his battle with brain cancer. And for Dr. Victor Levin's continuing friendship.

For my brother, Ronnie Barrett, who is wickedly funny...sometimes.

For Todd Brooks...and the Costa Rican flip flops I fell in love with.

For the Petro family (P.S. This is a long list because they're Catholic.) Madeline, Mike, the other Mike, Vicki, Nadine, Joe, Paula, Louis, Maria, Richard, Michelle, Bill, and super cool Joe. Am I missing anyone?

For the Barrett family: Dean and Anna Lee, Jim, Karen, Leslie, Chris, Kevin, Susan, Charles, Brandon, and Derrick.

And lastly, for my mother. For staying knee-deep in the trenches. Day after day.

Sir, if you were my husband, I'd poison your drink.

—LADY ASTOR *to* WINSTON CHURCHILL

Madame, if you were my wife, I would drink it.

—*His reply*

this is how

it happened

(not a love story)

Chapter 1

I never intended to KILL him kill him. I mean, actually kill him.
It started as a joke. Two women in a coffee shop talking about
their ex-disasters. And when Carlton's name came up, the pain
was so searing, so literal across my chest, I checked my stomach
to see if someone had sliced me open with a knife.

That's when I told my best friend, Heather, I wanted to kill
him.

"I'll hide the body," she said, taking a demure little sip from
her cappuccino. And we both giggled like schoolgirls. But then
she did something she's never done before. She put her hand
on my shoulder and shot me a look. It was one of those pitying
looks. The type of look a person gives a wounded dog before the
vet puts him down. She even crinkled her eyes and said, "Be
strong, Maddy."

And that's when I knew I was serious about killing him.

An hour later, after Heather and I parted company, I found
myself browsing the gardening section of Half Price Books. I was
looking for a book on poisons. And I didn't want to pay retail.

I felt angry. Angry as a tornado. Wild and swerving and unpre-
dictable. For some reason, maybe anxiety, my eye had begun to

twitch. I rubbed my eyelid and skulked up and down the book-store aisles.

The book I plucked from the shelf had a picture of a rat on the cover. I imagined Carlton's face attached to the rat's body. And then, for a split second, I imagined Carlton's *real* body, and us having sex on the kitchen floor, like we always used to do.

Another wave of anger swept over me and I shook my head back and forth, trying to erase the image from my mind. I was an assassin on a mission, after all.

I flipped open the rat book and began browsing through the pages.

Chapter 4: How to Exterminate those Pesky Pests.

"Making your own poison: The organic alternative," I read quietly to myself.

Am I really going to kill my ex? I thought. I blushed and glanced suspiciously up and down the bookstore aisles, as if half expecting a bunch of FBI guys to burst in and arrest me for Intent to Kill with Lavender-Scented Mouse Repellent.

I strolled to the register, casually, book tucked neatly under my arm.

"Cash or charge?" the longhaired clerk asked. He stroked his goatee and peered across the counter at me. I could smell the pungent scent of marijuana emanating from his clothes—particularly the hydroponic "kind-bud" variety preferred by the closet intelligentsia crowd of East Austin.

I winked at Mr. Greenleaf and slid a twenty across the counter. I'd seen enough movies to know I'd definitely be paying cash.

The first rule of killing an ex-fiancé: never leave a paper trail.

Chapter 2

The problem was, he was beautiful. When we moved in together, I'd watch Carlton slide open the kitchen window, place an ashtray on the sill, light his cigarette and let it drop to the side of his lips. He moved with a profound grace. And when he smiled at me—that sexy, sideways smile—my thoughts dropped away and everything I was became available to him. He's one of those men I would've jumped in front of a Greyhound bus for. And he made me believe he'd jump for me, too.

We met in graduate school at one of those young professionals happy-hour events. It was designed to be a casual meet-and-greet affair. A bunch of MBA students wearing jeans and nametags and drinking beer out of plastic cups.

Not surprisingly, it was held at an Irish pub. But not the real kind of Irish pub with plucky, fat-cheeked Irish people singing their lilting up-and-down songs, and dirty floors and the smell of stale beer. It was one of those newfangled Irish pubs. The ones with all the junk tacked up on the wall. Like street signs that say Sheperd's Pie Avenue. You know which kind of fake Irish pub I'm talking about. The kind that serves nachos.

I spotted him immediately. Shirt cuffs rolled up to his elbows. One leg dangling casually off a barstool. He had a certain movie star quality. A certain fluidity. The way he moved his hands as he spoke. The way he smiled that confident, sideways smile.

He was lounging at a cocktail table with another guy and neither of them wore nametags. I suddenly wished I hadn't plastered my own white sticker against my chest. And written MADELINE PIATRO in large, bold letters.

At the sign-in table, I apparently went to town with the black magic marker. I even put two exclamation points at the end of my name. So my tag read MADELINE PIATRO!!—as if I was excited about the notion of myself.

So, here I was. Wearing jeans and loafers. With a big, fat nametag affixed to my shirt. I mean, what a dork, right? I may as well have been wearing a pocket protector and a retainer.

So I stared across the bar at Movie Star Guy. And he must've felt my eyes boring into him because he looked straight at me and winked.

I remember blushing. A woman of my age. Blushing like a teenager. I glanced down at my loafers, took a deep breath and thought, "What the heck . . ."

And that's when I did it.

I, feeling full of bravado—after all, I was an MBA student!—marched right up and introduced myself.

"Hi. I'm Madeline. Madeline Piatro," I said, pointing to my nametag. "In case you couldn't read the billboard."

He seemed momentarily stunned. A woman approaching a man from across an entire bar was still rare in this circle. We were at the University of Texas—not some ultra-liberal northeastern school where the women weren't afraid of anything.

In Texas, the women still played a little coy. Cats on the prowl for unwitting husbands, if you will.

"I'm in your marketing class," I said, sticking out my sweaty palm. My motto, after all, had always been: *Leap Before You Look.*

"Pleasure to meet you, Madeline. Carlton Connors," he said in a formal voice. He took my hand and I noticed his palm was cool to the touch—not sweaty like mine. He had a firm handshake. Solid and manly.

He grinned at me, revealing perfect white teeth, and ran his hand through his perfect, movie star hair. "This is David," he said, motioning to his friend.

David rubbed his hand against his jeans and said, "Sorry. I've got beer hands. I think this table is wet."

I said, "Don't worry about it," and shook his sticky hand anyway. David had a flimsy handshake. Like a wet noodle.

"David was just talking about our marketing class," Carlton said.

I glance at David and see that Mr. Wet Noodle is smiling. The type of smile that comes from a guy who gets to hang out with the cool kid.

"Professor Morgan is always busting my balls, man," David says. "I've got a theory that she secretly hates men."

Carlton looks from me to David, then back at me. "Care to comment on that, Madeline? I'm sure Dave would love to hear a woman's perspective."

"Sounds like Professor Morgan doesn't hate men, she just hates David," I say.

I'm pleased when Carlton throws his head back in the air and laughs.

"Care to join us?" he asks, patting the empty barstool next to him. He's smiling the cocksure smile of a guy who's been around the block.

"Sure," I say, glad for the invitation.

I hopped up on a barstool and ordered a pint of pale beer that came with a lemon floating in it. And then I slept with Mr. Carlton Connors that very night.

Chapter 3

It was my usual Saturday afternoon routine. Have coffee with Heather. Check out the new paperback fiction. Maybe catch a matinee. The only difference—and it was a profound difference—was that I was alone. Carlton was no longer in my life. And I had a burning desire to kill him.

I brought the rat book home. Back to my empty townhouse. Free of Carlton's clothes, his belongings, our pictures as a couple. Once in a while I could smell his smell. The beautiful smell of the woods lingering on a piece of furniture. And each time I smelled it, my heart would drop. As much as I hated to admit it, part of me longed for the days when Carlton and I snuggled together in our big, comfy chair. The one with the oversized pillows. Drinking ice-cold margaritas with our legs intertwined.

And so, to get rid of his smell, I sprayed lemon freshener everywhere. Kept the windows open. Burned vanilla candles. Boiled cinnamon sticks in a pan on the stove.

Killing Carlton could be a futile exercise, I knew. I didn't have that kind of brio. But at least I could practice. Who knew?

I was Italian, so my blood ran hot. And I was a Texan to the core. (And everyone knows not to mess with Texas women.) But still. No matter what Carlton had done to me, and he'd done a lot, would I really feel better baking chocolate brownies filled with rat poison? Delivering them in an anonymous gift basket to the office we used to share? In the company we'd built? Together? Would this cheap, dirty trick make me feel better?

You betcha.

I wrestled a cast iron pot out of the kitchen cabinet. A beautiful Le Creuset 12-quart from Williams Sonoma. No black, bubbling witch's cauldron for me, thank you very much. I'm a gourmet assassin.

I don an apron that says, "Kiss me, I'm Italian," roll up my sleeves, and go to town. I follow my mother's old brownie recipe to a tee. Blending in the chocolate, slowly, so it won't burn. Melting salted butter in the microwave. Stirring the mixture hard and fast (at least fifty beats!) with a whipping spoon.

I imagine myself as a witch. Stirring my brew. Maybe I should join a Wicca group and burn incense and frog legs and chant incantations.

Or better yet, what about those Haitian voodoo witches? Perhaps I could learn the art of sticking pins in a Carlton doll. I'd dress it in a little biking outfit—and stick pins right through its little padded biking shorts.

Would Carlton feel the pain, I wondered?

It was worth a try.

I finish the brownie mixture, and like a good witch, I lick the spatulas. Then I pour the mixture into a baking pan. And for the final touch—

Arsenic, I think.

Chapter 4

The morning after I slept with Carlton Connors for the first time, I rolled over and was more than shocked to see a beautiful man in my bed. His body was perfect. A flat stomach with rolling muscles down his abdomen. Long, lean, muscular legs. Light brown, silky hair. A face like a Michelangelo. Strong nose. Dimple in the chin. And he smelled like a dream. A faint hint of cologne that reminded me of being in the woods. There was nothing offensive about Carlton Connors. Not a single blackhead on his nose. Not even a mole.

He opened a perfect eye. The color of a buttered almond— and he looked straight at me. I remember pulling the sheets up to my chin, hiding my nakedness. My itsy-bitsy flab. My poochy belly. My strong, yet somewhat stubby legs.

"I'll have you know, Mr. Connors, this is the first time I've ever slept with a guy I just met," I say, right off the bat.

"Sure. That's what they all say," he chuckles and strokes my hair. His touch is gentle but firm. And it sends me to the moon and back. I feel giddy as this man—this stranger—brushes my cheek with his finger.

"Good morning, beautiful," he whispers. He leans forward

and kisses me. Not a quick good morning peck, but a long, lingering kiss. The type of kiss you imagine might happen one day because you saw it in a movie once. But when it actually happens, you suck in your lungs because you're afraid you've got morning breath.

I pull back from Carlton, prop my elbow up on the pillow, my head against my hand. I shoot this new guy my most serious look. "I'm serious. I've never had a one-night stand," I protest, because I want him to know I'm not a slut. And because it's true.

"Who said anything about one night?" he replies.

I try to act cool at this point. No big, cheesy smiles or wild kisses.

I inform Carlton in my most neutral tone, "I don't know about you, but I'm serious about getting my MBA. I don't need a messy relationship getting in the way."

He chuckles, shakes his head, as if he can't believe my audacity.

"That rhymes," he says.

And then he surprises the hell out of me by singing in a woman's falsetto voice: "I'm serious about my MBAAA," he sings, "I don't need a guy getting in the Wa-aay."

"I don't even know you!" I say, lightly slapping his arm.

Carlton sticks his hand out and says, "Carlton Connors, pleasure to make your acquaintance, ma'am."

"Funny."

Carlton runs his hand through his hair, which I notice looks as perfect in the morning as it did last night.

I sit up in bed and prop a pillow behind my back, being careful to keep the sheets tucked up to my neck.

"Look, this was just a fling, okay?" I say in a strong voice. And I don't know why I say this, but I do. I guess it's a pride thing. Because I know this guy will never call me.

"Hey, I'm a nice guy, Madeline Piatro. So don't go breaking my heart," he says, flashing me his movie star smile.

I stare at this man in my bed. A hard stare. "You and I both know that this was just a one-night fling," I say, in my most business-like tone.

He presses his finger against my lips. "You're gonna need an army of bodyguards to keep me away from you, darlin'," he whispers.

I remember slapping my hand over his mouth, crawling on top of him like a rodeo cowgirl. And throwing caution to the fucking wind.

And so began our romance.

Chapter 5

I bend down and peer at my poison brownies. Poke them with a fork. Steam rises from the glass pan and the smell is mouth-watering. Like warm, molten chocolate. My stomach does a painful little flip-flop. I'm hungry. Famished, really. I haven't eaten since I had coffee with Heather. A few disappointing bites of a crusty, day-old scone. In fact, I haven't eaten in weeks. Not a real meal, anyway. Not four squares, whatever a square is. Come to think of it, I don't remember the last time I actually sat down and ate properly. Screw this "no carbs, Atkins, smoothie wheat-grass thing," —someone should write a book called "The Break-Up Diet."

I grab a beautiful knife from the wood block on my counter, and slice into the brownies. The smell is overwhelming, and when I pull the knife out, it's covered in rich, smooth, moist, chocolate. The kind of warm chocolate that feels good against the tongue. I stare at the knife a moment too long, then race to the sink and plunge it in water.

I couldn't find arsenic so I had to make do. Apparently, it's been outlawed for use in rat poison, ant poison, and weed killer. I also didn't have all the ingredients to make my lavender-scented pesticide brownies, so I've experimented with rosemary, sage, and furniture polish.

My brownies probably won't kill Carlton. But hopefully, he'll get a bad case of diarrhea. I consider the crime. It will be executed in the most elegant way. The delivery of a beautiful gift basket—anonymous of course—to Carlton's office with a little note. "Congratulations, you've been selected as a finalist for the Worst Man in the World Contest, and guess what—You've Won!" it could read. But then Carlton would know it was me. Perhaps just the basket with the brownies. I consider wrapping each one individually with Saran Wrap. Or do I slice them in cute little squares and tuck them neatly on decorative tissue paper?

Hmm—decisions, decisions.

The only kink in my plan, the only problem, and it's a doozy, is Carlton may end up sharing the brownies with his employees. And I know these people, because they used to be my employees, too. However, Carlton isn't much for sharing and I can see him stashing the basket under his desk. But still, I can't take the risk. What if someone sneaks into Carlton's office while he's away on his lunch break and grabs a brownie? Or worse, what if Carlton is feeling generous that day? What if he says, "Hey guys, someone sent me these brownies. Dig in!" The odds of this were small—Carlton was never one to be so chummy.

"Never get too friendly with the help," he used to say. The "help" being the employees.

I stare down at the brownies. God, they sure smell good. They even look tasty. This furniture polish thing may work out. I poke the brownies again with a fork. My stomach growls as more chocolate steam rises from the pan.

Hmm. I wonder if he'll taste the difference?

I cut off a tiny little chocolate edge, a sliver from the side of the pan. I hold it up to my nose and sniff. Smells like warm brownie, nothing more. I pop the sliver in my mouth. And chew.

Wow! Not bad. Not bad at all, actually.

I fork off another tiny bite, a morsel, really. Not even enough for a mouse. I let the warm chocolate melt on my tongue.

Uh-oh. I should've made a nonpoisonous batch for myself, I think. But what if I'd gotten the pans mixed up? Don't put it past me to do something brilliant like get my poison brownies mixed up with my yummy brownies.

"Maddy, what are you doing?" I hear a voice in my head ask.

"I don't know," I answer.

"This is nuts!" the voice says.

But this voice apparently doesn't know the power of warm chocolate brownie fresh out of the oven.

I use my fork to stab into the brownie pan and take a real bite. This time, I don't hesitate. Look out, Rachel Ray. I'm the anti-chef.

Hmm.

Maybe this furniture polish isn't as poisonous as I thought. I check the label.

CAUTION! HARMFUL IF INGESTED! DO NOT INDUCE VOMITING. CALL A PHYSICIAN OR POISON CONTROL CENTER IMMEDIATELY!

I grab the pan, walk out the back door, and dump the entire mixture in the trash. I come back inside, turn the sink on full blast so water sprays on my apron, pour liquid soap into the pan, and scrub-a-dub, dub.

And that's when I feel the nausea coming on.

I drop the pan in the sink, hit the water off, and race to the toilet. That's the good thing about throwing up. You get a small warning. Just enough time to turn the sink off because who wants to waste water, right?

I flip the lid up on the toilet, collapse to my knees, and begin fighting my body as it heaves and heaves. I try swallowing, but no dice.

The furniture polish and the chocolate are fighting a field battle in my stomach. The front lines have been breached. It's full-fledged, arm-to-arm combat now. I feel a searing pain in my esophagus. The final, killer blow. And I realize, as I moan over the toilet—I'm done for.

Chapter 6

The next evening, after my one-night stand with Carlton Connors, I got a singing telegram. From Mr. Connors himself.

He surprised me on my doorstep with a bouquet of yellow roses. "For my yellow rose of Texas," he said, with a cheesy grin on his face. And then he burst into the University of Texas college fight song.

"The eyes of Texas are upon us . . ." he sang, bent down on one knee, with his arms outstretched.

He brought a bag of groceries with him, and we cooked pasta and then had hot, sweaty sex on the tile floor in the kitchen.

From that day on, our one-night stands became a three-day-per-week event.

Within a month, Carlton moved out of his second-floor walkup, an efficiency that smelled faintly of mothballs, and into my small, but tidy, townhouse. Carlton figured it was cheaper and easier if we lived together in grad school. "We'll be more efficient if we're a team," he said.

He was having big problems in class and even bigger problems paying his tuition.

"I can't work and study and have any kind of social life," he complained. Bookwork and tests didn't come easily for Carlton.

We were both trying to hold down jobs while getting our MBAs. I had been working at the same company for fourteen years, if you include the time I'd spent interning in high school. Carlton was trying to hold down a low-level job at one of his father's warehouses.

Carlton's father, Forest Connors, was a millionaire several times over, and owned a company that sold medical equipment at high markups. Forest Connors was a well-known patron of the University of Texas McCombs School of Business, and had endowed a chair named after Carlton's grandfather.

Carlton first introduced me to his dad at an MBA event—a wine and cheese reception hosted by the economics department.

"This is Madeline—the girl I've been telling you about, Dad," Carlton had said, steering me in the direction of a tall, handsome man who vaguely resembled Carlton.

"Nice to meet you, Madeline. I'm Forest Connors," Mr. Connors announced, in a commanding voice.

I remember standing up straight and shaking Mr. Connors' broad, outstretched hand. He had a solid grip, just like Carlton. A winner's handshake.

"So, you're the woman who's keeping my son from concentrating on his work," Mr. Connors had said. And he was sort of joking, and sort of not.

"She's also responsible for the Gross National Debt, Dad," Carlton shot back, and we all laughed.

Later, when I asked Carlton why his father didn't help pay his tuition, Carlton said his father believed in "starting from the ground up." Forest Connors wasn't a man to spoil his son, and in fact, Carlton drove a rusty Honda that seemed to love to break down.

Carlton said his Honda had "personality," and it "loved to

buck the trend." He'd say this on mornings when he had the hood up, his hands covered in grease.

Carlton felt his Honda had single-handedly spoiled the Honda image—of the reliable, low-maintenance car that would run and run forever.

"Goddamn Asian prostitute!" he'd yell, kicking at the tires. When he went to work in one of his father's warehouses—gotta learn the business from the ground up!— he rode his bike. It got to the point where Carlton began leaving his schoolbooks at home. I was taking notes in class for both of us.

One night, after we'd had particularly good sex—sweaty, uninhibited, pornstar sex—he rolled me over, stroked my matted-down hair, and stared into my eyes. "I can't impress my dad at work *and* get good grades in school, and you're so great with marketing, Maddy—I mean, you're the number-one student in class."

"Say no more," I'd replied, pressing my hand against his lips.

The next thing I knew, I was doing all of Carlton's assignments. I wrote several knockout papers for him and he got A's on every single one. I felt like the girlfriend of the head football player. But I didn't mind. Carlton and I were madly in love. And that was all that mattered.

ᓂ Chapter 7

I spend the entire night in front of the porcelain throne, as they say. Throwing up like a drunk. Hurling out the small bits of brownie along with all of my acidic stomach juices. *This is my punishment.* For thinking these murderous, devil thoughts.

In the morning, after a restless, fitful sleep—a sweaty, tossing, turning sleep on my mattress—I use the bathroom and my pee smells like metal. Checking the mirror, I see my forehead is damp and my skin has a slight yellow pallor.

Hello, lemon face. I rinse my mouth with Listerine. I've rinsed it so much over the last eight hours the bottle is on its last drop.

I plod into the kitchen, rub my eyes, peer out the kitchen window and see a black, furry thing lying in my driveway.

Terrific.

I'm a murderess after all.

I pad down the driveway in my tatty robe and bare feet. A dead raccoon is next to my garbage can, the trail of brownie crumbs leading directly from its slack-jawed, wide-open mouth.

I stare down at the mess in my driveway, at the poor, dead animal, and the first thought that enters my head is: *There's never a man around when you need one.* Stepping back inside, I don a pair of yellow rubber dishwashing gloves, my flip-flops, and waltz out to the driveway once again in my outfit du jour—my shaggy purple bathrobe. I pick the raccoon up by the tail, and swing its dead carcass into the garbage. It's a little heavier than I thought, so at first, I accidentally bang the raccoon into the side of the can, before heaving it up and over.

"Rest in peace, little fellow," I say, in case there exists some kind of raccoon Karma.

I sweep up the brownie crumbs. Then, I roll the garbage can out to the street, because tomorrow is garbage day, thank God.

Here I am, on the street in a purple bathrobe with throw-up stains on the front. I've almost poisoned myself and I've killed an innocent raccoon. And hey, it isn't even 10:00 a.m.

I pull the rubber gloves off my hands, open the lid to the trash, and drop them in. I let the lid fall back down . . . but then I make a huge mistake.

I open the lid and peek inside.

The raccoon, its dead black eyes wide open, is staring straight up at me.

"It was an unintentional crime, it really was . . . little guy," I murmur. Followed by, "I'm sorry."

I drop the lid back down and use my body weight to slam it tight, like I'm slamming the trunk of my car. The garbage men are coming tomorrow, but still. I don't want to risk having an entire dead zoo out here.

God help me if Pamela Anderson and her PETA pals saw this, I muse, as I plod back up my driveway.

I think of Pamela Lee Anderson and I start to get pissed off. I mean, sure. I buy lipstick that hasn't been tested on lab monkeys, and I fully support the whole dolphin thing, but c'mon. Enough is enough. Some of us have to work around here.

What? Like Pamela is some kind of saint because she survives on berries and seeds? As if she's never opened a can of tuna fish?

Are her shoes made of plastic? Her belts of eco-friendly twine? Has she never accidentally run over a squirrel or hit a bird?

I pad back into the house. And swing the front door shut. Slam!

Carlton, by the way, was a huge Pam fan.

Chapter 8

I never thought that I'd be the type of girl who waited for some guy to marry me. It seemed old fashioned. To be that girl.

And yet a part of me wondered what was taking so long? Carlton and I were both in our thirties. We'd lived together for four years. I'd assumed marriage was right around the corner.

Of course, I wasn't bothered by the idea of "living in sin." I didn't need the ceremony, the gleaming diamond ring—my girlfriends fawning over me in a sleek, white Vera Wang gown.

Carlton and I could live together for the rest of our lives, as far as I was concerned. The love between us was so great the idea of *not* getting married seemed terribly romantic.

We'd be modern. Like movie stars. Susan Sarandon and Tim Robbins. Goldie Hawn and Kurt Russell. Hugh Grant asking Andie McDowell in *Four Weddings and a Funeral,* "Will you promise never to marry me?"

And besides, I couldn't complain. Behind closed doors, Carlton referred to me as his "fiancée." As he put it, we were "unofficially" engaged.

He hadn't asked me to marry him in the traditional way. There was no candlelight dinner. No diamond. No bending down on one knee. Rather, he'd told me late one night, and I might add—after sweaty, post-coital sex—that he "intended" to marry me.

This is how it happened:

One night, as we lay breathless and sweaty on my mattress, stark naked with the damp sheets kicked on the floor, he'd reached over to the side of the bed, grabbed my hand, and slipped a ring on my finger.

"I intend to marry you," he said, simply. Instead of a diamond, he'd given me a simple white-gold band he'd bought at Zales.

"It's beautiful," I whispered. I twirled the ring around my finger. I loved the way it felt, heavy on my hand.

Carlton took it off and showed me the inside.

"Read the engraving," he said.

I peered at the ring. Then I turned and threw my arm over his chest. Kissed him full on the mouth.

"Oh Romeo, Romeo. Wherefore art thou?" I said, my eyes misting up with tears.

"Right here, baby. Right where I want to be," he said, stroking my hair.

I wasn't being a complete cheeseball. There was a reason for the Romeo, Romeo thing.

A few weeks earlier, on one of those gloriously lazy Sundays, Carlton and I had been walking down the street hand in hand when an older woman started waving her cane at us.

"Your love is so bright, kiddos, I've gotta wear shades," she'd called out. Then, she donned a pair of hip, funky-looking sunglasses and blew us a kiss.

"To Romeo and Juliet!" she said, in a strong voice, as she hobbled away.

From then on, Carlton had called me "his Juliet." And sometimes, I'd call him "Romeo," too. We both knew it was cheesy and overused, but we didn't care.

It was our little secret.

"Thank you, Romeo," I said, as Carlton kissed my ring finger and slipped the ring back on.

"Do you like it?" he asked. He cupped my hands in his and brought them to his chest. I felt his skin, still warm from the sex, and noticed his shoulders were a splotchy pink from all the exertion.

We lay on the bed, naked, facing each other. It was the most intimate moment of my life.

"I love it," I said.

And he grinned.

In truth, most girls would've probably hated the ring. It was plain Jane. The kind of ring you buy in the mall, as an afterthought. And much too thick for my finger.

But I loved it. I wore it every day. Even in the shower. I didn't care if Carlton ever bought me a diamond. And besides, I wasn't the type of woman who was a Nazi about carat, cut, and clarity. I didn't care to wave my finger in front of friends and co-workers and brag out loud, "Look what Carlton gave me," as I flashed a huge, sparkling rock. No, what Carlton and I had was special. A special bond between us.

This ring was different.

I took it off my finger and read the engraving almost every day.

"Forever, my Juliet," it read.

Chapter 9

I've got to get the hell out of Dodge, I think. I stare at my empty house. My Carlton-free Zone.

A few weeks ago, I packed up all our photographs and everything else that reminded me of Carlton, and I cried the proverbial river of tears. I boxed up everything, even a postcard he'd sent me from a trip to New York City that said, "Someone in the Big Apple loves you." I hid it all in my garage, behind some paint cans. I couldn't bear to throw it out. Most women probably would've torched the stuff, but deep down, I was a softie. I mean, sure, I'd just killed a raccoon. But that was a total accident.

It's hard not to feel alone when you've lived with a man for the past four years. And then one day, that man is gone. And he's taken your self-esteem with him.

I have only one thought on days like this. And that thought is: *Get Out!* Weekends are, most certainly, the worst. What I like to call my "Very Lonely Saturdays" are followed by my "Self-Pitying Sundays." The biggest problem with weekends is they keep rolling back around.

I've considered flying someplace where I'd lose time. Like

Costa Rica. I imagine an open wooden beach hut. A soft bed with white mosquito netting. The sounds of the waves rolling in. Me sopping up alcohol like chicken soup. Not knowing the day of the week. Not caring about the time. Maybe I'd take up surfing. And have sex with some hot, Tico guy. You never know. It could happen.

I pick up the phone to call Heather, but then put it back down. She's probably sick of me, and besides, she's happily married. And sometimes it isn't healthy being around a smiling, doting couple. So I've got to turn to my last resort—my family.

I call my brother.

He answers with his usual flair.

"Hullo?" he says.

"Hey, what's shakin' bacon?" I ask, jumping in.

"Same shit, different day," my brother says. He's got a knack for words, that guy.

"I was thinking we could get some burgers," I say. This tactic, the burger tactic, usually works. My brother is a sucker for a free cheeseburger. And he knows that when I call him, it means I'm the one who's paying.

I'm paying for Ronnie Piatro's company because I'm lonely and I've just killed a small animal.

"I'm kind of tied up," Ronnie says.

"I just killed a raccoon!"

"With your car?"

"No, I accidentally poisoned it. I was trying to make these poison brownies to deliver to Carlton's office but I ended up killing a small, innocent animal," I say, and I realize I'm talking fast. Like a crazy person.

I hear my brother take a deep breath into the phone.

"I'm going to pray for you, Maddy," he says. And he means it. He pauses and I can almost hear him praying for me.

We're both silent on the phone, and I don't interrupt. Because I know my brother is a serious prayer freak. He takes prayer *very* seriously.

Finally, he sighs into the phone, "I'll meet you at The Tavern in one hour."

Bingo.

Chapter 10

The Friday after Carlton gave me the Juliet ring, we packed up my Volvo with suitcases and drove to Houston for the weekend. Carlton's Honda was still on the blink, but instead of buying a new battery, Carlton said he was going to splurge on our hotel.

"Houston's expensive as shit," he'd said, in a caustic voice. "But we're not staying at some fucking Hampton Inn when the rest of the wedding party is staying at the Houstonian."

Carlton's father was getting married again. His fifth or sixth time around—I couldn't remember which. And neither could Carlton.

"Let's see. There was that waitress from Denver," Carlton said, counting on his fingers. "But that only lasted a month. So I think they annulled it. That makes five," he said, flashing me all five of his fingers.

"Getting married five or six times is a very *Texas* thing to do," I said.

"Well, howdy fucking doo-dah," Carlton replied, gunning the accelerator. We cruised down I-10, past the Katy outlet mall, the strip centers filled with Home Depots, Walmarts, Exxons, and McDonald's—the sprawling concrete jungle that stretched like open arms into the city. A green sign on the side of the highway said HOUSTON 17 MILES.

I shrugged my shoulders. "Don't hold it against your dad, Carlton. Some men are the marrying type."

Carlton shook his head, a bitter look on his face. "My dad is the RE-marrying type," he said, simply. "But at least he's got a pre-nup that's tighter than The Donald's."

"Who's the lucky bride?" I asked.

"Some flight attendant. Holly something or other. She works the first-class section. Dad met her on a flight to New York. They spent their first weekend together at the Ritz in Central Park." Carlton put his hand to his ear and said, "Can't you hear the wedding bells, Maddy?"

"I'm sure she's a very nice person," I deadpanned.

"They're all nice," Carlton said. "Especially when they see the checking account."

"C'mon, babe. Give us some credit. All women aren't gold diggers."

Carlton rolled his head dramatically in my direction. "Not all women. Not you," he said. "You fell in love with me despite my Honda."

"That's right, Romeo," I said, plugging my finger into his arm. "And don't you forget it."

An hour later, Carlton and I checked into our luxurious king-sized room at the Houstonian Hotel. We "christened" the bed first, with quick athletic sex, and then showered and got ready for the wedding.

I wore a tight aqua-blue dress I got on sale at Saks. It wasn't ugly aqua like something a mermaid would wear; it was the softest, palest blue you could imagine. And it really brought out the color of my skin, which being a Piatro, was on the olive side.

Carlton wore his favorite Italian suit with a blue tie. When we were finished getting ready, he said, "Sorry, sweetie. I forgot your blue wrist corsage."

I giggled and covered my mouth. "I forgot your blue boutonniere."

He grabbed me and swung me around in a dance circle.

"We're not too matchy-matchy, are we?" I asked, wrapping my arm around his waist and posing in front of the bathroom mirror.

"Who cares?" he mumbled. He suddenly spotted the Juliet ring on my finger. In one quick motion, he grabbed my hand and rolled the ring off my finger.

"Hey!" I said.

"Don't wear this tonight," he said, holding the ring in front of my nose. "I don't want my dad to think we got engaged without telling him. This is *his* night."

I smiled at Carlton and nodded. For now, the Juliet ring would be our little secret.

The entire wedding was held inside the Grand Ballroom of the Houstonian Hotel. The ceremony itself lasted four minutes. Carlton's father recited his vows as if they were second-nature. Like a hiccup.

The reception, on the other hand, was just like Carlton's dad. Big and bold, and a little on the wild side. A lavish, Texas-sized affair, complete with rib eye steaks the size of footballs, and strolling mariachis singing "La Cucaracha."

Forest Connors greeted us underneath one of the sprawling chandeliers. He smiled his big-tooth, politician's smile and waved his broad hand. He was wearing a black suit instead of a tuxedo. And black cowboy boots.

El Diablo.

"Madeline," he said, inclining his head in my direction.

"Mr. Connors," I replied.

"Glad you could make it, son!" he said, clapping Carlton on the back.

Carlton gave his dad an awkward sideways hug, and said, "You know I never miss one of your weddings, Dad."

"Aw, shucks, son! Cut your old man a break." Forest Connors chuckled.

"I read somewhere that married men live longer," I piped up.

Forest Connors looked down his nose at me as if I were some kind of flea or tick.

"Hell, Madeline! Why would anyone want to *grow old*?" Forest Connors boomed. He pointed his finger and stabbed it in my direction. "Better to lead a fast life, die young, and look good in your coffin. Right, Son?" he said, nudging Carlton.

"Whatever you say, Dad."

"Life is short, Madeline. I can always make more money. But I can't make any more time," Forest Connors said. He winked at Carlton and walked away.

It was disarming. The way Forest Connors walked and talked. With his snakeskin cowboy boots and Texas twang. On the outside, he had the genuineness of a pure country bumpkin—the type of guy you see driving a tractor on the side of the road. Chewing on a sprig of mint.

And yet, it was his eyes that bothered me. When I looked into his hawkish dark eyes, I saw that Forest Connors was a solid force of a man. Those eyes held sheer raw, unadulterated power.

For the rest of the night, whenever I was around Mr. Connors, I felt uneasy. When I laughed, I laughed too loudly. That type of thing. Secretly, I thought Carlton's father believed women should be seen and not heard.

Perhaps it's because he had a slew of ex-wives. And Carlton told me they were each less challenging than the previous.

Forest Connor's latest addition to the Connors clan was a blonde bombshell named Holly. She was thirty-nine years old, a former Miss Texas pageant finalist, and a plastic surgeon's wet dream.

Whenever Carlton saw her blazing toward us in her fire-engine-red wedding dress, he'd look at me and say, "Holy Shit. Here Comes Holly!"

"Talk about eye candy," I said, conspiratorially.

"Stale eye candy," Carlton said, and we both laughed like criminals.

I know he secretly resented the silky white Mercedes convertible his father had given Holly as a wedding gift—parked outside the hotel entrance for everyone to admire, with a big red bow wrapped around it—especially since Carlton still bumped around in his rusty Honda.

But there was more to it than that, I thought.

"I don't understand why my dad is never satisfied with one woman. I guess my old man prefers the all-u-can-eat buffet," Carlton said, as we danced to the wedding band playing an awful rendition of "Brown Eyed Girl." He encircled his arms around my waist and held me tightly.

"Apples don't fall far from the tree, babe," I teased.

Carlton smiled his sexy, sideways smile. "Don't worry, darlin'," he whispered. "I'm a single entree kind of guy."

And I, of course, being the sucker that I am, totally believed him.

Chapter 11

I arrive at The Tavern early, of course. I'm dressed in wrinkled jeans and a stained white T-shirt that says, "South Padre Island." On the back of the shirt, in tiny blue letters, it reads, STAND STRONG 2 THE WINDS OF CHANGE.

So here I am. In a smelly bar. Waiting for my brother. And standing strong to the winds of change.

The bartender approaches me armed with this smarmy smile.

"You look like you could use a drink, Missy," is his opening line.

"Thanks, but I'll just have a coke."

"Sure you don't want me to pour a shot of Jack on top?"

"It's not even noon," I say.

"Time is what you make of it."

See, here's the problem with Austin, Texas. Everyone's a closet intellect. No one is who they seem to be. Your barman is probably a PhD in Philosophy or English Lit; your waitress, a budding filmmaker.

My closet intellect bartender slides the glass toward me. He looks a little disappointed that I'm not DRINKING drinking.

I sit on the barstool and sip my coke. Ronnie is a former alcoholic and drug addict so I never drink alcohol around him. He tells me it's okay. "Don't worry, Maddy. You won't get me back off the wagon," he says. But I figure if I was a chocoholic, I'd be pissed if someone wolfed down a Snickers right in front of me.

My brother strolls in the door. He's wearing a Longhorns shirt, of course, because he bleeds burnt orange. His hair is messed up on top. A serious case of bed-head.

"I've been staring at my computer for the past nine hours," he says, rubbing both his eyes like he used to do when he was a little boy.

"Trying to save the world again?" I ask.

He shoots me a look. "One teenager at a time, Maddy. That's my motto.

My brother is a rehab counselor for troubled teens. And he takes the hard cases, because he used to be a hard case himself. He says he feels lucky to be alive and that the rehab business is his "life calling."

I've seen him in action. Three nights a week my brother lectures for free at the local community center. He's gotten quite a following and even started a Monday night volunteer crisis-counseling hotline—where neither he nor any of the crisis counselors get paid. They work all night long. And the phones ring nonstop.

I know because I've volunteered. Not a lot. But enough to know my brother is making a difference.

He counsels kids who have abused more alcohol and street drugs than anyone cares to think about. Kids with dim, weary, aging eyes. The kind of eyes that have seen too much in their short time.

My brother calls these kids his "Miracle Teens."

"Every one of them needs a miracle," he says.

I motion to the bartender and order a coke, two cheeseburgers, onion rings instead of fries, and extra pickles.

My brother and I have been doing this burger gig a long time.

"So, you want to kill Carlton?" my brother says, most bluntly.

"Yes."

"With poison brownies?"

I slurp my coke out of the straw and don't answer.

"Like some Grim Reaping Martha Stewart?" my brother asks.

The bartender slides two greasy red baskets in front of us.

I rub my hands together and dig in.

"You're not answering me," my brother says.

"Off with his head!" I say, biting into my juicy cheeseburger. I wipe my mouth with my napkin. My brother watches me, carefully.

"Don't you dare tell me I have to be strong," I say.

"You have to be strong," Ronnie says. He's ignoring his food, which is odd for him, because that guy can really pack it down.

"How long has it been, Maddy? three, four months? And you're still obsessed. You think killing Carlton is going to bring you closure?"

"I know it sounds crazy, Ronnie, but I think it's the only sane thing to do," I mumble.

"Ask yourself why," my brother replies. He likes to do this. It's a counseling technique.

I decide to ignore the question.

"Mange, mange," I say, pointing to his food.

He pushes the basket away from him. Okay. Stop the presses. My brother *never* does this. He can usually pack away a cheeseburger, maybe two, and still manage to stay rail thin.

He swings around on his bar stool and stares at me, his fist pressed against his thigh. His green eyes are bright and flashy so I know he's upset.

Ronnie and I are both full-blooded Italian on our father's

side, and while we each got the naturally tan olive skin and thick dark hair, my brother got these flashy green Italian eyes—while I was stuck with boring, run-of-the-mill hazel. Ronnie's eyes are so expressive when he's angry, he could make even the biggest felon in a motorcycle gang take two steps backward. My brother isn't a big guy, but he's got enough Italian Stallion in him to make other men think twice.

"What's going on with you, Maddy?" he says, slapping his hand against the bar. "You've never been like this. You're the bounce-back kid, remember? Always Miss Positive. Where's the person who says if life gives you lemons, put on a party dress and go out for cocktails? What did you do with my big sister?" he demands, and his face is dead serious.

I swirl an onion ring around in ketchup. Pop it in my mouth. Chew.

"You don't know all the facts," I say.

"I know Carlton was a shit head," Ronnie says. "I knew it from the first day I met Prince Charming."

"You should've told me!"

"I did. Remember? I said, 'Maddy, watch out for this cat.' I wouldn't trust a man who looks at himself in the mirror for that long—especially after he takes a freakin' piss. I swear we were in the john together and he was gussing around with his hair like he was the Prom King!"

I think for a moment. I don't remember my brother saying this but I was so blinded by Carlton's sun, it wouldn't have mattered.

"You don't understand, Ronnie. I can't sit back and let him railroad all over me!"

"Cut your losses," my brother says. "Start a new life—without dick face."

I shake my head back and forth.

"You've gone through way more trauma than this, Maddy! Remember when Mom and Dad died? You told me it was God's will. And that they were in a better place. You were solid as a rock. What are you saying? That you got taken by some lousy guy. So what? So now you're a wet noodle? Some weak-willed, whiney-ass girl?"

"I'm unemployed, Ronnie! I sank everything I had into that company!"

"You got sucker-punched by that bastard. But what are you gonna do? Lie down and let him kick dirt in your face? Or stand up, brush yourself off, and tell him to go fuck himself? I mean, c'mon, Maddy. You can get a new job. A woman with your talent and credentials. Fuckin' A, Maddy—you started that company from the ground up and ran with it. You made him successful. He was the face of the operation. But you were the brains. The woman behind the scenes. You can do it again."

This is, apparently, my brother's idea of a pep talk. He doesn't realize how hard it is to jumpstart a brand new company. How I spent four years working my tail off—day and night. And how, after this sucker-punch, I just don't have it in me.

I realize, suddenly, that I need a major chocolate fix.

I raise my arm in the air, wave crazily at the bartender, and say, "Yo!" The bartender strolls over.

"Have you decided to get shit faced?" he asks.

(P.S. I really hate it when people say this.)

"Do you have chocolate milkshakes?" I ask.

He wipes his hand on a bar towel and informs me, "I've got milk and ice cream but none of that chocolate syrup. So I can make ya' vanilla."

My brother reaches down and pulls a Hershey bar from his messenger bag. "Use this," he says, slapping it down on the bar.

"This is my little brother and my hero," I tell the bartender.

"Aw, how sweet," the bartender says in a deadpan voice.

My brother shoots me a look.

"You know, Maddy. Real assassins don't drink chocolate milk-shakes," he says.

I guess he has a point.

"If you want me to kick his ass, I'll kick his ass." Ronnie grabs his basket and finally bites into his cheeseburger.

I try to imagine my brother and Carlton scuffling around on the ground. My brother would win, of course. Assuming that it was a fair fight. But I wouldn't put it past Carlton to use some cheap, dirty trick. Like throwing sand in Ronnie's eyes and punching him in the kidneys.

"I don't want you to get involved," I say.

"I don't want you to get involved," my brother chirps, mimicking my voice.

"Maybe I should hire someone."

My brother sits back on his stool and claps his hands together. "Bravo, Maddy. That's just what you need. A hit man. Good idea."

"Do you know someone?" I ask. And it's not an off-the-wall question. My brother knows some shady characters from his drug-running days. He used to work for a man named Snoop Santino, one of the most notorious drug kingpins in South Texas.

"What about . . ." I hesitate. "What about Snoop?" I ask, finally.

I've got Ronnie's full attention now.

"I'm going to pretend you didn't say that," he says, in a soft tone. When my brother is infuriated, he speaks in a hushed tone like this. It's entirely frightening.

"You don't know what you're messing with when you throw out a name like Snoop Santino," Ronnie says.

"Well, we've both known him since we were kids."

"Yeah, Maddy. That was back then. Before he got damaged. Before he decided to nose-dive into a life of thieving and drug dealing."

Then Ronnie does something that he rarely does, ever. He pulls up the side of his T-shirt, and points at the bullet wound. It's on the left, near his rib cage. "Clean entry and exit" is what the surgeon told me that night. When Ronnie was fighting for his life.

"Remember who I was with when I got shot, Maddy?"

I'm quiet. Maybe bringing up Snoop Santino's name wasn't such a good idea. But deep down, people envy criminals, don't they? Isn't that why the Sopranos was so popular?

After he got shot, my brother found God.

Now that Ronnie's on a mission to save every teenager from drugs, he sometimes meets up with street dealers and asks them to stay away from schools.

"Leave the kids alone," he'll say to a small-time street dealer. Ronnie tries to reason with drug dealers. He travels to the periphery of the city, to streets where the cops don't even go, and meets the dealers in person. And they respect him because he used to be in the trafficking business himself. He used to be in the employ of Snoop Santino, so Ronnie's name is known around certain circles, as they say.

My little brother meets with street dealers and lays out both a moral and logical argument for why they shouldn't sell to minors. And after each meeting, he says, very sincerely, "Thank you for your time."

He's got cojones, my brother.

I've asked him how he gets the dealers to agree to stay away from schools. "What do you offer them, Ronnie? Besides a moral argument?" I ask.

"I cut my own deals," my brother says, simply. So I haven't pressed the issue.

The bartender shoves a milkshake in front of me. It's good and thick. I can see pieces of Hershey bar stuck in the sweet sludge. I reach for the glass, but Ronnie swipes it away from me.

"Hey!" I protest.

"Not so fast, sister."

He takes a sip from the straw and smacks his lips, as if he's just tasted heaven. He slides the glass toward me, because, for all his bark, my brother is really a big, fat softie.

I take a sip from the straw, but nothing comes out. So I use a spoon instead.

Delicious. . .

"Let's forget about Snoop, then. You know of anyone else with muscle for hire?" I say.

Ronnie puts his cheeseburger down, licks his fingers. "You can't be serious," he says.

I stare at him, with my plain-Jane hazel eyes.

My brother shakes his head. "I'm gonna pray for you, Maddy," he says. And just like that, he lowers his head, curls his fingers underneath his chin, and begins to pray.

Ronnie prays a lot. But usually not in public. So he must think this is an emergency.

The bartender sees my brother with his head bent low over his cheeseburger basket. He raises an eyebrow, and starts to walk over, a worried expression on his face.

I hold up a single finger and mouth the words, "One minute." The bartender considers me, and then turns back to his bottles. I sit quietly until Ronnie finishes. My shake is melting but I don't touch it. My brother, by the way, does not take kindly to prayer-interruption.

His head finally jolts up and he looks at me.

"All better?" I ask.

"There is great power in letting go, Maddy," he says.

My brother, the Sensei. God, how I love that guy.

Chapter 12

After Carlton gave me the Juliet ring, I expected us to announce our engagement. I practiced saying my name aloud in the bathroom mirror. "Madeline Connors," I'd say, trying it on for size.

But Carlton wanted to wait. And I understood why.

He'd been married before. His "starter marriage," he called it. She was seven years younger. A blonde bombshell. And a Mormon, of all things.

I'd found a photograph of her once, in a shoebox Carlton kept high in the closet. Unlike my dark, Italian features, she was tall, with sumptuous blond hair running in long waves down her back. Bright blue eyes, gorgeous, supermodel smile, and dimples the size of Lake Erie. In her lap, she held a Labrador puppy.

She was the kind of woman who looked like the perfect wife, actually. Not stubby and dark-haired and tragically ethnic like me. Not to sell myself short. I mean, I was a powerhouse on two legs, a firecracker, as they say. And I was pretty in a way, if you looked closely—but I was certainly no knockout. No one had ever suggested I be prom queen. Or a Victoria's Secret model. In fact, men usually dated me for my "personality," my "flair," my "Piatro pizzazz." But I wasn't boring in bed, either. I knew my way around a man, let's put it that way.

That very night, I cooked Carlton's favorite dinner. Herbed salmon with new potatoes and asparagus. I splurged on a bottle of Chianti that was much too expensive for my just-out-of-grad-school starting salary. And I had my nails done with French tips.

Carlton came in from work and we sat at our makeshift "bar." A card table with two stools I'd put in the kitchen.

I poured his wine.

He tasted it.

"Fancy," he said.

I walked around the table and rubbed his shoulders.

"Ahhh," he said, as I dug my thumbs into his muscles. I took this as my cue. And asked him casually why he'd gotten a divorce.

Carlton sat up, suddenly. I walked around the table, plopped down across from him and waited.

"I bought Megan fake tits," he replied, finally. "And she still wasn't happy. She was the type of woman who'd never be happy."

He raised his wineglass. Clinked it against mine. "Why are you so curious all of a sudden?"

"I thought you hated fake breasts," I said, crossing my arms over my own chest. It's not like I was flat as a cookie sheet or anything. But I was no double D.

He sighed. "Hey sweetie. I just walked in the door and you're already wearing me out."

So I dropped it.

But I didn't drop the engagement thing. I stood up and served both of us plates of salmon, new potatoes, warm French bread, and salads with blue cheese crumbles.

We sat across from each other and ate in silence until I couldn't hold it in any longer.

I sucked in my breath and blurted: "I don't understand why

we're not telling anyone about our engagement." Carlton looked up and I flashed him the Juliet ring on my ring finger.

He rubbed his forehead, a man under pressure. "Look sweetie. I don't want to introduce you as my fiancée to my family yet. Because you have to understand, Maddy, they'll think I'm crazy to be engaged again. So soon after my divorce."

"You've been divorced for two years!"

"Separated," Carlton corrects me. "The divorce was just finalized, remember? And I don't want my dad lecturing me about moving too quickly. He wants me to focus on work, so we can start our own company, sweetie. Don't you want to hit the ground running? Instead of spending all our energy planning some ridiculous, over-the-top wedding?"

"I was thinking we'd do something small," I say. "Intimate."

Carlton rolls his eyes. "Please. With my family. As-if," he huffs. "I mean, my dad'll have to invite all his goddamned employees. We'll be lucky to have less than eight hundred guests."

"Sounds like a circus," I murmur. I wonder if Carlton and the supermodel Mormon had eight hundred people at their wedding. But I don't ask.

I look down at the table, and I can't help but think of my parents. See, that's the problem with drunk drivers. They really take the fun out of weddings. I mean, I wonder if the guy who slammed into my parents' car realized that if their only daughter ever were to marry, the friends and relatives on the "bride" side would be slim pickin's. My brother will walk me down the aisle, of course. When the time comes.

But jeez. Eight hundred people? I'm lucky if I could score twenty people. The church would topple over to one side, it would be so uneven. I can hear the ushers now, "Bride or groom? No wait! Let me guess—Groom, right?"

I pour more wine in my glass.

Bottoms up.

Carlton looks up and says, "Easy with the vino, Maddy," but I ignore him.

We eat for a few minutes in silence and then Carlton says, "Look, Maddy. We've just graduated and gotten our MBAs." He scrapes his fork along his plate. "It's time to do *Something Big*, Maddy. Start our own company. Not dick around with caterers."

"You're absolutely right," I say. "And on that note—"

I stand up, excitedly, and hustle around the kitchen. I take Carlton's plate away from him, clear the entire card table.

"Hey! I wasn't finished with that," he says, playfully, but I ignore him.

I've come up with a novel idea for a company. In fact, I've been working on it nonstop for a month. Tonight is the night to surprise Carlton.

In between my day job as a marketing consultant for a top-notch firm, I've been sweating over my computer, working up spreadsheets and models for a new company concept I've developed.

I grab my portfolio book and spread a few news articles in front of him.

"What's this?" he asks. I look at him and can tell he's getting excited. This kind of stuff is totally Carlton's thing. He lives for it.

"See all these news articles. They're talking about how unhealthy the school lunch programs are around the country. All these kids are eating really crappy food every day, right? And that's what might be causing this child obesity epidemic," I say, and I'm talking quickly now.

"And now—look at this—" I spread more articles out across the table.

"Whole Foods is the fastest growing organic foods grocery store in the country. They've got a sixty-thousand-square-foot store here in Austin, and are opening stores all around the country. Organic food is becoming more affordable and popular as people are concerned with their diets. So my idea is to combine this organic food craze with busy parents who don't have time to pack their kids a lunch. These parents want their kids to eat something healthier than the awful slop that the school is doling out."

I'm in full presentation mode, now. I raise my hands in the air, like I've just shouted Boo!

"My business idea, Carlton, is Organics for Kids. An organic lunch program for parents on the go."

Carlton is silent a moment. I pass him all the charts and spreadsheets I've been working on. I go over all of the numbers. It takes us a long time. When I'm finished, an hour has ticked past.

"See, it can work," I say. "All we need is a major infusion of cash, and it can really work."

I stare down at the table, cluttered with all my data.

Carlton sifts through the papers, silently. He reads everything. And then he sits quietly a moment, closes his eyes. Like a sleeping Buddha.

Suddenly, he jumps up, knocking his chair over on the floor. He grabs me and swings me in a circle.

"Christ, you've done it, Maddy! This is it! No one—I mean no one—is doing this. I've gotta call my dad, pronto! He can get us the cash we need. He knows tons of investors. Oh my God, Maddy. He's gonna love this. I'll set up a meeting with him and some of his buddies. We'll develop an entire presentation. Something formal. We need more data showing the potential market for this. Pitfalls, expenses, marketing projections—an entire business plan!"

I pull a cream-colored bound notebook from my bag and hold it in the air. I've done the cover myself. Using crayons and several different colors from the box, I've printed out the title: ORGAN-ICS 4 KIDS: A BUSINESS PLAN BY CARLTON CONNORS AND MADELINE PIATRO.

"Surprise," I say.

Carlton stares at the notebook. "You put my name first," he says.

"Alphabetical," I shrug.

Carlton grabs the notebook out of my hand and lifts me in the air again. He throws me over his shoulder like a sack of potatoes and carries me into the bedroom. He topples me onto the bed, unzips his jeans, and crawls on top. I can feel his hot breath against my neck as he whispers in my ear.

"My little Einstein is about to get poked," he says. He's rough and crude and the zipper on his jeans scratches my leg, but I can't help myself.

I love every minute of it.

Chapter 13

Carbon monoxide, I think. *That's the easy way to go.*

I pick up the phone and dial my best friend. Heather picks up on the first ring. She's a housewife so she can get to the phone that fast.

"What do you know about carbon monoxide poisoning?" I ask.

I know it's not good to have all these witnesses. But I introduced Heather to her husband. So I figure the least she can do is lie for me on the stand.

"Carbon monoxide? I think it's fatal," Heather says. (She's really helpful, my friend.)

"Why? Is your stove out again?" she presses. "I told you to get it fixed, Maddy. Your old gas stove could be leaking and you'd never know until it was too late."

"You're going to make a great mom," I say. Heather is five months pregnant, but she's still a goddamn size 2.

"Thanks!" she says, with utter earnestness. "So, it's Friday night. What cha up to?"

"I've got a date with Matthew McConnaughey."

"Gag me," Heather says.

"C'mon. He's not that bad," I say, because I don't want to knock a fellow Texan. Especially a guy who went to my same Alma Mater.

"Be sure to bring the body condom," Heather says and giggles into the phone. Heather, by the way, is a real girly girl. In college, she was even president of her sorority. Tri-Delt, I think.

"I've actually got an exciting evening planned at a lovely place called Blockbuster," I say. "I swear the video guy's seen me so many times, he's starting to recommend movies. Last night he suggested a documentary about some guy who gets eaten by bears."

"I hate it when they do that," Heather says. I think she's talking about the video guy recommending bad movies, but she's actually talking about the bears.

"You know, people think bears are friendly," she informs me, "but they're really quite dangerous."

"God, if it's not leaky gas stoves, its killer bears. When will the madness ever end," I say.

Heather ignores me. "Why don't you come over for dinner?" she says. "Michael and I are *doing* Shabbat." She sighs into the phone. "Oy Vay. I've got a lot of cooking to do."

"Did you just say, '*oy vay*'?'"

"Why, do I sound stupid?"

It surprises me to hear Heather talk like this, especially considering she's not Jewish. But her husband, Michael, is. So Heather, bless her heart, is in the process of converting. The problem is, she doesn't have the Jewish thing down quite right. The religion, the culture, the tradition, the language—are all far beyond her grasp. As much as she tries, Heather can't seem to shed her Tri-Delt self.

She took Yiddish classes and spent a summer in Israel doing a Kibbutz. But still, it's as if becoming a Jew is beyond her conditioning.

Heather's husband, on the other hand, could pass for a Bible-belt Baptist if he wanted to. Michael is a rising star trial lawyer in South Texas. The type of guy who argues the plight of the common man against the large, faceless corporate monster. So, he's tailored his accent, a deep Southern drawl, and his image—jeans and cowboy boots—to appeal to the South Texas courtroom.

"To the fine men and women on the jury who prefer the Southern sensibility," he likes to say. If I didn't know better, I'd think Mr. Wasserstein rode to the courthouse each morning on a horse.

Thirty minutes later, I'm sitting at Heather's kitchen table. She's made me a cup of Earl Grey tea. And she's rustling around the kitchen. Getting everything in order. Michael swings in the front door, and drops his briefcase.

"I'd sue my own wife if she weren't so darned beautiful," he says, in his pitch perfect Southern drawl. The drawl he's perfected for the jury. Michael never goes out of character. Even at home.

He bounds into the kitchen, grabs Heather, kisses her on the forehead, and puts his arms around her waist.

Michael is a bundle of raw energy. We call him "Mr. Fun."

"How's my little Super-Jew?" he teases, squeezing Heather's waist.

She smiles broadly, her clear blue eyes gleaming. "You're *my-sugar-na*," she says.

"Mishugina," Michael corrects her. "It means 'nuts.'"

"You're nuts," Heather repeats.

He rubs her belly. "And how's Baby Wasserstein today?" he says, putting his ear against her stomach.

Heather giggles like a schoolgirl.

Michael pretends to listen to his baby. He nods his head against Heather's belly and says, "Your mom is gonna be mad, but I'll see what I can do."

"Our son wants whiskey," he says.

"Stop it!" Heather shrieks and slaps Michael playfully on the arm. He smacks her on the bottom and pours himself a small glass of Jack Daniels.

It's painful for me to watch them like this. And I see how perfectly comfortable they are. Heather's hair is greasy and she's got yellow stains on her shirt. Michael is sporting day-old stubble.

Carlton and I were never this real.

"How was work, Michael? Did you dazzle them with your Texas twang, today?" I ask.

"Sheee-it," Michael says, taking a swig of his cocktail. "I'll be anyone that jury wants me to be. I'll wear a cross on my suit like Johnny Coch-RAIN if it helps me win a case," he drawls.

"I saw your picture in the paper. The Top Fifty Trial Lawyers in Texas. Pretty impressive," I say. "So I guess you're famous."

"I'm signin' autographs after dinner." Michael chuckles at himself and smiles his clever cat smile.

"So I hear your wife is going to be a Jew," I say. Sometimes I like to stir the pot. And I know Michael likes it, too.

"We both want the baby to be Jewish," Heather explains. "Under traditional Jewish law, the mother should be Jewish," she explains.

"I don't know if you can shed the South Carolina in you," I say, making a face.

"She ain't sheddin' nothin'. She's augmentin'," Michael says.

This is how we always are, Michael and I. We always butt heads and Heather is the middleman. But Michael loves the tête-à-têtes. And so do I. Sometimes we argue about the Middle East and I stick up for the Palestinians. Just to play Devil's Advocate. It really gets Michael riled up. His face turns beet red and he starts sweating buckets. Heather's afraid it'll give him a heart attack. But I've known Michael longer than she has. He loves to debate. I mean, he really lives for this shit.

"Can't you bring up your child in the Jewish faith without actually converting?" I ask.

Heather is standing in front of the stove, stirring a pot with a wooden spoon. "I want to convert," she says, wiping her hand against her pants.

"Deep down, she's one of the tribe," Michael says.

"Yes. Deep, *deep* down," I say, and we all laugh.

If you saw Heather, you'd know she was white Anglo-Saxon Protestant. She's got all the WASP features. Blue eyes, pale skin, and blond hair cut in a cute bob at her shoulders. She seems almost Norwegian, with her long, straight nose.

Heather grew up Methodist. Her maiden name is Smith. And she looks like she used to be both the head cheerleader and the prom queen, which she was. She bakes low-fat oatmeal cookies. She eats salad like it's a meal. She pays retail for her clothes. She drives a Saab. I mean, she's from Charleston, South Carolina, for chrissakes.

As much as she tries to observe Jewish laws and customs, she can't seem to get it quite right.

"What are you cooking?" I say.

"My new specialty," Heather says. "I call it: Lotsa-Matzoh Ball Spaghetti."

I break out into a smile.

Michael shoots me a look, puts his fingers to his lips and shakes his head no.

I get the message. We're not supposed to poke fun at Heather. At least she's trying. The little pregnant Size 2 WASP is trying.

Before dinner, we stand around the table. Michael pours kosher wine.

"It's the good one," Heather assures me. "Not the icky, grape-juicy one," she says. Always the terrific hostess, my girlfriend. Michael cuts the challah bread and chants a prayer in Hebrew or Yiddish, or something.

We sit down. Michael and I go to town on the food. Heather nibbles here and there. She's eating for two, which means Michael and I must be eating for four. I say something about the Gaza Strip and send Michael into an hour-long rant.

We hold our wineglasses in the air and toast the baby, Heather becoming a Jew, and Michael's picture in the paper. Finally, we toast our friendship. All in all, it's the best night I've had in a *very* long time.

Chapter 14

Carlton is adamant about not introducing me as his fiancée. We've gotta keep it "under wraps," he says. And I respect his wishes. After all, I don't want his family to think I'm simply a rebound girl. So, to his friends and family, we remain boyfriend, girlfriend. A typical live-in couple, just out of grad school, and trying to make ends meet. But to strangers, Carlton always introduces me as his fiancée.

"Meet my fiancée," he'd say, looping his arm over my shoulders. It was at those moments I felt the proudest.

I should've paid more attention when Carlton's old school friends, David and Elizabeth, paid us a visit.

"Watch out for ol' Carlton," Elizabeth said, in her rolling drawl. "He loves bein' in love."

At the time, I'd taken it as a compliment. Carlton loved me, after all. I was his Juliet. I never realized what she meant—until it was too late.

What Carlton loved—was beginnings. The honeymoon phase, as they say. When we first started dating, he brought me flowers every night. But when he moved in with me, things started to slip. The flowers tapered off. I figured this was normal. He was no longer trying to seduce me. He'd captured his prize. Flowers would come on birthdays and anniversaries, and what was so wrong with that?

But there was more to it.

It was when things started to "get real" that Carlton panicked.

"I'm going to the drugstore," Carlton had said once. "Need anything?"

"Toothpaste," I'd said. "Oh, and some tampons if you don't mind."

He'd cringed. Visibly cringed. And I immediately regretted my mistake.

"Just kidding, babe," I'd said, quickly. But the damage had been done. I remember walking up to him and stroking my fingers through the back of his hair. And it could've been my imagination, but I think he pulled away. Slightly.

After that, I tried my best to keep reality out of our tiny house. I didn't want to spoil his image of me as a sexy minx—a woman he desired. So, even though my townhouse had only one small bathroom, I waited until Carlton was gone to floss my teeth, or use the toilet in any major way.

I became obsessive about keeping the cold, grim facts of my womanhood away from Carlton. I wrapped my used tampons in enough toilet paper to embalm a mummy. I threw them in the outside garbage, so he'd never see them in the bathroom trash bin. Each month during my period, I hand-washed my stained panties, but I never let them dry in the shower. I put them in the dryer—shrinking them a size too small.

I never burped, passed gas, or left smelly socks on the floor. I showered immediately after the gym. I shaved my legs and armpits religiously, kept my hair washed, wore makeup on Saturday mornings, and spent every other week with Maria—my Mexican bikini waxing Senorita—who was painfully kind.

I plucked errant hairs from my eyebrows and once in a while, my neck. I relentlessly accessorized. Matching my belts to my purses to my shoes. I wore jewelry and uncomfortably tight jeans. Because once he'd said, "Hot jeans."

I wore high heels that gave me blisters. Once a month, I bought a new piece of lingerie—either a red thong or black lace teddy—to surprise him with.

One thing I did not do, however, was diet. I was happy with my body. Sure, I was short. Five foot three, to be exact. I had average breasts and a size 6 figure. I could've gone to a size 4, which would have better suited my height, but hey, weren't women supposed to have hips? Thighs? An ass?

Stick figures were for doodling, in my opinion. And besides, I was Italian. I loved to eat. And I ate with gusto. None of this dainty, set the fork down after each small, mousy bite for me, thank you very much. When I dug in, I literally *dug in*.

I could wolf down a hotdog in less time than a grizzly bear at a campground. And I didn't see anything wrong with it.

Food, after all, was meant to be eaten.

One night, I fix Carlton a light, Mediterranean-inspired supper. Roasted chicken, hummus, tabouli, grape leaves, and cucumber salad. It's Greek night. Just call me Athena. Goddess of Pita.

Carlton and I have eaten so much take-out lately, the restaurants are on my speed-dial. Plus, I'm getting sick of the same ol', same ol'. Pizza, Chinese food, and cold Subway sandwiches. So tonight, I'm splurging. I've even bought a bottle of genuine Napa Valley Cabernet. Not the cheaper stuff from Chile.

I set the "dining room" table—the card table—uncorked the wine to let it breathe, and waited for Carlton to show up. His Honda has broken down again so he's on the bike. It'll take an extra half hour for him to ride home but he loves the wind in his hair after a long day at the warehouse.

Ever since Carlton signed off on my business plan idea, my

schedule, thus far, has moved with warp speed. I work night and day, seven days a week. I drink coffee by the bucket, type on my computer keyboard until my wrists ache, and smack my own cheeks to keep from dozing off at my desk.

Carlton and I are starting a brand new company. And my life has never been more exciting. We're using the name I came up with: ORGANICS 4 KIDS. And it's up to us to get it off the ground.

Carlton's got two more classes until he "officially" finishes grad school but he's still working at his dad's warehouse. He's enrolled in two evening classes, which conflict with his work schedule, but I happily accept the extra study load. Because it comes easier for me than it does for Carlton. And besides, he's helping me pay the utility and cable bills I used to pay myself.

Carlton says he needs an MBA if he's going to be a CEO. It helps with his credibility. Especially with new investors.

I say, "Why don't I be CEO?" and watch as Carlton's face changes color. He quickly nixes the idea, tout de suite.

"My dad will never agree to that," he says. "And besides, Maddy, you're the secret weapon."

So the secret weapon stands in her kitchen and crumbles feta cheese over a cucumber and tomato salad. Squeeze a lemon, twist some fresh cracked pepper over the whole deal, and voila! It's like the Mediterranean in June.

Carlton bursts in the door. He's holding his biking helmet in one hand and a paper bag in the other. He drops the helmet and it bangs against the floor. With one arm, he whisks a bottle of wine from the bag and says, "Time to celebrate, Maddy!"

I mosey on over to the man of the hour and give him a nice wet kiss on the lips. I can smell the woodsy scent of his cologne mixed with sweat from the bike ride. It's a really good smell. Masculine and musky.

"What's the occasion?" I say, in my huskiest bedroom voice.

"We got the meeting, sweetie! My dad set the whole thing up.

It's gonna be him and like five other investors. It's next Tuesday. In Houston. So we've gotta be prepared."

I cup my hand against my mouth to keep from screaming. "You're kidding!"

Carlton plunks his biking helmet on the counter. "Nope. And if they think our idea is as promising as we think it is, we'll be in business. My dad says we can get three million to start."

"You mean a bunch of complete strangers are going to give us three million bucks?" I ask, incredulously. "For our company?"

"Ooh. I love it when you talk dirty," Carlton says. He sets the wine bottle down, tackles me onto the kitchen floor, and unzips his pants.

Carlton pushes up my skirt and rubs inside my thighs. He does this little trick of his, where he pulls my panties down with his teeth. I stare up at the ceiling and the tile feels cold and hard under my skin. But when in Rome—

Chapter 15

So, how to create a fatal carbon monoxide poisoning? A good death, if you ask me. There's no struggling, no pain, no fear. You just fall unconscious, right? And what's so wrong with that?

I grab a broom and swat my carbon monoxide detector until it falls to the kitchen floor. Picking it off the tile, I check the instructions.

Hmm. No instructions. I pull the plastic cover off and look inside, at the guts of the machine.

A tiny red sticker says, "WARNING! DETECTOR WILL NOT BEEP IF BATTERY IS REMOVED." I bet it's pretty easy to dismantle one of these. Not like a nuclear warhead. Here, you just slip out the battery and stick it back up on the ceiling. Then start a slow leak in a leaky gas stove and boom! You've got your man.

I think back to the brownie incident—my glamorous night of hurl—and wonder if I could accidentally carbon monoxide myself.

I know it's some kind of gas. But where does it come from? Like, originally?

I pad into my living room, drop down in front of my laptop,

and Google it. I can do this sort of thing now. Now that I've got so much free time on my hands.

I type in **carbon monoxide poisoning**. There are 1.6 million sites so I'm guessing I'm not the first person who's thought about this.

I choose a website called **Fatal Carbon Monoxide Poisoning**.

I rub my palms together. Like a praying mantis or one of those evil villains you see in the movies.

Now we're talking, I think.

Carbon monoxide is a colorless, odorless, and extremely deadly gas—

Hmm. How can something be *extremely* deadly? I mean, are there degrees of deadliness? If it's deadly, it's deadly, right? Ain't no *extreme* about it folks. Extremely deadly is extremely redundant in my humble opinion. But I guess I'm nit-picking.

Gas appliances should have a blue flame, not an orange one, it says.

I plod over to my kitchen stove. Turn the burner on. The flame shoots up and it's blue.

The likelihood of Carlton's new fancy-schmancy townhouse having a faulty appliance is pretty slim. Even if I knew how to block the ventilation, the guy never cooks for himself. I'd be lucky if he turned on the stove once a year to fry an egg.

I read further.

Fireplaces!

Terrific. I know Carlton has one. It's not as if I've been doing late-night drive-by's like a stalker, but I've been doing late-night drive-by's like a stalker.

A fireplace where the flue is blocked is especially dangerous. If the flue is clear, the deadly gases will escape. But with insufficient ventilation, the gases enter the room. Even a bird's nest blocking a chimney can pose a significant risk. A person who is asleep can die within several hours of exposure.

Okay. So all I've gotta do for this carbon monoxide thing to work is climb into Carlton's chimney, a la Santa Claus, stuff it with a bird's nest, and hope that Carlton builds himself a nice brisk fire. In the middle of summer. In Texas. And that he'll fall asleep in front of the fireplace, on that ridiculous bear rug of his.

Carlton Connors, my sleeping beauty.

I think back to the bear rug. Complete with a bear head at the top and bear claws at the bottom. Carlton shot it with his father on a weekend hunting trip in Minnesota. Then he had a rug made out of the poor gal. (It was a female bear, go figure.)

At the time, he told me it was a clean shot, but I know Carlton didn't have that kind of concentration. If anything, he probably took her down with a club and an Uzi for all I know.

I hated the rug, but Carlton loved it. So I made do, and placed the rug right in front of the fireplace.

One night, when we first started our company, Carlton came home late. I was waiting for him. Stark naked on the bear rug. Feeling sassy. I'd just hired a graphic artist, and together we'd designed a hot new company logo. Organics 4 Kids in rainbow colors. The 4 turned around in the opposite direction. Like a kid drew it.

I took the new logo to a local tattoo artist and had him draw it as a temporary henna tattoo across my bottom. Then I propped my buck-naked self on the rug and waited.

"Well, well, what do we have here?" Carlton had said, coming in the doorway. Dropping his briefcase.

"I wanted to show you our new logo," I said, quietly. Then I turned over. Flashed him my bare bottom. "How do you like it?" I asked, in a sultry voice. I had candles burning, the lights low, the whole shebang.

"I need to take a closer look," he'd said.

And we did it like animals on the awful bear rug. Afterward, I told him it was the best sex I'd ever had. The sad part is . . .

It was true.

❀　❀　❀

I sit quietly at the laptop and breathe in and out. The house feels quiet and I can hear my own heart beating.

I hate that.

I decide to get some air.

I mean, why should I sit around and mope?

I hop in my car. Drive around aimlessly. I head toward an area of town that's considered a hot spot. An "action" area. There's a bookstore, a coffee shop, a spa. The usual suspects.

I park my car and stroll into the spa.

The woman at the counter looks up at me, and I must look a wreck, because she breaks out into a polite smile. The kind of smile you give to a disabled person when they roll by you in a wheelchair.

"Can I help you?" she asks, raising a pencil-thin eyebrow. She reminds me of Cruella Deville—or Sharon Stone. She's got that cool, cold, polished look.

"I'd like a facial," I say. And then I add, "Or something."

Cruella looks me up and down. Sizes me up. I'm clad in jeans and Nikes, no less. But at least they're my good Nikes. And not the muddy ones.

"Do you have an appointment?"

Ah, I see how this works. They're going to hit me with a technicality.

"No." I shove my hands in my pockets and rock back and forth on the balls of my feet.

Cruella shakes her head. Flips through her appointment book. "We don't take walk-ins," she says, crisply. "But I can fit you in next Thursday. Say seven o'clock?"

"That's all right," I say. I turn and push the door open. A little bell tinkles. Cinderella has left the building.

I plod through the parking lot.

Now what? I wonder. I was going to turn this into a Day of

Maddy. Get a facial. Maybe even a massage. But somehow, Cruella managed to cock-block me.

"Miss—MISS!"

I turn around and well, well, well. Speak of the Devil. Cruella Deville is racing toward me, her Chanel heels clomping hard against the asphalt. "Miss!" she yells. She's got her arm in the air like she's hailing a cab.

I turn around and go, "Ye-ss?"

"We just had a cancellation. We can take you now," she says, breathlessly, her face cracking into a smile.

"I'd recommend our most popular treatment. The rainforest facial," she says. I turn and walk with her back into the building.

"You've got a wonderful olive skin tone," she says. She's fawning over me now. Kissing my size 6 ass.

"I'm Italian," I reply.

Cruella looks at me and flutters her eyelashes in a buttery sweet way. So I cut her a break. I reach the door and hold it open for her.

"After you," I say.

Twenty minutes later, I'm lying on my back in a soft, white terrycloth robe. The aesthetician is exfoliating my nose with a coarse scrubbing pad.

"So why is it called the rainforest facial? Does this mud actually come from the rainforest?" I ask, as she packs this funky-smelling green clay on my face.

"Not exactly," she says. "But the product line was 'inspired' by the rainforest."

"So none of this mud actually *came* from the rainforest?"

"That's right. But it's got rainforest names. Like this mask is called the Costa Rican Howler Monkey Mud Mask."

"Huh. So where's this stuff actually made?"

She looks at one of the bottles. "Looks like New Jersey," she says.

"What a scam," I say.

She plops two cucumbers on my eyelids. I guess to shut me up.

But, oh well. I pay twenty bucks more than a regular facial and get to enjoy the background sounds of howler monkeys and toucans. From the rainforest "inspired" CD.

All in all, it's a pretty good hour. An indulgent hour, but I figure I owe myself. And afterward, as I'm milling around the relaxation room, I feel shiny and gleaming, but still an interloper among the glossy women breezing by.

Like a used car in a new-car lot.

Cruella sees me and claps her hands together once. "Well don't you look refreshed," she croons, handing me a small bottle of Evian.

She heads to the cash register and taps her long, blood-red talon fingernails on the countertop.

Yes, this woman is definitely channeling Sharon Stone. And not the young, sexy Sharon. The older, scary Sharon.

"So is this going to be cash or credit?" she asks.

"Credit," I say. "Always credit."

"Tell me about it, hon," she says, rolling her eyes. "I'm a bank's wet dream."

And that's when I decide I like this woman. I like her very much.

Chapter 16

In preparation for the big investor meeting with Carlton's father, I arrange a meeting with my own boss, Henry Wrona. Henry is Polish and like a father to me. And for these two reasons, but especially the Polish-ness, I decide to tell him what's what.

Henry says Polaks don't like surprises. He's big into what he calls the whole "respect" thing. So he'd be offended if he thought I was holding out on him.

Fair is fair. And I don't want to leave Henry in the lurch. Plus, I've worked for him for fourteen years. His company, Capitol Marketing, is one of the most prestigious public relations firms in town. It's a boutique firm, a small but venerable powerhouse, owned and operated by a firecracker of a man who's "been in the biz forever," as they say. Henry Wrona is a walking, talking institution.

And the best boss I could ever imagine.

But if Carlton and I get the seed money for Organics 4 Kids, I'll have to quit. Which is unfortunate because I'm a rare breed of employee. I love my job.

I started working for Henry as an intern when I was still in high school. Then all through college and grad school. Part-time during the school year, and full-time in summer.

As corny as it sounds, business and marketing is in my blood. I love it.

Henry was a friend of my father back in the day. A long time ago. Before the car accident.

"Your father was a prince of a man," Henry used to say, before I told him I didn't like to be reminded of my dad.

Sometimes, especially in cases of extreme trauma, a person needs to shelve certain emotions. Tuck them away in a drawer. It's a good way to get through the day. Because reminiscing, sentimentalizing, all that crap, leads to alcohol and pills and other bad stuff. Stuff to make you forget, anyway.

It's not like I want to forget my parents; it's just that it's easier not to remember all the details. Like the way my mother used to sing and brush her hair. Upside down. Her head almost touching the floor. Bobbing as she sang along to Mick Jagger. "I'm a honkey tonk woo-man!" she'd sing.

That kind of memory. It kills me.

I walk over to Henry's office. Peek inside. He's at his computer. Typing like a madman. He's got a shock of white hair on his head, twinkling blue eyes, and an ornery smirk.

I tap on the door even though it's open.

Henry is one of those bosses with an open-door policy. "My door is always open," he says, his blue eyes twinkling. He's like Santa Claus, without the beard.

He really is.

"Madeline!" he roars, looking up from the screen. "Come in, come in. How's my FAVE-rite gal?"

I walk into the office, a big smile on my face. "I'm fine, Henry. Great, actually."

"Good to hear, good to hear. Sit, sit," he says, motioning to a chair in front of his desk.

I sit.

He swivels around and faces me. "You, my dear, are a genius," he starts in, pointing a stubby finger at me. "The marketing plan you came up with for the Meyers Group—pure gold, kiddo."

The Meyers account was the largest account Henry had ever entrusted me with. When the call came in, from Mr. Meyers himself, Henry informed him that I was in charge. He was putting his full faith in me.

"Aren't you going to be involved at all?" I'd asked.

"I need a fresh mind on this one. Not my crusty ol' ideas, kiddo. And I know you won't disappoint me," he'd added.

So, I met with the client. Mr. Meyers and twelve of his staff. I was the youngest person in the room by twenty years. And the only woman.

"She may look young, but she's my top gun," Henry had said, in the introductory meeting.

I spent several sleepless weeks devising a campaign. They needed something lightning-fast. And Henry promised them I would deliver.

Mr. Meyers was the CEO of an investment bank—J.P. Meyers and Company. He'd founded J.P. Meyers in 1964 but had recently suffered a massive heart attack. And since the stock price had fallen on the news, the company was trying to do split-second damage control.

My tag line for the marketing campaign I developed was: IF YOU THINK YOU'VE GOT TO TEACH AN OLD DOG NEW TRICKS— THINK AGAIN. Pictures of Mr. Meyers came on the screen, first as a young man, and then growing older as the company grew into one of the most revered firms on Wall Street, along with statistics of his accomplishments. We did a commercial and a glossy brochure for the company's quarterly report to shareholders.

The bottom of the brochure read: J.P. MEYERS AND COMPANY—OUR CAPTAIN HAS WEATHERED THE SHIP FOR THE PAST 40 YEARS. HOW LONG HAS YOURS BEEN AT THE HELM?

"I'm glad you liked it, Henry," I say. "I worked hard on that."

"Like it? I LOVED it, Maddy! And so did the client. Mr. Meyers actually clapped when he saw the commercial." Henry drums his knuckles against the desk. "Rest assured, my dear. As soon as they pay their bill, you're in for a very significant raise. Soon you'll be making more money than yours truly," Henry teases, his blue eyes moist from his morning hot toddy. I know he's splashed some Irish whiskey into his coffee. I can smell it on his breath.

"Drinking before 10:00 a.m.?" I ask. "On a Monday?"

"Medicine, my dear," Henry shrugs, with his smiling eyes. He's got bright, shiny, mischievous eyes. The type of eyes that seem to know everything. And so even when I put on my game-face, he knows immediately something is up.

"But you're not here to talk about Mr. Jack Daniels, I can see that," Henry says. He folds his hands underneath his chin.

I take a deep breath. "Carlton and I have a new business idea. Organics 4 Kids. It's a healthy school lunch program. He's gotten his father and a bunch of investors together. They're planning to invest three million dollars in start-up money. The meeting is next week. I didn't expect it to happen so quickly, Henry. So, things are already off the ground and running."

Henry whistles through his teeth. "Woo-wee. Must be some phenomenal business plan," he says. "If they're making that kind of financial commitment."

I hold up my thick black binder. "I thought you might like to see it," I say, plopping it down on his desk.

He adjusts his bifocals and peers down the end of his nose. I wait as he flips through the pages, slowly. Sopping up each word. Taking it all in. The clock ticks away. Fifteen minutes go by. Then twenty.

Finally, Henry looks at me over the top of his glasses. "You're a piece of work, Madeline Piatro," he says, shaking his head.

"Thanks Henry. That means a lot."

He bites his bottom lip and I can see his mind whirling. He's devising something. "Are you sure you want to give this away to Carlton's dad and all his cronies? I mean, once they invest their money, Maddy, you won't be in control. You'll just be a hired gun. Like a consultant. And the company will belong to them."

"Carlton and I talked about that. We're both going to protect our interests."

"Well of course Carlton will be protected. Daddy Warbucks will make sure of that. But what about you?"

I twirl the Juliet ring on my finger. Look down at it. Remember the engraving. "Forever, my Juliet," it reads.

I look up at Henry and smile. "Carlton and I are in this together," I say. "And plus, a lot of this was his idea."

Henry shoots me a look. A real zinger. "Sure," he says, his voice dripping with sarcasm. "You can use that line on other folks, but I know My Madeline." He slaps my notebook down on his desk. "And this has her name written all over it. Christ, it's brilliant, kiddo! Why don't you let me set up a few meetings on my end? I know some angel investors who may step up to the plate. I mean, it probably won't be three million dollars, but it'll be something."

"That's a great backup plan, Henry. If this meeting doesn't work out. You know, Carlton's dad and his investors could always say no."

"They're not gonna say no to this," Henry says. "By the way, who is Carlton's old man? He must be a man of consequence if he can arrange this kind of cash."

"Forest Connors. Heard of him?"

Henry smacks his palms on the desk. Whap!

I jump in my chair.

"Heard of him? Jeez Louise, Maddy! What do you think? I was born yesterday?"

I watch Henry as his face reddens from exertion. He's really getting riled up.

"I can't believe you never told me Carlton's father was Forest Connors!"

"I didn't think—"

"Forest Connors would steal from his own mother if it helped his bottom line," Henry informs me, crossing his arms over his chest.

"Wow, Henry. So you have no strong feelings whatsoever," I say.

Henry is a little dramatic sometimes. And stubborn as a bull. He doesn't like a lot of people. "I'm not a people person, Maddy," he always says. To which I reply, "That's odd considering you own *a p.r. firm*." Which gets him every time.

So this doesn't surprise me.

"What did Forest Connors ever do to you, Henry?" I ask.

Henry's face is red and blustery now.

Uh-oh. Here comes the rant.

"Listen up, Maddy. Forest Connors was a client of mine. A long, long time ago. We were both young bucks. Bull-headed back then. I was running my own one-man show and I was happy for the business. So I gave him a great deal on my usual hourly rate. In the end, he ditched on my bill. Got some vampire lawyer involved. Calling and threatening to sue me for breach of contract and all this nonsense. Cause I was two days late with his marketing plan.

I decided it wasn't worth the headache to fight him, Maddy. Come to find out later, he used my entire marketing plan. Word for word. Every inch of it. Didn't pay me a dime."

I sit back in my chair. "Wow," I say. "I barely know Mr. Connors. I've only met him a few times."

Henry pokes his finger in the air. "An old Polish proverb is 'forgive your enemies, but never forget their names.' I'll never forget Forest Connors. Granted it was twenty-five years ago," he says. "But I hear he's still a ball buster, plain and simple."

Henry sighs and leans back in his chair, hands behind his head like an executive. "I wouldn't trust him with my dry cleaning, kiddo."

"What should I do?"

"Cancel the meeting. You don't want to get in bed with these guys, Maddy. They're in the big leagues. And they play dirty."

"Carlton set up the meeting. I can't cancel it. And what about the company? You said it yourself. It's almost impossible to get that kind of start-up money."

Henry put his hand in the air, like a stop sign. "Don't say it," he said. "Don't tell me I'm about to lose the best marketing and P.R. person I've ever had to Forest Connors. Look, kiddo. I'll do anything. I'll pay as much as this shop can afford."

"I'm sorry, Henry. But Carlton needs me. And this company is my baby. You always told me if I had the opportunity to go in my own direction, I should take it."

Henry sighs, puts his hands to his forehead and rubs his temples. "Well I don't want to stop you. But beware of the Connors clan. Apples don't fall far from the tree, my dear."

"Oh come on, Henry. It was twenty-five years ago. Don't you think Forest Connors has changed? I mean, everyone makes mistakes."

He gives me a pointed look. "If you think you can teach an old dog new tricks—think again."

"Clever," I say.

I stand and walk toward his door. Then pivot on my heel. "I guess Polaks aren't as dumb as they look," I say.

Henry pulls a bottle of Jack Daniels from his drawer and pours a small shot into his coffee mug. "How do you sink a Polish navy ship?" he asks, flashing me his trademark smirk.

"Put it in water," I reply. Because I've heard them all before.

Chapter 17

Some poisons aren't all they're cracked up to be. But cyanide. Cyanide really does the trick.

You think I would've learned my lesson from the brownies. I mean, really. But here I am. On a cyanide research binge. Clicking away at Web page after Web page. Cyanide this, cyanide that. I'm becoming an expert in the stuff. Here are a few fun facts about cyanide: number one, it's deadly. Like deadlier than arsenic and strychnine and a new song by Britney Spears.

Number two, it's been around a long time. The Russians tried to kill Rasputin in 1916 by feeding him cyanide-laced wine. In World War II, Hermann Goering, Heinrich Himmler, and Adolph Hitler were reputed to have used cyanide pills to commit suicide. Even U.S. spies were issued cyanide pills to be ingested if they were captured.

Number three, you can't buy the "poison pill" on E-bay. Which is a shame, because I'm sure there are lots of women out there, lots of frustrated wives and girlfriends, who'd put up a highly competitive auction. Let the bidding begin, ladies.

I stand from my desk and shuffle into the kitchen to make a pot of breakfast tea. It's ten o'clock on Saturday morning and I'm already antsy. How will I fill my day? With cyanide Web pages?

I know I should feel liberated and free as a bird. But unfortunately, the silence, my dear friends, is deafening. I'm alone. Alone with a capital "A." Alone in my kitchen. I grab my phone and clutch it against my chest. I swear if I don't reach out and touch somebody, I'm going to lose it.

I dial Heather's number.

"Pick up, pick up—" I say, hopping up and down. Doing a rain dance as the phone rings and rings. Heather always answers on the first ring so I'm worried she's not home.

"Hey Maddy!" she chirps into the phone. She sounds out of breath. "Sorry. I was painting the second bedroom. It's going to be the cutest little nursery when I get finished!"

"When can I see it?"

"Maybe a week," she says. "So what's up?"

"You've been studying the Talmud. What does it say about murder? Is there ever any justification?" I ask.

"No," Heather says, flatly.

"You sure? I thought the Jews were big into the whole 'eye for an eye' thing."

"Hang on a sec," Heather says. I can hear her rummaging through a book, flipping pages. "Here. It says something right here," she says.

"What does it say?"

"It says—Get *Over* It, Maddy."

"Okay. I just want you to think about all the murder throughout history that was considered justified. Like Clint Eastwood in *The Unforgiven*."

"That's a movie," Heather says. "Not history."

"So you're saying the military can bomb villages and kill hundreds of innocent women and children, but I can't OFF one lousy ex-fiancé?"

"He wasn't technically your fiancé, Maddy."

Oh. So we're back to this again. Heather, by the way, is big on technicalities.

"What was the Juliet ring? And the 'I intend to marry you?' What was that all about?" I ask, and my voice sounds whiney. I'm even starting to annoy myself.

"It was a promise," Heather says. "But it didn't work out. You can't hold it against him for changing his mind."

I want to tell Heather about the worst thing Carlton did to me. I want to bolster my argument. Lay out my case. But I can't. I'm too ashamed. Embarrassed. Humiliated. Repulsed.

"Forever, my Juliet. Yeah, right," I grumble. "Forever sure isn't what it used to be."

"He's a bad seed, Maddy. But at least you found out before anything worse could happen."

Something worse did happen, I think.

Heather starts talking quickly now. She's on a roll.

"Imagine if you did marry Carlton and have his children, Maddy. Then what? Then you find out he's a schmuck, but you're stuck with a mortgage and a bunch of rug rats."

"Good point," I say. I'm resigned to accepting her advice. I know it will make her feel good. As if she's accomplished something.

"Thanks for the advice," I say, magnanimously.

I grip the phone and stare up at the ceiling. Thinking of ways to poison Carlton without poisoning the other employees.

I look around the kitchen. At the refrigerator. The freezer.

The freezer! Carlton always kept a vodka bottle in the freezer and took a nip after work. Maybe I could start with that. Cyanide meets Grey Goose.

A-ha!

Perfecto, I think.

"What do you know about cyanide?" I ask, swinging my toe in an arc across the tile floor.

"Oy Vay," Heather sighs into the phone. My friend, the sorority girl from South Carolina.

"You think I can buy cyanide on the black market?" I ask. I'm really nutty this morning.

"Where is the black market?" Heather says.

"I don't know. We could Mapquest it."

"You could get a heat-seeking missile launcher," Heather pipes up. "You know, since Carlton's so hot."

I giggle. God bless my friend Heather.

"Cyanide smells like almonds," I say.

Heather ignores me. "Come over," she says. "I'm making a traditional Israeli breakfast."

"Ooh. Sounds de-lish," I say. "I'll be there in a jiffy. Want me to bring anything?"

"Just your appetite," she says.

Heather loves to cook and I love to eat so, in a way, our friendship revolves a lot around food.

I jump in the shower, wash my hair for the first time in three days, and shave my legs because I don't want Michael to say I'm "going native."

Throwing on a pair of cargo shorts and a T-shirt, I hop in my car. I zip over to Starbucks and buy a pound of Kenyan roast. A gift for Heather. And a little baby Starbucks mug. It's an eensy-beensy little toy coffee cup for kids. She'll get a kick out of it.

I arrive at the Wasserstein residence. A quaint one-story "fixer upper" Michael bought when he was still in law school. The house used to be crumbling around the edges, a bachelor pad that smelled faintly of spoiled milk; but after he and Heather got married, she turned the place into a little jewel. She's got a knack for homey stuff—potted plants, frilly curtains, tassel pillows, the whole nine yards.

I buzz through the screen door and see that Heather's outdone herself in the kitchen. On the table are heaping plates of food. She's got olive bread drizzled with honey, and a platter of creamy, white cheeses. I also spot a salad of cucumbers, fresh mint, and vine-ripened tomatoes. And for Michael, sausage and biscuits, of course.

Michael is sitting at the table, pounding his fork and knife down.

"Food, food," he chants in a booming voice. "The King requires food."

"Hey Maddy!" Heather says, rushing over to give me a hug. She smells good, my friend. Like peaches. And her face is rosy and healthy looking. Even pregnant, my girlfriend could be in a Pond's cold cream commercial.

I notice she's wearing a Star of David around her neck.

"That's beautiful," I say, peering closely at it, and turning it over in my hands.

"A gift from my adorable husband," she says.

"What's the occasion?"

"I don't need an occasion to tell my wife how darned beautiful she is," Michael says, in his Texas twang.

I give Heather a meaningful look.

"I know, I know," she says. "I'm the luckiest woman in the world."

"Hell, I'll be the luckiest man in the world if I get to eat!" Michael booms.

"The necklace suits you," I say. "It's perfect."

Heather sets a plate in front of Michael, wipes her hands against her shirt and goes, "Ta-Da! Breakfast is served."

"It's Tel Aviv with a dash of South Carolina mixed in!" Michael says, pouring thick white gravy over his biscuits, and licking his fingers.

Heather spoons a small dab of hummus onto a slice of bread

and takes a tiny bite. The problem with my pregnant, size 2 girl-friend is she eats like a ballerina.

Meanwhile, Michael and I shovel—I mean, literally shovel—food down our throats. We clean our plates. Michael scrapes gravy and licks his fork, before Heather even sits down with her small portion of cucumbers and yogurt.

He leans back in his chair and pats his belly. "Ahh, that was real terrific, honey," he says, in his Southern drawl.

Heather beams at him in that way that makes my stomach twist. If only I could have that, I think, as the Perfect Relation-ship kisses each other and smiles at me from across the breakfast table.

"So when do you officially become Jewish?" I ask Heather. "Does it happen before the baby is born?"

Heather looks at me and I can tell she's nervous because she twists her napkin in her hand.

Michael rubs her on the back. "The conversion exam with the Rabbi is next week. She doesn't think she's ready," he says.

"I'm not ready," Heather repeats.

"Of course you're ready," I say, pointing to the stack of books on the kitchen counter. "Look at all these books you've read—*How to Become a Jew; So You Want to Convert; The Book of Jewish Customs*—"

"It's not sticking," Heather says. She bites her lip and stares down at her empty breakfast plate. "Becoming a Jew—is so hard," she says, in a quiet voice.

"Come on, Heather. You graduated from the University of South Carolina with flying colors," I say. "So what's the process? What is it? A written test?"

"Oral," Heather says. "I have an oral exam with the Rabbi."

Michael pipes up, "Then she'll go through the rituals of con-version. She'll be immersed in a Mikveh—which is the ritual bath used to purify the spirit. And she'll be given a Hebrew name."

Heather drops her head in her hands. "But I haven't turned our home into a real Jewish home yet!" she says, exasperated. She stands up, suddenly, and bolts to the front door. She swings the door open with a flourish. "Look at this! We don't even have a Jewish Bazooka outside the doorway!"

Michael shoots me a look. "Mezuzah, hon. It's called a Mezuzah. And what's the reason that Jews hang a Mezuzah outside the doorpost?"

He's quizzing her. For her oral exam with the Rabbi.

Heather stands up straight. Like she's been called on by the teacher.

"Jews hang a Bezooza to remind us of God's presence and our duty to fulfill God's commandments," Heather says. I can tell she's memorized this. "The Bezooza contains two portions of the Torah in a small, protective case."

"Very good," Michael says. "But remember. It's Mezuzah. With an 'M', hon."

"Mezuzah," Heather says, twitching nervously.

"You're going to do fine," I say.

Heather pats her stomach. "Oops, duty calls," she says. She shuts the door and hurries toward the bathroom. "When you're pregnant, you've always gotta go," she says, glancing at us from over her shoulder.

Michael shoos her away with his hand. "Too much information, hon," he says.

Michael turns to me at the table.

"Women are crazy," he says, matter-of-fact.

We push our plates away, and Michael pats his stomach. "That hit the spot."

I take a sip of coffee, pause, put my coffee cup delicately on the table. "So tell me about this eye-for-an-eye thing? Does Jewish law allow for revenge?"

"Aw, c'mon, Maddy. Don't tell me you're still hung up on ol'

Carlton," Michael says. For a moment, when he was teaching Heather, his Southern drawl disappeared. But now Mr. Texas Twang is back.

"I'm not hung up. I'm obsessed," I say.

Michael grins. "The passage goes like this: *Life shall go for life, eye for eye, tooth for tooth.* It's in Deuteronomy. And it means a punishment in which the offender suffers the exact punishment as the victim suffered. Exact retribution."

He sits back in his chair and puts his feet up. "But don't get your hopes up. Jewish law doesn't justify revenge, Maddy. In fact, the Torah strictly warns against taking revenge." He looks down his nose at me. Like a professor.

"Don't take vengeance and don't bear a grudge against the members of your nation," he says. *"Love your neighbor as yourself.* That's in Leviticus."

"What happened to the eye-for-an-eye thing?"

"It's outdated. Civilization has progressed so that we no longer punish rape with rape, murder with murder. And besides, Carlton didn't kill anyone."

"He killed my spirit," I say, in a glum tone.

"Ah," Michael says. "Ain't that a bitch."

I throw a napkin at him. And he laughs. "I've seen enough snakes in the courtroom to know a snake when I see one. And Carlton is a snake, Maddy. No matter how goddamned good his hair looks. But I hate to say it—"

I shoot my arm in the air. "Don't say it."

Heather walks back into the kitchen and crosses her arms over her chest. "We told you so," she says. "Michael and I both told you so."

I look at them and shake my head.

"Jews," I say.

And they both laugh.

Chapter 18

It's typical to see a great-looking woman with an average-looking guy. It's highly unusual the other way around. (Unless the woman is super rich and the guy is like her chauffeur or something.)

But that's how it was with Carlton and me. Carlton was, in all senses of the word, gorgeous. Breathtakingly gorgeous. The type of man who caused you to tuck in your tummy and stand up straight when he smiled at you from across a room. And he chose me. Five-foot-three, size 6, *la bella donna*, Madeline Jane Piatro.

I never should've fallen in love with a man so far out of my league in the looks department. He could have whichever woman he wanted. The only thing standing in Carlton's way was money. A hefty bank account to keep up with his silver spoon tastes. And then he'd have it all. The looks . . . and the Porsche.

Carlton's father, while enormously wealthy, was one of those men who believed in making Carlton "work for it." Plus, Mr. Connors had a gaggle of ex-wives and court-ordered support. Over time, these women had managed to ratchet down his sizable wealth. Forest Connors was still a safe multimillionaire. Many, many times over. But, according to Carlton, he'd once had a whole lot more.

Forest Connors also loved showering expensive gifts on the new women in his life. Carlton said his dad once bought a quarter-million-dollar diamond necklace for a woman he'd only known a month. A hairdresser from Abilene.

This drove Carlton nuts. The trophy wives, trophy diamonds, trophy cars, and trophy alimony payments. One thing Forest Connors did give Carlton was a wristwatch. A rare Patek Phillipe he'd bought at a Sotheby's auction. Carlton wore the watch every day. Even when he rode his bike. It was like a talisman of power handed down from father to son. The watch symbolized Carlton's future. A future filled with wealth and privilege. Carlton knew it was just a matter of time before his father's jet-set lifestyle became his own. It was waiting for him like a trust fund—it was right around the corner.

And so, because of Carlton's status as The Man Who Walked on Water, sometimes I liked to take him down a notch. Show him that I, too, was a force to be reckoned with. While I was neither rich nor drop-dead gorgeous, I still had chutzpa, as Michael would say.

And that's why I liked to beat the pants off Carlton in tennis.

It's the one area where I truly excelled. My body seemed made for smashing forehands and backhands low across the net. I might trip while walking in a pair of high heels, but on a tennis court, I was pure grace.

I'd been playing for as long as I could hold a racquet. It was my dad's thing to enroll me in tennis camp as soon as I could walk. I guess he dreamed of sitting on the sidelines of the U.S. Open one day, clapping as I went head to head with Venus Williams. For an amateur, I wasn't just good at tennis, I was great.

And so, because of Carlton's healthy ego, sometimes I had to show him a thing or two. It was all in fun, of course. But I had more fun than Carlton did. He was ultra-competitive and couldn't believe each time he lost to a mere pint-sized woman and got run ragged in the process. I was no Amazon woman, that's for sure. But despite my size, I was fast as hell. And I liked to make Carlton chase the ball. It was good for him.

It was a source of entertainment, a joke we told at parties among friends. "Maddy may look like a sweet lil' thang on the outside," Carlton would say, "but I dare any of you guys to play her on the tennis court." I'd watch Carlton as he'd push a perfect lock of hair off his perfect forehead. "Talk about brutal," he'd say. "She kicks ass." Sometimes he'd place bets. Challenge his buddies to a "Game with My Maddy."

He won money, sometimes. But mostly, he won free beer.

The night before our big investor meeting with Carlton's father, Carlton decided he wanted to play tennis.

"I need to let off some steam," he said, holding up the racquets. "Care to rise to the challenge?"

I grabbed my Slazenger out of his hand. Shook it playfully in front of his face. "Let's see what you got, girly-man," I said. So off we went. To the public courts.

The Slazenger was a birthday gift from my dad. I got it after he died. He was having it specially fitted for me and the pro shop called three days after the funeral. "This is a message for Mr. Piatro. Your daughter's racquet is ready," it said on the answering machine.

The Slazenger was just like my dad. Classy. Old School. With a little bit of zing. Carlton sometimes wanted to borrow it, and I let him. But it didn't make a difference. I'd beat him with a Wilson, too. It really didn't matter.

Carlton said my racquet had the "Magic Juice." But deep down, he knew it wasn't the racquet. As a man, he had the power, but I had the finesse. And like my dad used to say, "Nothing beats a ball down the line."

I could place the ball wherever I wanted it to go. Carlton's only hope was to hit it fast and hard, and get it past me before I could react.

Carlton was naturally gifted. A born athlete. He was what you'd call an outdoors "enthusiast." He ran, biked, kayaked, and played soccer on an intramural league.

I knew this tennis thing really bugged him, but I refused to be a wilting flower. The type of girl who "let the guy win." Carlton didn't need a confidence booster. He had a solidly healthy ego, to say the least. But I never beat him as badly as I knew I could. I always held back.

Still, Carlton tried every trick in the book; he even taunted me from the other end of the court.

This was the tactic he was trying now. Now that he was down, four games to zero. I guess it was time to let him win one.

It was my turn to serve.

"Look out!" Carlton shouted, "Here comes the noodle!"

He always did this when he was losing. Tried to get my head off the game.

I watch him as he makes a big production of walking closer to the net. Because he knows I don't have the strength to ace him, to get the ball past the baseline. He's in a ready stance, bouncing slightly on his feet, his tennis racquet in both hands, peering at me. Waiting for my serve.

"Come on, Maddy! I don't have all day!" he shouts. Which is bad tennis etiquette. And poor sportsmanship. But he looks damn good in his white shorts.

I throw the ball into the air, arch my body back, and whack it. Immediately, I know it's a good serve. I can hear the ball ping against my racquet strings—it's a good sound, that ping.

I watch Carlton swing at the ball like he's playing baseball. It's ugly, but it goes over the net. I return it. He returns it. We get into a competitive volley. Each hitting the ball at different angles with different spins. I'm in motion, now. This is my thing. Back and forth. Front to back. Whap, whap, whap—

I watch Carlton race for the ball. He's struggling, I can tell. Thinking to himself, "Don't hit it in the net, don't hit it in the net." Which, by the way, he does.

"Goddamnit!" he shouts. He throws the racquet on the ground, stalks around in a circle. A pissed-off wildcat.

Perhaps I should bring it down a notch.

"You're cheating with that racquet!" he says.

Hmm. Perhaps not.

I walk to the net. Calmly. Like a pro.

"Here, babe. Let's switch," I say.

He storms toward the net, grabs the Slazenger from my hand, and thrusts the Wilson over.

"I bet this'll turn the tide of things," he snaps. I watch as sweat drips down his forehead. He wipes his face with the edge of his shirt.

"Jesus H. Christ! It's hot as a bitch!" he yells.

"Nice," I say.

Carlton looks down at his New Balance tennis shoes. "You're getting me riled up," he says, apologetically.

"Your serve," I say, tossing him a ball. I try not to laugh as he tries to catch it on his racquet, but he overcompensates, and the ball bounces off. "Sonofabitch!" he yells, chasing after it.

Granted I'm no Billie Jean King or Martina Navratilova, but I'm better at this game than Carlton. So I'll be damned if I'm going to flit around in a short, white tennis skirt and let his attitude get to me.

I happen to be wearing a short, white tennis skirt, but that's a minor detail.

Carlton walks to the baseline, a man ready to win. He waves my Slazenger in the air and says, "Now who's got the Magic Juice?"

He arches his back and serves. The ball speeds past me.

Carlton raises both arms in the air. "Yes!" he says, because he's just aced me.

He kisses the racquet.

"Fifteen-LOVE!" he shouts.

I move back way behind the baseline because I know what's coming next. It's time to have a little fun.

Carlton whacks it again. Harder this time. But I'm prepared. My racquet catches the ball squarely on and I hear the familiar ping. The good ping. The ping that means it's sailing down the line.

I watch Carlton run for it, swing, and miss.

He stares at me. "Lucky shot," he says. "Fifteen-All."

Yeah right, I think.

I know Carlton is nervous about the investor meeting, and about impressing his father, but I'm nervous, too.

I debate whether to let Carlton win as he rips another serve past me.

"Thirty-fifteen, BYYYATCH!" he shouts. He never calls me names like "bitch," so I know he's saying this as a joke. But still. Byyyatch or no byyyatch. I'll show him a real byyyatch.

I see Carlton smiling this huge grin at the end of the court. Mr. Perfect. Thinking he's about to win this game.

Think again.

I bend down, prepare for another serve, keeping the racquet loose in my grip. Carlton rips another serve and I hit it short over the net and watch him run for it. He pops it up, and I easily hit it back. He runs and hits it back. So I decide to do this sneaky thing. This thing where I hit the ball from side-to-side and make Carlton sweat it out. I watch as he runs to the left, then the right, then the left again. Until finally, he hits it in the net. We do this a few times until I win game. And a few more times until I win the whole set.

Carlton curses at himself because he got beat, yet again, by a mere Maddy.

Game, Set, Match.

I watch Carlton as he flops down on the bench and drapes his neck with a towel. He hangs his head low. His face red and sweat dripping from his forehead. Totally spent.

He looks at me. "I think we're ready for the meeting," he says. And then adds, "You're definitely ready."

I plop my leg up on the bench and stretch, a little ballet stretch, with my arm over my head.

"I think you should be the one to make the presentation, Carlton. It's your father. His investors. They know you. Plus, you're one of the boys," I say.

He shakes his head, slaps the towel on the bench. "No one knows the business model like you do, Maddy. If you can make the presentation like you just played tennis out there, we'll be as good as gold."

"Tennis is easy. Boardrooms make me nervous," I say. "Especially since I'll be the only woman."

"Hey now. You just knocked it out of the park with the Meyers account. And that was all men. So this should be a piece of cake. Besides, I want my dad to see you in action. He can be kind of a dick, sometimes."

I want to tell Carlton what Henry told me about Forest Connors. About how Carlton's father didn't pay Henry, and even got a nasty lawyer involved. But I hold back because I know what Carlton will say. He'll say his father probably did take advantage of Henry, but that was a long time ago. Business is business. And maybe Henry should let bygones be bygones. That's what Carlton will say.

"So what are you gonna do while I'm making the presentation?" I ask.

He slaps me on the bottom with his towel. Hard.

"Hey!" I say.

"You've got a great ass, you know that, Maddy?"

I smile and sit on his lap. Then I writhe around a little. Like I'm a stripper giving him a lap dance. I'm a saucy little tart sometimes.

Carlton reaches around and cups my breast in his hand. I can feel him getting aroused. I turn and kiss him on the mouth.

"Let's take this home," he says.

"There's no one around," I say. I slip my hand inside the front of his pants.

"Jesus, Maddy. We're going to get caught."

I lift up my white tennis skirt, put the towel over my lap, and let Carlton enter me from the back.

"No one can see a thing," I say, as his breath gets faster and faster.

"I love you, Maddy," he whispers.

I rock back and forth on his lap, going faster and faster.

"Good game, sport," I say, breathlessly, in his ear.

Carlton moans. He grabs my waist and pumps me up and down on his lap. Hard. Like a man who's had his ass handed to him on a tennis court. He's gotta make up for his bruised manhood so he's decided to punish me.

I kind of like it.

"You're a naughty li'l thang," he says, and his voice is hoarse in my ear.

"I haven't even gotten started yet," I say.

And we do it like animals, right there on the tennis court.

Chapter 19

Wednesday morning rolls around and I'm desperate. I log onto the Internet and search revenge books on Amazon. There are more than I expected. The titles all sound alike:

10,000 Dirty Tricks to Pull on Your Ex-Husband

Down and Dirty Revenge Tactics for the Scorned Woman

Screw Him—The Ex-wife's Guide to Getting Even

A sample chapter is called "Five Revenge Tactics to Get Him Good."

The advice borders on obnoxious:

1. Kidnap His Dog.
Hmm, Carlton hates animals.

2. Put a For Sale Sign in Front of His House When He's Away on Business.
But Carlton's renting.

3. Place a Singles Ad for Him in a Gay Newspaper.
That's pretty funny. But Carlton will think it's a prank from an old fraternity brother.

4. Cast a Revenge Spell.

Hmm. Good one. A revenge spell. Despite my occasional fantasies when baking brownies, I'm no witch. But I bet I can hire one.

I type in the words "witchcraft spell" and arrive at the website of the California Astrology Association. It reads:

Want to right a wrong?
You've come to the right place.
We guarantee you won't be disappointed!
Now it's your turn to fight back!

Now we're talking, I think. I scroll down the page.

The Retribution Spell is a powerful way to get even with someone who has no regard for others.

Has someone insulted you, tricked you, embarrassed you? Do you feel powerless? Well now there's something you can do. For only $19.95, we will cast a retribution spell on your behalf.

Hmm. Twenty bucks. Not a bad price. I guess witchcraft has gotten cheaper these days. Even witches give a good bargain.

I keep reading. This witchcraft website has me mesmerized:

A retribution spell will lower his self-esteem, deplete his energy, and throw him off-kilter.

Perfect, I think. Just what Carlton needs. A little lowering of his huge, blimp-sized self-esteem.

I click the "ORDER NOW" button and a shipping information page comes up. I type in my name and credit card info. In the last box, it says, **Details for the spell.** And **Please be specific!** I pause for a moment and then type:

Carlton Connors.

Austin, Texas. 36 years old. Manipulated and lied to me. Deserves retribution spell and more! Incantation should include the fact that he's seeking a trophy wife to match his trophy life. P.S. Please make sure he never gets the sailboat he always wanted.

I hit the send button and get an instant reply. **Your spell has been cast.**

Good, that should do it, I think, sitting back in my chair. I can't help it. I begin to cry.

Rushing to the bathroom, I lean forward and stare in the mirror. My eyes are puffy and dark underneath. I feel swollen, bruised. Angry. Overwrought.

And fat.

The pores on my nose look dirty. Like someone threw pepper in my face. Rainforest facial, my ass. I would've been better off with a giant blue tub of Noxzema. A cheap three-dollar fix.

Oh well. So I got ripped off at the spa. So what? I guess this calls for chocolate. Maybe a milkshake. Or some comfort food. I consider dialing my brother, but I call Heather instead. Heather is light and airy. My brother would probably start praying for me. And I'm really not in the mood for a Hail Mary today.

Fifteen minutes later, I hear a light tap on the door. Heather's such a lady. The way she knocks. So politely. As if she's a little unsure of herself.

It's sweet.

I swing open the door and see my best friend is wielding a large potted plant. She's dressed head to toe in a little flowery dress and little matching flowery flip-flops. She's even got flow-ery barrettes in her hair. It's as if Laura Ashley threw up all over her.

But Heather can pull it off. She looks adorable, of course.

"For you!" she titters, hoisting the plant into my arms.

I stare down at the plant like it's my enemy.

"You know I'm a black thumb," I say. "Remember what hap-pened with the last plant you gave me?"

Heather bites her lip. "That one was touchy."

"It was a cactus!"

My best friend squeezes past me into the living room and takes a seat on the couch. She crosses her legs and folds her hands prettily on her knee, like she's on an interview.

"Relax," I tell her. "You're pregnant. Take a load off." (P.S. When I'm at home, I prop my feet up on the coffee table.)

"I *am* relaxed," Heather says, smiling perkily. She's sitting erect, her back as straight as an ironing board. I imagine her presiding over a Tri-Delt sorority meeting.

I set the plant down next to the front door. "You're taking this with you when you leave," I say, pointing my finger at her.

"C'mon, Maddy. You could use a little greenery in this apart-ment," Heather says. She stretches out both her arms and mo-tions around like a game-show hostess. "It's like a morgue in here," she says.

"Thanks."

"No, I mean. It's nice to have a plant. A plant is *Life*, Maddy."

"I killed a cactus, remember?"

"Even a cactus needs a little TLC," Heather says. "You left it on the windowsill and forgot to water it."

"Since when does a cactus need water!"

Heather shrugs. "Everything drinks," she says, simply.

Jesus, I could learn a few tricks from her.

I sink down on the couch next to my friend and try to sit up straight and tall, but it's too much damn effort. I fall back into the cushions. A heap of grungy sweat pants, stinky T-shirt, and stringy hair.

"What's wrong, Maddy?" Heather demands. She whirls around and gives me a worried look. The type of look the ambulance driver gives the gunshot victim.

"Allergies," I say. I grab a Kleenex off the coffee table and dab underneath my nose for effect. "I'm stopped up tighter than Martha Stewart's bed sheets."

Heather rolls her eyes. "Don't make fun of my Martha," she warns. "I love that woman. In fact, you remind me of her."

"Why? Because I'm so damn prickly?"

"No, because she's a great businesswoman. She's got a great mind. And so do you."

"Aw shucks," I say.

"I'm serious," Heather says.

"Look, if I was a great businesswoman, I would still be in charge of Organics 4 Kids. Instead, I'm stressing about what movie I'm going to rent tonight."

"Come over for dinner," Heather says. "Michael and I are doing Shabbat. I've hired Rabbi Moscowitz to come over and cut the bread for us."

"You've *hired* him?"

"You know what I mean, Maddy. Don't give me grief."

"Sorry."

"He's coming over and he's slicing the holler bread."

"Challah bread, Heather. Not holler."

"What?"

"Never mind."

"Ooh!" Heather claps her petite little hands together. "And I bought some kosher wine," she titters. "But don't worry, it's the good stuff," she says, nodding her head approvingly.

"Ah, a good Manischevitz."

"Oh yes," Heather exclaims. She presses her hand against her chest. All prim and lady-like.

"There are wonderful vineyards in the Golan," she gushes. "In fact, Michael says all the fighting for the Golan Heights—it's really for the wine."

I look at Heather and see that, bless her heart, she's completely earnest. She doesn't even realize when her husband is jerking her chain.

Don't get me wrong, Heather's a smart girl. But she's not book smart. She's smart in more subtle ways. Like she knows how many fat grams are in tomato bisque. She knows Brad Pitt's birthday. She knows if a Hermes scarf matches a certain pair of shoes. She's that kind of smart. Girly Smart. And that's no small thing, believe me. I'm the last person on Earth who could pick out the differences between off-white, cream, and taupe.

But she still can't seem to find her inner Jewishness. She doesn't have that keen Jewish wit, as they say. She's a little slow on the uptake.

Heather leans back on the sofa, finally, and pats her small belly. "I'm a size 4 now," she sighs.

I could kill her, I really could. If she weren't so damn sweet. And my best friend to boot.

"Wow, almost time for Plus-Sizes," I say, sarcastically.

Heather looks at me and I see her eyes twinkling. "I don't mind, Maddy, because my boobs are fabulous!"

Great. My pregnant size 4 girlfriend has fabulous boobs, now.

I look down at my own boobs. I'm not wearing a bra so they seem a little droopy. Like they belong on an old lady.

Heather shakes her head. "Oy Vay. I'm so nervous about my conversion test," she says.

"You're going to do fine. The Rabbis just want to see that you're committed to this."

"Oh I know, Maddy. It's just that—I can't seem to get anything right. I mean, I went to the grocery store last night and asked the manager where I could find the Filtered Fish."

I chuckle and pat Heather's shoulder. "Look, you're doing your best. And Michael loves you for trying. I mean, c'mon. You spent August in Israel. It was 120 degrees in the shade."

"Small price to pay," she murmurs. I notice her mood is changing. Her face seems dark, suddenly.

"Hey, that reminds me!" I say. My mood has just changed too—for the better. I jump up and rush to my bedroom. I return with a book and hold it up in the air. Like Moses with the Ten Commandments.

"Voila!" I say. "We're going to practice."

I flash Heather the title.

"The Idiot's Guide to Becoming a Jew," she reads.

"I figured out what your problem is," I say.

Heather stares down at the floor. "Yeah, I'm an idiot," she mumbles.

"Beep! Wrong! You're trying to learn too much from a bunch of complicated books," I say. "It's time to simplify!"

Heather looks at me with a hopeful expression.

"Look, I made flash cards," I say, holding up a stack of note cards.

Heather's face brightens and she claps her hands again, a dainty little clap. "Ooh, I love flash cards!" she gushes.

"You're going to pass this test with flying colors," I say. "Okay, first things first." I pull up the first flash card. "What's a matzoh ball?"

"The Rabbis aren't going to ask me that, silly," Heather giggles.

"We're getting into the swing of things," I explain.

"A matzoh ball is made with egg whites and matzoh meal. You roll it and put it in a chicken soup broth," she says.

"Very good." I show her the back of the flash card where I've printed a recipe for matzoh ball soup from the Internet.

When I was making the flash cards, I decided to start with a cooking question because I didn't want Heather to be scared right off the bat. Testing her Jewish I.Q. will pose a challenge.

"Next question. Why do the Jewish people celebrate Passover?"

Heather chews her lip. "Passover comes from the Hebrew word, "Pesach," meaning to pass over, to exempt, or to spare. It refers to the time when God "passed over" the houses of the Jews when he was slaying the firstborn of Egypt. "Pesach" is also the name of the sacrificial offering, or lamb, that was sacrificed in the temple."

"Wow. Very impressive," I say. "And absolutely correct."

"I've been reading up," Heather informs me.

She leans back on the couch and I can tell she's really getting into this flash card stuff.

"Hit me again," she says. And her face is beaming.

I playfully punch her in the arm. A light little tap. "There, I'm hitting you."

"You're a goof," she says.

"I'm Martha Stewart," I reply.

Chapter 20

"How do I look?" I ask Carlton. I do a comical supermodel strut across the bedroom, swing around with my hand on my hip, strike a pose, and pout my lips.

He chuckles and straightens his tie. "Like a champ," he says.

I watch him walk into the bathroom and lean in toward the mirror.

"Jesus, I need a cigarette," he says. He finishes fumbling with his tie and admires himself in the mirror. I see a hint of a smile streak across his lips.

I sashay up to him, in my best suit, my interview suit, and wrap my arms around his waist.

"We're going to get this money today, don't you worry," I say.

He turns around and pecks me quickly on the lips. I smell his cologne, the faint smell of burning wood, like a fire out in a log cabin, and my knees go momentarily weak. God, he's gorgeous. This man I love. I stare up into Carlton's beautiful eyes.

"I've been waiting for this moment my entire life," he says. "To present a phenomenal business idea in front of my father. In his boardroom."

"That's why *you* should make the presentation," I protest.

Carlton puts his hand to my lips. "Shhh. We've already been over this," he says.

I notice he's sweating slightly. A few tiny droplets forming above his upper lip.

"You're nervous," I say, pointing to his face.

He peers into the mirror and wipes his mouth with the back of his hand, self-consciously.

"It's hot as a bitch in this house," he says. "Why don't you ever turn on the AC?"

"It's your house, too, you know," I say.

"Please, Maddy. You own this place. It's your name on the title, not mine."

"If you want me to add your name to the title, why don't you just say so?"

Carlton rolls his eyes. "Because you know I can't help with the mortgage payments. Not on this goddamn hourly wage my dad is paying me. You'd think the son of the CEO would make more than your average day laborer! But he's paying me the same as all the other Mexicans working the shit-shift!"

"He's giving you a great hands-on experience, babe. I mean, it makes sense for you to experience every aspect of running a company, from the ground up. And how would it look if you made more money than those other guys? They'd hate you."

"I don't care. After today, I hope I'll never have to set foot in that shit-hole of a warehouse again," Carlton muses. He swings back around to the mirror. I watch him as he adds gel to his hair and combs it back in a crisp, formal style.

"After today, you're going to be CEO of Organics 4 Kids," I say. I put my arms around his waist and hug him from behind.

He cups his hands over mine. I feel him fingering the Juliet ring on my left hand.

"You better take this off," he says, holding my hand up. "I don't want my dad thinking we got engaged overnight."

I stare down at the bathroom floor. "Don't you think it's about time we told him? I mean, I've had the ring for months, Carlton. He knows we live together. We're in our thirties. Jesus! We're adults," I say. And I realize my voice sounds whiney. Child-like.

"Maddy," he says, softly. He slips the ring off my finger and places it gently on the bathroom counter. "Today is not the day. You know that, sweetie. We want my dad's mind to be strictly on our business plan. I swear if he sees this ring, all he'll be thinking about is pre-nups."

"I already told you I'd sign one," I say. "Especially if it makes Daddy Dollar-Sign feel better."

Carlton loosens my arms from around his waist. "Don't call him that," he warns.

"Sorry," I murmur. I walk into the bedroom and slip on my heels. I'd prefer to wear a conservative pair of loafers since I'm going to be standing up during my presentation, but heels make me taller.

Carlton's dad, Forest Connors, is a big man. An assuming presence in a room. So I need all the height I can get.

My ring finger feels bare without the Juliet. I rub the tan line where the ring used to be. Something is missing.

Carlton strolls into the room looking like a Calvin Klein model in his dark, tailored Italian suit. He grins at me—his famous, winning grin, and takes me by the arm.

"You ready?" he asks.

I sigh. "Ready as I'll ever be."

He taps his watch, the watch his father gave him, the Patek Phillipe. "It's do or die time," he says.

"Leap Before You Look," I reply.

Three hours later, I'm at the head of the boardroom, standing in front of Carlton, his father, and a group of six men in serious suits. My new heels are causing blisters on the back of my feet. I'm aching, but I smile through the pain.

"As you can see, gentlemen, the only possible competitor will be Giganto Foods," I say in a confident voice. "But they haven't even begun to enter the organics market for kids. So our company—Organics 4 Kids—will be the first to enter this new niche market."

I smile and make careful eye contact with each man around the table. Carlton's father nods at me, in a clipped, no-nonsense fashion.

"That concludes our presentation," I say, motioning toward Carlton. He's sitting at the end of the boardroom and he smiles, nervously.

"We've worked out all the angles, Dad," he says, a sheepish grin crossing his face.

I see a shadow cross Forest Connors' face when he hears Carlton refer to him as "Dad." It's inappropriate for Carlton to say this in such a formal setting and Carlton immediately realizes his mistake. He assumes a professional tone and says, "Madeline and I have prepared an investor prospectus for each of you."

Reaching down into my messenger bag, Carlton pulls out seven navy blue folders. He stands and passes them around to each man at the table.

I take a seat at the end of the table. As Carlton walks by me, he whispers, "Great job," in a muffled tone.

Forest Connors flips through the prospectus. The room is suddenly quiet. I hear a clock on the wall ticking. Everyone waits until the Big Man on Campus speaks. He swivels around in his chair and stares at me, his eyebrows raised. "You're proposing Carlton as CEO and yourself as Chief Operating Officer?"

"Correct," I say.

"And you are also proposing a 15 percent ownership stake for each of you in the Class A shares?"

"That's right."

"The problem as I see it, Madeline, is you don't have any skin in the game," Carlton's father says, crossing his arms over his linebacker-sized chest. "You're not risking any of your own money."

I shift around in my chair. I'm wearing my best dress suit. My interview suit. But I've got a run in my panty hose. I see it. Right below my skirt. Heading dangerously close to my knee. I tug the skirt down.

I glance at Carlton. He's taken a seat next to me at the table. He takes a sip of coffee from a Styrofoam cup. I can tell he's nervous. The cup quivers a little in his hand. We anticipated this question, Carlton and I, but Carlton was supposed to answer it. So far, he's sitting quietly in his seat, staring down at the table. And leaving me high and dry.

"I'm quitting my job, Mr. Connors," I say. "That's a risk."

Forest Connors glances at the other men in the room. His other investors. He takes a deep breath. Like a man about to deliver bad news.

"Yes, and to compensate you, we're willing to pay you a generous salary and give you any title you choose. But quite frankly, I feel uncomfortable issuing you a seat on the board, or voting power with the company. You're what we call 'sweat equity.' You've got to earn your shares in the company by working for them."

He shrugs his bullish shoulders. "It's business 101," he says.

"I wrote this business plan," I stutter, holding up my black notebook. "The concept for Organics 4 Kids is my idea."

Carlton's dad flutters his hand, as if shooing away a fly. "Could've been a work-for-hire," he says.

"But I'm quitting my job with Henry Wrona," I say. "I've worked for him fourteen years! All through college and grad school."

Carlton's father leans forward in his chair. "How is ol' Henry?" he asks. He's eyeing me like a vulture eyes a wounded baby deer.

Before I can answer, Forest Connors says. "Problem with Henry is he's a small fish. He thinks and acts like a big fish, but he ain't. It's a shame, really. Cause the man's got talent."

I glance at Carlton and see he's fiddling with his watch.

Fantastic.

"Well, I like Henry as a boss very much. In fact, I've never had to worry about getting my paycheck," I say. "Henry always pays his bills on time."

Forest Connors' eyes harden and he stares at me. A cold stare. He's wondering if I'm sassing him. Which I am. So I play it off. I mean, what the hell am I doing? Forest Connors has the power to make or break Organics 4 Kids. What am I doing? Shooting myself in the foot?

I flip my hair, giggle, and do the girl thing. Right in the boardroom. Like the boardroom babe that I am.

"And heaven knows I need to pay off my student loans," I say.

I look over at Carlton. He's staring at me, but he suddenly breaks out into a relieved smile. "Maddy's always worried about her monthly student loan payments," he says, backing me up.

Forest Connors nods quietly.

The clock ticks by and no one says a single word.

Carlton shoots me a look from across the table as if to say he's sorry. But it's too late.

Finally, Forest Connors speaks. "I'll back this venture, but only on certain terms. First, Carlton is President and CEO. Second, I'll hold one-third of the shares, Carlton will hold one-third, and these other fellows will hold one-third. We can design a plan to award you shares, Madeline, based on performance over time. I'll have my lawyers write up the paperwork," he informs us.

I glance at Carlton and see him trying to hide a smile. This is the moment he's been waiting for. His father passing down the torch, if you will.

"We enjoyed your presentation, Madeline, and I'm sure you'll make a fine addition to the company," Forest Connors says.

I suddenly realize Henry was right. In one swift move, I've lost all control. I've been sucker-punched.

I remember Henry telling me about Forest Connors. "He made all his money in medical supplies," Henry said. "The man positively 'minted money,' with these incredibly high markups on wheelchairs and oxygen tanks."

At the investor meeting, I look helplessly from Carlton to his father and around the table at his father's cronies. Forest Connors is a shark, all right.

Carlton walks around the table and sits down in an empty chair next to me.

"I don't feel comfortable being *just an employee*," I say.

Carlton grabs my knee under the table. He whispers in my ear. "Don't worry, sweetie. You'll own some of my shares in the company soon."

Which is a hint toward a wedding date, I guess.

"Very soon," he says, winking at me.

Carlton leans back in his chair. Eyes the men around the table. "Dad, I don't want Maddy to get the short end of the stick here. Even if you won't give her the title of Chief Operating Officer, I want her to be Director of Marketing and P.R. And I want her to be free to hire whomever she wants."

Carlton's father looks at me. Regards me like he's looking at a strange new species of bug.

"Fine," he says, finally, slapping his palm on the table. THWAP! "We've got some housekeeping issues to cover. Let's move on."

Chapter 21

My brother calls himself an "addiction specialist." I've seen his speech. It always begins the same way. He walks to the microphone, steadies himself, and says in a low voice, "When I was fifteen, my parents died in a car wreck. That was the night I took my first drink."

The room is always crowded with hardened drug users and alcoholics. And everyone is usually under twenty years old. Ronnie Piatro deals strictly with teenagers. "Gotta catch it before it starts," he always says.

Ten years ago, I remember kidnapping my brother out of the filthy, drug-infested apartment he'd been sleeping in. There were a few dogs, some feral-looking cats, the smell of urine and burning drugs. Like sulfur and marijuana and other smells I couldn't identify. I remember seeing all the tools for cooking drugs on a dirty coffee table, littered with cigarette butts and beer cans; broken light bulbs; what looked like a camping burner; propane gas; even syringes.

I kidnapped my brother. He was barely conscious. I drove three hours from San Antonio to Houston and dumped him in the Medical Center. Every few hours, I checked on him and brought him food and water. He went through the throes of coming down. The detox process. He screamed, sweated, overturned the furniture, smashed all the lamps.

At one point, he attacked me with his fists and threatened to kill me. I knew this wasn't Ronnie. This was the drugs. My brother was a good soul. A kind, gentle, funny person. Four days later, he agreed to enter a three-month, inpatient, rehab program in Jackson, Mississippi.

And that's where he hooked up with Snoop Santino. Why bother snorting it or shooting up, he and Snoop decided, if you could sell the stuff and make a killing instead.

Snoop and Ronnie devised several legitimate business fronts to mask the drug deals, and soon became a fearsome team.

It took a bullet, thirty-seven hours of surgery, and a drug deal gone bad to finally jar Ronnie out of the criminal life.

That night in the hospital, I cornered Snoop Santino.

"My brother is *finished* working for you," I'd hissed, pointing my finger in his thick chest.

"Your brother knows too much," he'd replied, like a threat.

"Ronnie will never talk, and you know it," I'd said, and then I did something I never imagined I would do. I leaned into Snoop Santino's face.

We'd had a stare-down contest—me and Snoop Santino—one of the most feared drug dealers in the state. He'd shrugged, finally, and skulked out the hospital door, with a few of his henchmen in tow.

"Best day of my life," my brother now says. When speaking to his troubled teen groups. He lays it all out for them. Rolls up his sleeves and shows them his arms, where the needle marks used to be.

"I'd go to Mexico and shoot up twenty times a day," he'd say. "It's a miracle I'm still alive. But I believe God kept me here for a reason." Then he points around the room. "And that reason is you," he says. "And you, and you, and you," he says, pointing at each kid throughout the room.

Unlike other rehab counselors, my brother is still in close contact with what he calls the "bad element."

"Why ignore the street dealers?" he'll say. "They control supply." He tells me that he doesn't trust law enforcement to do the job. "I meet up with the dealers myself and tell them to lay off selling to these kids," he says.

When I ask my brother how he does it, he says he appeals to their inner morality. "Drug dealers are businessmen," he'll say. "I just call them up and remind them that I used to work for Snoop Santino. This gets their attention real fast. Then I tell them the obvious, i.e., they've got plenty of adult users. They don't need to take a child's lunch money."

"Does it work?" I ask.

My brother shrugs. "No one wants to feel like a child molester," he says.

I drive to see my brother. His official full-time job is at an inpatient rehab campus outside Austin. It's nicknamed "the farm."

The place is surrounded by a grim wall. I wish someone would paint the wall blue, or pink. Something better than cold, embattled gray. I drive through the main gates.

The guard checks my purse for drugs. And then surprises me with a full-on check of my car.

"Go ahead," he says, clicking open a locked gate.

I walk to my brother's small office. It's got a poster on it. A bunch of people smiling and holding hands. Rehabbers. My brother is in the picture, too.

"Today is the first day of the rest of your life," it says.

Terrific, I think.

I pause outside the door. Ronnie opens it, wide. He's grinning. He's never been touchy-feely, the type of guy who needs a hug, but he grabs me anyway and squeezes me tightly.

My little brother.

"Maddy-go-laddy," he says. He ushers me into his office, clears a stack of files from a chair, and motions for me to sit.

Over his desk is the Serenity Prayer:

GOD GRANT ME THE SERENITY TO ACCEPT THE THINGS I CANNOT CHANGE, COURAGE TO CHANGE THE THINGS I CAN, AND THE WISDOM TO KNOW THE DIFFERENCE.

On his shirt, he's wearing a nametag. It says, "HELLO, MY NAME IS RONNIE. AND I'M AN ADDICT."

I point to the nametag. "Subtle," I say.

He chuckles. "These kids need to know they're not alone. And let me tell you, Maddy, they feel a lot more comfortable when they know their counselors aren't just blowing a bunch of hot air up their asses."

My brother sighs. He looks older than his twenty-nine years. The by-product of hard drugs and fast living.

"How's it going?" I ask.

I watch as he reaches across his desk and grabs at a pack of Marlboro's. I think he's about to light one, but he just sits there, with his hand on the pack.

"I had a girl o.d. on me last night. She escaped over the wall, hitched a ride with some jerk-off, and then did a bunch of crystal-meth."

He shakes his head back and forth. "I swear that stuff is the devil." He looks up at me suddenly, remembers I'm there, and smiles. "Sorry. Let's talk about something light. What's going on with you?"

"I've been dreaming of Carlton," I say. "And every night it's the same dream. We're alone. On a beautiful sailboat. Having sex. And then he tries to strangle me. Like in the movie *Dead Calm*."

My brother slides a cigarette between his lips. Flicks his lighter.

"That's fucked up," he says, exhaling smoke through his nose.

"It gets worse. I've been researching cyanide websites. I even paid a witch twenty dollars to cast a spell on him."

"You went to see a witch?"

"Actually, you can hex someone over the Internet, now."

"Holy Mary! You're worrying me, Maddy! Do I need to get one of my crisis counselors in here?" Ronnie asks, and he's looking at me like I'm the weird one.

"No. I'm not really going to KILL him kill him. I'm just—venting."

My brother points to a crucifix on the wall above my head. "What would Jesus do?" he asks, and I think he's kidding, but he's dead serious.

"Turn the other cheek, I guess," I say, staring at my shoes.

"That's right," my brother says, slapping his knee with conviction.

"What's happened to this society!" I protest. "When did we get to be such pushovers? I mean, what happened to an eye for an eye?"

My brother shrugs. "We've evolved," he says. "There's no such thing as vigilante justice."

"But Carlton broke—" I stop.

"There's no law against breaking someone's heart," my brother says, solemnly. "There's no law against screwing someone in business. There's no law against sleeping with someone and not telling them you have an STD."

I raise my finger in the air. "Michael said it's called Reckless Endangerment."

"That's for HIV," my brother says.

I don't know how Ronnie knows this. But he does.

"Look, Maddy. There's no law against being a shitty person. And we all know Carlton's shitty. So move on. Count yourself lucky you didn't have his kid."

I cringe. Hearing my brother say this makes me think of the one thing I haven't told him. *Or anyone.*

My brother holds his cigarette between two fingers, casually —a man who's done it ten thousand times before. He muses as the smoke curls into the air. "This is the worst drug of 'em all," he says, stabbing the cigarette into a black tray. He pushes the tray aside as if he's angry with it.

"I know you can find someone to help me," I say.

My brother sighs. And it's a profound sigh. Long and weighty. As if he's got the world resting on his shoulders.

"Look, Maddy. You've always been the logical one. The person who thinks through every decision. If you want someone to beat Carlton's ass black and blue to make yourself feel better, I'll find someone. Or I'll do it myself. But I think you're being irrational. And that's not you. That's not the sister who saved my life," he says, steadying me with his gaze.

"You saved your own life, Ronnie. You made the choice," I say.

"Bullshit," he says. He raises his hand to his head and salutes me.

I stare down at the floor in my brother's office. At the institutional-looking carpet. Carpet the color of burnt oatmeal.

"What's happened to you, Maddy? What's happened to my positive, high-on-life sister? The sister who always says, 'Leap Before You Look?'" Ronnie asks. He shakes another cigarette from the pack and tucks it behind his ear.

"That's what I did with Carlton, Ronnie! I did the whole 'leap before you look,' thing—"

My brother doesn't answer.

I glance over at him and see that he's bowed his head in prayer.

I really shouldn't involve him in this, I think. But I can't help myself. Carlton Connors haunts my every waking moment.

And even my dreams.

Chapter 22

A week after the big investor meeting, I found the pill bottle. In the bathroom, in a side pocket of his dop kit. I was looking for a condom. We usually didn't use them because Carlton hated the way they felt.

"Don't make me bag it," he'd say, flashing me his sexiest grin.

But tonight was different. I was in the dangerous part of the month and—as much as Carlton professed his control—the rhythm method seemed risky.

I wasn't a candidate for birth control because of a hormone problem I'd had since childhood. So I did what every good Italian Catholic woman does.

I prayed. And counted the days, keeping a meticulous calendar of every time I thought I could possibly be ovulating. In the fifteen years since I'd started having sex, it had somehow, miraculously, worked.

Heather told me I was "playing with fire."

"You should make Carlton wear one Every Single Time," she said. "He'll get used to it."

But I didn't listen. I wanted him to feel good. I wanted sex between us to be natural. And besides, ripping open a condom always seemed to be a bit of a buzz kill.

No matter how creative I got—extra sensitive, glow-in-the-dark, lambskin, and the occasional French tickler, Carlton still acted as though I'd dumped a bucket of ice over his head.

He suffered through it, sure. And he'd smile when I'd make jokes. Trying to find humor in the situation. Lighten the mood, as they say.

"Look out, babe! I think this thing is trying to suffocate you," I'd say, as I fumbled around. Trying to unroll it. My hands nervous and slippery.

The moment we finished, he'd tear it off, throw it on the floor, a look of disdain on his face.

I always—always picked it up. Wrapped it in toilet paper. Threw it away. It was the least I could do, I figured. After all, he was the one making all the compromises.

So, finding the condom box empty, and knowing Carlton was on his way home, I began a frantic search. For an errant condom. The one that got away.

I dug through every drawer in the bathroom.

A-ha! I thought, flicking my finger in the air. Carlton's dop kit. Under the sink.

The pill bottle was one I'd never seen before.

It said: *Carlton Connors. Take one in the morning. With food.* I checked the date on the bottle. Hmm. Two weeks ago. Carlton never told me he went to the doctor.

Just then, Carlton walked in the door.

I held up the bottle. "What's this? What's Valtrixo?" I asked, reading the name off the prescription.

His face turned a shade of crimson I'd never seen before.

"I love you," he said, immediately.

"Oh . . . Kay," I replied.

"Seriously, babe? What's this for? Jock itch? Hemorrhoids?" I giggled and covered my mouth with my hand. "I think it's cute you're embarrassed," I said, kissing him on the cheek.

He grabbed my shoulders and steered me over to the bed. "Sit," he said.

I was suddenly nervous.

This was no jock itch.

"What is it, Carlton?" I asked, almost in a whisper.

"There's something I've been meaning to tell you for a while, Maddy."

"What? Ohmigod, Carlton. What!"

He stood up and began pacing the bedroom. "You're going to be mad, but I want you to hear me out. First things first, I want you to know I love you. I want us to get married." He swung around, knelt down on his knees, grabbed both my hands, and kissed them. First one. Then the other.

"I didn't tell you because I didn't want you to leave me."

I sit on the bed, still as a statue. Carlton is on his knees, on the floor in front of me. I wait for the bomb to drop.

He stares past me. "After Megan and I got divorced, I was in a state of confusion. Depressed, you know. So I went out with the guys a lot. To different bars. To Vegas. We all got hammered. And I had a few girls . . ." he trails off. "I don't even remember most of their names, Maddy."

"Nice," I say.

Carlton takes my hand and kisses my ring finger. He notices I'm not wearing the Juliet ring.

"Where's your ring?"

"You wanted me to take it off before the investor meeting, remember?" I say, in a caustic voice.

Carlton rushes into the bathroom, spots the ring on the counter, and comes back into the bedroom. He kneels down on one knee and pushes the ring back on my finger.

"Tell me more," I say.

Carlton stays on his knee. He doesn't look at me. "There was this one girl," he says, taking a deep breath. "I found some pills in her medicine cabinet but it was too late. I'd already been infected."

"Infected?" I pull my hands away. Carlton looks up at me, a wounded dog.

God, he's gorgeous, I think. I don't want to think this way, but with him staring up at me with his movie star eyes, I can't help myself.

Carlton runs his hand through his hair. "Genital herpes. It's not that serious, Maddy. Sixty percent of American men and women in our age group have it."

"And you've got it?" I ask, even though I know the answer.

"Yeah."

"We've been having unprotected sex, Carlton! We LIVE together! When were you planning to tell me?"

"I've been careful, Maddy. You've got to understand. Whenever I've had a flare-up, I haven't slept with you. I check myself every day. In the shower. Scouts Honor." He raises his hand, like a boy scout taking an oath.

"I swear to you, Maddy. I would never, EVER put you at risk."

"But you did put me at risk, Carlton. No matter how careful you were!"

"If you don't have any symptoms, you probably haven't been infected," he says.

"Probably?" I stand from the bed, abruptly, and pace the room. "First you leave me high and dry in the investor meeting. You completely accept the fact that your father basically robbed me of any power in Organics 4 Kids—my idea!—and now—this!"

I stare into Carlton's eyes and see that they're surprisingly moist.

"Maddy, I'm going to marry you. And you'll get a huge share of the company, no matter what my father says about it. I promise you." Carlton lowers his voice. "Please understand that the reason I didn't tell you about the herpes is because I love you so much. I didn't want to risk losing you." He kisses my ring. "Forever, my Juliet," he says, softly.

I push past him and march into the living room. Clutching a pillow and blanket under my arm.

He follows after me. "Don't sleep on the couch," he says.

But it's too late.

I'm already pulling out the mattress.

⌒ Chapter 23

Heather has invited me over for the Big Day. The "unveiling of the nursery," as she calls it. I swing by with an early baby gift. Something I bought from the Internet. Now that I'm officially an Internet warrior, whatever that means.

It's a Hanukah bear with a little wood Dreidel around its neck. I got it off a website called "OyToys For Jewish Joys."

Heather rips the bear out of the gift bag and literally squeals. "Oh my Gaaahh, Maddy! I absolutely One Hundred Percent Adore It!"

She cradles the bear in her arms, like a child herself, and nuzzles it against her chin. "Let's show Michael!" she says, leading me from the kitchen to the living room. Heather calls it the "sitting room," but it's nothing fancy. It's just a plain ol' comfortable television room filled with the typical starter-marriage furniture. Mismatched stuff that looks like it came from Pottery Barn or IKEA. Heather's decorated as best she could with a few lamps and throw pillows to make everything nice and cozy. Her piece de resistance is an antique prayer rug she brought back from her summer in the Middle East. But this doesn't compare to Michael's finishing touch—a gigantic, 60-inch, big-screen plasma TV that barely fits in the room. Michael calls it "his baby."

I see him sitting on the couch, a bucket of popcorn in his lap.

Heather says, "Look at this adorable little Hanukah bear Maddy gave us!"

"Cute," Michael says, staring at the TV. He points to his movie-theater-sized screen. I can see Julia Roberts. An almost life-sized Julia Roberts onscreen.

Julia says, "They're called boobs, Ed."

"They're called boobs, Ed!" Michael squeals, hooting, and honking, and slapping his knee like a hillbilly.

Heather turns to me and rolls her eyes. "He's watching *Erin Brockovitch*. AGAIN!" She sighs and pats Michael's head as we breeze by. "Some husbands dream of speedboats and swimsuit models. My husband dreams of medical malpractice."

"McDonald's coffee," Michael corrects her.

Heather turns to me. "You know the big lawsuit where McDonald's was serving its coffee too hot?"

I nod. Sometimes Heather and Michael do this jive where they both talk at the same time. Finish each other's sentences, that type of thing. They start to do this now. Talking over each other. Something about McDonald's coffee.

Michael swings around and flings a piece of popcorn in Heather's direction. It hits her shoulder and falls to the floor.

"Mature," she says, crossing her arms over her chest.

"I'll pick it up," he drawls in his fake Southern accent. "Don't git your knickers in a twist, darlin'."

"What about the McDonald's case?" I ask, because I know Michael wants to tell me. He likes to be the center of attention, which is why he loves standing up in front of the jury box and telling twelve fine citizens of Travis County what's what.

Michael says, "Well, Maddy, if you must know, I dreamt of that woman calling me and telling me she burned herself because the coffee was too damn hot— And in my dream, I say, 'well, where'd ya get the coffee?' And she says, 'McDonald's.'"

"You should have heard him moaning in his sleep," Heather says.

"Yeah," Michael says, "Can you imagine the lawyer that got to sue Mickey D's? I bet he smiled his way to the bank," he says, with his Southern drawl.

Michael turns back to the TV. "You know. Julia Roberts is one hot tamale in this movie," he says.

Heather tosses some popcorn kernels on the floor near Michael and stomps on them. I hear the kernels crunch under her sandal.

"That's not nice," Michael drawls. But even as he says it, he looks up at his wife and smiles.

I look at Heather with her supermodel face. *I guess a man will forgive anything with a face like that*, I think. Heather is a real knockout. She's got the body of a young Twiggy or Kate Moss, and a face that makes most red-blooded American men do a double take. When I'm with her, I'm the invisible friend.

Heather leads me into the new nursery.

"Ta-da!" she says, flicking the light on. "Well," she says, swinging her arms out like a game show hostess again, "What do you think?"

I look around. At the walls painted a soft, robin's egg blue. At the white crib in the corner. At the miniature Alexander Calder mobile hanging over the crib from the newly painted white ceiling.

Armed only with a paintbrush and a shoestring budget, I see Heather's done a tremendous job.

"Wow," I say. "Make that double wow."

"You like it?"

"Did you hand-paint all these little bears?"

"Stencils," Heather says.

"You're going to be one terrific mom."

Heather smiles at me, beatifically.

Saint Heather.

"I may not be the brains of this family," she says, "but at least I've got an eye for color."

"Hey. Stop selling yourself short in the brains department," I say.

Heather always does this. And it gets annoying. My best friend may not be the brightest bulb in the room, but she's certainly not dumb. And I think having a heart of gold counts for something. Not to mention her looks. A girl as beautiful as Heather could probably get away with being a bitch. But Heather is a "pure soul," as my brother likes to say.

Heather looks around the room, admiring her handiwork. "I'm glad you like it," she says, flicking off the light. She motions for me to follow her. "C'mon. Let's give Michael some more grief," she says.

"Gladly."

Heather waltzes into the living room, grabs the bucket of popcorn, and dumps the entire thing over Michael's head.

"Hey!" he says, jumping up. He grabs my pregnant girlfriend, lifts her off the ground, and tosses her softly on the couch. "Looks like someone needs a spankin'!" he says, as he gently manhandles her.

"Michael stop!" Heather shrieks and begins giggling uncontrollably as Michael turns her over in his lap and begins patting her bottom.

"Who's been a bad girl?" Michael asks.

(Oh Lord. I guess this is their idea of foreplay.)

"I was just leaving," I say, letting myself out the door.

"Bye, Maddy!" Heather and Michael both shout, in unison.

I tread out to my car, haul myself into the driver's seat, and slam the door.

I drive slowly, wishing there was someplace else to go. Like maybe a movie. But I've seen everything worth seeing. Plus a few not worth seeing.

I drive in silence and try not to think the unthinkable. The "maybe Carlton will come to his senses and come crawling back to me" thought. I picture him on my doorstep, on his knees, the Juliet ring in his hand.

"Marry me, Maddy," he says. When I say yes, Carlton stands, and proceeds to strangle me.

Such are my dreams. Every single night.

Which is why I really don't know why I'm pulling into my garage right now. I mean, it's not even dark yet. And I'm already dreading going to sleep.

I ease the car inside, put it in park, and just sit.

Hmm. How long does it take this carbon monoxide thing to work, I wonder? Punching a button on my dashboard, I watch in the rearview as the garage door closes down behind me.

The engine is still running. I unlock my seatbelt. Could I kill myself in a matter of minutes? Hours? How long does it take? I crack open a window and let the engine idle.

I could probably sit here for days and it wouldn't matter. And then I suddenly remember what I learned from the carbon monoxide websites . . .

Carbon monoxide is a silent killer. The odorless, colorless, poisonous gas attacks before you even know what's happening.

The next thing I know, someone is shaking me.

"Jesus, Maddy! Are you trying to kill yourself?" I crack open my eyes and see a vision in pink. It's Heather. And she's wearing a pink jogging suit.

"You can't kill yourself before my baby shower! I need you!" she screeches.

"Huh? What happened?" I ask, and my voice is dry, clogged.

Heather jerks open the driver's side door and pulls me out of the car. My head is pounding like someone's got a jackhammer to my ear.

"You're asleep in your car! In the garage. And the car is running!" Heather shouts. Her voice sounds far away. "I'm taking you to the emergency room!"

I'm confused. Groggy. And I've apparently almost gassed myself to death.

"You left in such a rush, you left your purse at our house," Heather says, her voice in a panic. "Oh my God! I never should've finished watching *Erin Brockovitch!*"

I swing my legs out of the driver's seat. Try to stand. I see the garage door is up. Michael is standing with his arms crossed over his chest. Looking really pissed.

"We saw the light on in the garage," he announces. "It's a good thing Heather knows where your extra key is hidden."

"I—I'm sorry?" I say, and my voice is hoarse.

"I told my wife if the fumes didn't kill ya, I was gonna do it," Michael says. He's looking at me the way he does sometimes. Not mean. Just pissed.

"I think we should call an ambulance," Heather says. I watch as she rummages in her purse for a cell phone.

"Water," I croak. "No ambulance."

Michael disappears and returns with a bottle of mineral water. "Drink," he says.

I drink the water, quickly. Too quickly. Suddenly I feel the signal. The gurgling in my belly. I rush to my front yard and vomit on the sidewalk.

Michael doesn't say a word. He grabs my garden hose and washes the puke into the street. Then he picks up his cell phone.

"No! I'm begging you! No ambulance. My health insurance has lapsed!"

Michael holds up his finger to shut me up.

"Hey Dad. Sorry to bother you so late," he says. "I've got a question about carbon monoxide poisoning." Michael turns his back to me and I hear him speaking to his father in a hushed tone.

His dad is a doctor, which comes in handy. So Michael's done this routine before. Calling his dad when I thought I had a mole that looked like skin cancer. And the time when Heather thought she had Lyme disease because she was feeling "extra tired" that week.

Dr. Wasserstein calls us the "Hypochondriackers."

I flop down onto the ground and clutch my stomach. Heather sits next to me and rubs my back. Gently. Like the extra nice person that she is.

"What's happened to you, Maddy?" she asks, in a soft voice. "You were always so positive about everything. Remember when I was stressed out about getting pregnant? You're the one who assured me it would all be okay. You always told me to *leap before I looked*, remember?"

I nod and stare down at the grass. "Maybe you shouldn't have listened."

"Nonsense," Heather says.

Michael hands me the phone.

"Talk to my dad," he orders me.

I shake my head no, but he opens my hand and slaps the phone into my palm.

"Dr. Wasserstein?" I ask, and my voice sounds meek.

"Do you have a headache, Maddy?"

"Yes."

"Nausea?"

"Oh yeah."

"Is your vision impaired?"

I squint my eyes and look at Heather. She still looks pink. But it's not blurry pink. It's just pink pink.

"No."

"Okay, I think you've been exposed to an elevated level of carbon monoxide. But I don't think you need an ambulance. However, if you start experiencing irregular breathing, dizziness, fainting—any severe symptoms—then I want you to call 911. And then call me on my cell. Michael will give you the number."

"Thanks Dr. Wasserstein," I say, and I sound like I'm a kid, again.

"In the meantime, Madeline, I think you should see a therapist."

"I'll consider it," I say.

"You know, I could put you on suicide watch."

I laugh into the phone. But then I realize Dr. Wasserstein isn't joking. Is that what everyone thinks? That I'm trying to kill myself?

Well, what were you doing? a voice in my head asks.

"It's not what you think," I say in a cool-as-cucumber voice. My head is ringing, my ears are popping and I think I'm going to throw up again. But I've got to save face here.

"I'm glad to hear it," Dr. Wasserstein says. "Just remember, Madeline, my door is always open."

"Thanks."

I pass the phone back to Michael. Heather turns to me and says, "I'm not leaving you alone tonight."

"Tryin' to steal my wife," Michael says, shaking his head. He's not mad anymore. I can see it in his eyes. He's back to his old whimsical self. If anything, Michael probably finds this mildly amusing.

"It's okay, guys. I'm just going to bed," I say. I hoist myself off the ground and brush off my jeans. "Thanks for bringing over my purse. You're a lifesaver," I say.

Heather says, "No problem."

Michael says, "Lifesaver! Ha! I get it."

We all have a good laugh, Michael orders a cheese pizza, and we sit around my kitchen till the wee hours talking about old times. So the night doesn't end up sucking after all.

God, the lengths I have to go.

Chapter 24

When Carlton felt he was in the doghouse, he wooed me with tons of flowers. Cards. Chocolates. Candles. The whole shebang. Every day he'd surprise me with little gifts. It was as if we were back in our honeymoon period.

I craved the extra attention. And I loved the man who was giving it. He was my soul mate, if ever there'd been such a thing. If we were going to be together forever, I'd protect myself. And Carlton would protect me, too. He swore to it.

"Why do I love you so much?" he'd say, tweaking me on the chin.

"Just because I'm me," I'd say, and we'd laugh.

Everyone made mistakes, I figured. And this was Carlton's. His love was his Achilles' heel. He'd been ashamed to tell me of his STD. That's how much he wanted us to stay together.

So I forgave him.

That very week, the Carlton-Coming-Out-About-Herpes Week, I made an emergency appointment to see Cheryl, my gynecologist. In the waiting room I read all the pamphlets on STD's, HIV, gonorrhea, syphilis. I read them all.

Apparently, if you have your pick of the litter, genital herpes is the way to go.

It's the STD with the least amount of trouble. A minor offender in a roomful of felons.

I wait more than an hour for Cheryl. She's a lesbian, my ob-gyn. And I know this because her life partner, Bernice, works in the office next to me at Henry's marketing firm. She keeps Cheryl's picture in a frame on her desk.

"How can you go to a lesbian?" Heather asks me.

"Because she happens to be *a doctor*," I reply.

When Heather snickers, I say, "You know, Jewish people are supposed to be *liberal*."

"You mean they vote Democrat?" she'll say, with all the innocence in the world.

"That too," I'll say.

It kills me when Heather scribbles this in her book. The "How to be a Jew" logbook she keeps, filled with helpful hints, recipes for knish and latkes, that sort of thing.

Cheryl is actually the best gynecologist I've ever been to. When I finally see her, she tells me genital herpes is almost impossible to test for.

"You have to wait for a break-out. Then we test the open sore," she says.

"How long until I have a break-out?" I ask. I'm up on the examination table, my feet in cold stirrups. On the ceiling is a poster with a cat dangling from a tree limb. "Hang in there!" the poster says.

It's really bad.

Cheryl pokes and prods. Digs her fingers into my abdomen. "Could be years," she says.

"If I'm infected, what happens to me?" I ask.

"The worst part of this disease is the social stigma associated with it. But you should know, Maddy, there is no cure—it's a disease you have for a lifetime. But rest assured, people can lead normal lives with herpes."

"All finished," she says. "You can sit up."

I sit up in my thin paper robe. The white paper crinkles underneath me. She takes her glasses off and lets them hang from a beaded chain around her neck. "There are topical lotions, and of course, pills, to control flare-ups. The only significant danger is for pregnant women."

"How so?"

"If a woman gives birth during a flare-up, and the newborn gets infected in the birth canal, it can be fatal for the baby. Women with genital herpes are advised to have cesarean sections rather than risk natural childbirth."

"How will I know if I've contracted it?"

She stands, walks to the sink. Washes her hands.

"You'll know. The sores are often painful during the first flare-up. And you'll most likely run a high fever. Come see me if that happens."

"Okay."

"Oh, and Maddy," she says.

"Yeah?"

"Be careful who you sleep with."

Before I can utter a word to Cheryl about being in a monogamous relationship with a beautiful man for the past several years, she walks briskly out, letting the door click shut behind her.

"Got it," I say to the empty room.

Chapter 25

It's time to buck up, Maddy, I tell myself. I practice smiling in the mirror, but it doesn't feel right. My lips are lopsided. And kind of dorky looking. Like a person trying to smile.

I decide to shake off my depression with a good healthy dose of the outdoors. My tennis club is offering discount lessons. I figure I could use some work on my serve. Plus, since Carlton and I broke up, I haven't had anyone to hit the ball around with. I'm rusty. Out of shape. And a tad flabby in the middle.

I could use a few hours outside, practicing my forehand with some individual one-on-one attention. So I sign up.

The next evening, I jog out to the court. It's brisk and clear. A cool breeze sweeps across my cheeks and I glance up to a sky sparkling with stars. Perfect tennis weather, as my dad used to say.

I'm wearing tennis whites. My favorite white tennis skirt with pleats, a white Addidas sports top, and white shoes. My only playful item is my socks. Polka dot.

The court lights are on and I see a few people warming up. The instructor is dark-skinned, and thin. He tells me his name is Deepak and he's from New Delhi, India. When he speaks, it's in that exuberant, up-and-down singsong voice. I love the Indian accent.

The tennis class is filled with couples. Deepak pairs them together. I'm the odd man out, of course. The only single. So Deepak pairs me with himself.

I'm dismayed at first, but then I realize it's good for my game to be paired with the tennis pro.

Deepak asks me why I'm taking lessons. "You do not need," he says, generously, as I whap the ball to the corners. Give Deepak a little challenge. He saves face by hitting a thunderous ball down the middle. I swing for it and miss. A beginner's mistake.

"Good game," he says, chuckling. We each walk to the net and shake hands. Like me, Deepak is a tennis purist. He only wears white. Strict white. None of these crazy colors. Like Andre Agassi or Venus Williams.

I like Deepak and notice he's wearing a gold wedding band. "Do you have kids?" I ask, as we gather around the cooler. I chug my Gatorade. Wipe sweat from my forehead. Deepak takes an Ozarka bottle and squirts water over his neck, then shakes his head, like a dog coming out of a lake.

"Two kids," he says. "A blessing in many disguises. And you?"

I end up spilling the beans about Carlton. Telling Deepak everything about the break-up.

Well—not everything

"Do not worry about this man," he says, in his deep, lilting voice. "We have a saying in India—What goes around—" he swings his arm in a wide arc to demonstrate a circle, "comes back around!"

"Yeah, but sometimes Deepak, you need more than Karma. You need a professional," I say.

He laughs and says, "Good one." He doesn't realize I'm serious as a heart attack.

Chapter 26

I thought quitting my job with Henry would be hard. Putting in notice and packing up my office, and so forth. But Henry makes things easy for me. He paves a smooth road, as they say. And turns my last day into a party.

He has helium balloons and cake and catering by Manny's Mexican—my favorite enchilada people. Afterward, we pack up my office together and Henry takes small nips from a Jack Daniels bottle he's hidden behind my desk.

"I still can't believe I'm losing you to Forest Connors," he says, flashing me his twinkling blue eyes. He's wearing a pale, butter-colored suit today with a pink kerchief in the breast pocket. It's a dandy—the kind of suit that only Henry can get away with. He loosens his tie and I can see he's waiting for me to say something.

I debate whether to tell Henry the arrangement I've been forced into. The sweat equity, stock options–to-ownership, work-for-hire thing. It's been such a nice day I don't want to get him into a rant.

I decide to stick with the positive.

"I'm starting *my own* company, Henry. Can you believe it!"

"If anyone deserves it—you do, kiddo. Just remember what I told you about Mr. *You Know Who.*"

"I know, I know. I couldn't even trust him to mow my yard."

Henry lifts the whiskey to take a quick nip. He points the bottle in my direction. "Just make sure you don't end up doing all the work and getting none of the reward."

"Hey, I've got free reign to hire whatever employees I need. And plus, Carlton and I are splitting the workload."

Henry raises his eyebrows in that clever, know-it-all, way. "I know what you're capable of, my dear. As for Carlton . . ." he stops and shakes his head.

"Always the cynic," I say. And I don't mean to say it. But I do. Because sometimes Henry is a bit much.

"It's never good to mix work-life with love-life," he says, matter-of-fact.

"At least we're not sharing an office," I say. "Carlton found this amazing office space for a great price. Fourteen bucks a square foot and we get almost the entire floor! We're moving in next week." I say. "Organics 4 Kids is about to have a home!" I squeal and clap my hands. It's something Heather would do, but I don't care.

Henry laughs. "I bet this company will be more successful than you ever dreamed."

I grab the tape and roll it across one of the boxes. "You know, our only competitor will be Giganto Foods," I say. "But they haven't even begun to scratch the surface of the organics food market. Especially for children's food."

Henry nods. "Maybe you should bring your idea directly to Giganto. I bet they'd pay a fine penny to hire someone like you."

I stop and look at him. He's eyeing me in that way where I can tell he wants to say something.

"C'mon. Out with it," I say.

Henry pulls a white envelope from his pocket and thrusts it into my hands.

"A little going-away present," he says.

I feel my eyes beginning to tear up. "I—I can't accept—"

Henry raises his finger to his lips and goes, "SHHHH! You're the best employee I've ever had, Madeline. You've made this company a whole lot of money and kept my clients very satisfied. And you knocked it out of the park with the Meyers account. Take the envelope, my dear."

Henry grabs my hand and squeezes it. "Promise me something, kiddo."

"What?"

"Don't spend it. Just put it in a savings account for a rainy day. You never know when you'll need to break open the piggy."

"So this is my 'break glass in case of emergency' money?"

Henry slaps his palm against the desk. "Exactly."

I look down at the envelope, and turn it over in my hands. I don't open it because I know it's a significant amount of money. And I don't want to cry.

After all these years working for Henry, on my last day, I want to be all smiles.

"Thank you, Henry. I don't know what to say." I walk over to him and give him an awkward sideways hug.

Henry chuckles and I can smell the alcohol on his breath.

"I have a little something for you, too," I say. I walk over to my desk and pull out a finely crafted, leather-bound keepsake book. Over the past few months, I've constructed the interior of the book, by carefully pasting together all of the newspaper articles, glossy magazine photos, and client confessionals—every single mention of Henry Wrona since the company's inception. I've created something Henry would never create for himself. It's a book of his accolades, his accomplishments, his lifetime of success in the business.

"What's this?" he asks, almost in a whisper. He sets the book on the table and begins flipping through it, slowly. Taking it all in.

"This is a gift for a man who taught me almost everything I

know about business. A man without an ego. And the best boss anyone could ever ask for," I say, quietly.

Henry looks up at me, and his eyes are filled with tears.

"Did you hear the one about the Polish loan shark who loaned out all his money?" he asks, his voice cracking.

"He had to skip town," I say.

Henry smoothes back his streaked white hair and wipes his eyes. "I know I've got a joke you haven't heard."

"I doubt it," I say. I grab my portfolios and slip them in a box. Grabbing a black magic marker, I label the box "Important!"

I've arranged all of the client work I've done over the past fourteen years in several black, bound portfolio books. I made the portfolios in case I ever needed to interview for a big firm. The Big Firms require portfolios. So I spent years working on mine. I crafted them during grad school and updated them with all my new work every year.

Henry watches me as I put the box with my portfolio books on the top of the stack.

"You mustn't lose your portfolios, Maddy," he cautions. "They're the gatekeeper to the entire industry."

"Don't worry," I say. "I won't let these babies out of my sight."

Henry helps me lift a few boxes and we walk toward the office door. I turn and give the place one last look.

I feel my heart drop into my stomach.

Henry notices, so he says, "Why don't Polish women ever use vibrators?"

"Henry!" I say, slapping him playfully in the arm.

"Because it chips their teeth!" He throws his head back and laughs up at the ceiling.

"You're right," I say, shaking my head. "I haven't heard them all."

He claps me on the back and we both buzz out the door.

Chapter 27

I have a theory. And here it is . . .

Breakups are better in winter.

Yes, it's better to break up in the winter than in the summer. Let me share my logic. In the summertime, people are outdoors, the sun is shining, and you look like a big fat loser if you're sitting alone inside your house moping on a beautiful day. But if it's wintertime, you can watch Blockbuster movies and sit inside and eat pizza after pizza and complain about the weather.

The problem with living in central Texas is that even in February, it almost always feels like summer. The sun is always shining. I mean, it's not New Jersey here.

And therefore, I'm not getting the benefit of the winter breakup. I mean, the sky is blue, the sun is shining, and here I am, moping around my house, wishing for a freak ice storm.

Sometimes you've got to pull yourself out of the funk. So when Sunday rolls around, I treat myself to a Day of Maddy. First, the do-it-yourself spa. A fabulous three-dollar Noxzema facial, complete with sounds of howling monkeys and screeching birds in the background. I have to admit something here. I ended up buying the rainforest "inspired" CD, so I figure I should get some use out of it. It's an indulgent afternoon, me taking a long bubble bath in my glorious tub, but I figure I owe myself.

Afterward, I eat lunch at my favorite pit-stop. Manny's Mexican. I order the chicken enchiladas with extra cheese and extra Guac.

"You want hot or mild salsa?" the Mexican waiter asks.

I say, "Surprise me."

He brings me the hot stuff, surprise, surprise.

I read the newspaper. The Sunday *New York Times*. From cover to cover. (Well, almost. I skip the Arts and Entertainment Section. I don't need art. And I don't need entertainment. What I need is a gun. Ha, ha.)

But seriously. I'm on my own. For the first time in almost four years.

I consider calling Henry. Begging for my old job back. Especially now that I'm sitting in Manny's Mexican—it reminds me of the big going-away party he threw me. And the big going-away check. My "Break Glass In Case of Emergency" check that I'm now living on.

Good ol' Henry. He was right all along, and I guess, deep down, I knew he was right. I don't mind conceding the point, but it would be awkward. When I was working at Organics 4 Kids, I never kept up with him like I should have. I was always busy. We had a few lunches together, exchanged e-mails, that sort of thing. But our relationship, during my stint at Organics, fizzled.

Now that I've got so much free time on my hands, I feel the loss. And it's an acute pain. I know I'll call Henry one of these days. Let him know the scoop. And then I'll have to listen to a big, fat "I Told You So," speech.

But not today. Today is Maddy Day.

I decide to take a nice stroll.

I walk to the Public Library. The Park. And the Museum District. There's a new exhibit about the Constitutional Congress. And I'm somewhat of a Revolutionary War buff. So I figure, what the heck?

I walk inside and realize it's been a while since I've set foot in a museum. It's a shame, really, because I love museums. They make me feel as though life is so fleeting, that our time on Earth is so precious, that we've really got to live it!

Yes, museums make me hokey.

The exhibit is neat. It starts with letters from the Founding Fathers. A sign on the wall reads: *Welcome to the National Archives Experience.*

I peruse some of the letters. The museum feels cold. And a little dark inside. "Probably to preserve these letters," I think.

There were fifty-five delegates to the Constitutional Congress, but only thirty-nine actually signed on the dotted line. I stroll around the glass cases reading letters by our Founding Fathers: Alexander Hamilton, George Washington, Patrick Henry, and Benjamin Franklin.

The usual daddy-o's.

All of the letters appear with a typed, translated version, in case me olde tyme English is rusty. The translated version is helpful.

I stop at the letters from Abigail Adams to John Adams. Abigail is the only female writer in this exhibit, as far as I've seen. She's written a letter to John Adams for his journey to the Continental Congress. I peer down at the letter. It's magnified and under glass. And it starts with:

"Remember the Ladies."

Remember the Ladies . . . in the new Code of Laws. Remember the Ladies and be more generous and favourable to them than your ancestors. Do not put such unlimited power into the hands of the Husbands. Remember—all Men would be tyrants if they could.

—*Abigail Adams*

Letter to John Adams in Philadelphia. Braintree. March 31, 1776.

I straighten my shoulders and stare off into space.

All men would be tyrants if they could?

Wow. You got that right, sister.

I leave the museum with my head in a fog. The museum lady says, "Have a nice day," as I amble out the door. I wave to her, absently.

On my way home I consider my role in Carlton's crimes against me. If anything, I was certainly an accomplice. I mean, what did I do to protect myself? Nothing. And in the end, I suffered.

I did it. Me! Carlton never put a gun to my head. He simply asked, cajoled, persuaded, and gave me the type of mind-boggling sex that made my head spin and my eyes roll back. But in the end, wasn't I to blame? Didn't I put all my eggs in the Carlton Basket? And watch, as a mere bystander, a sniveling victim, while he crushed those eggs, not one by one, but with one swift kick?

I consider this. And I consider Abigail Adams. For a woman of her time, Abigail Adams had some spunk.

Chapter 28

After Carlton and I moved into the new Organics 4 Kids head-quarters, we hit the ground running. The company will be top-notch, we decide, so we hire the best people to design our website, network our computers, and do all the general dirty work of getting going.

I spend night and day designing our marketing and public relations program. To really capture the theme, I have the Organics 4 Kids logo emblazoned on T-shirts, bumper stickers, lunch boxes, and even on our refrigerated delivery trucks. The rainbow-colored logo becomes so popular, the local news does a feature story on us.

I hatch an idea to have school kids participate in our focus groups. We discover that parents want healthy organic school lunches at a reasonable price. Kids are all about taste. So we compromise and develop a unique school lunch program to make everybody happy. Our organic cheese pizzas or chicken tenders might be paired with snack-pak carrots, micro greens salad, an apple, a healthy cookie, or Vitamin C–enhanced fruit juice.

We hire a famous nutritionist to help develop weekly menus

so we can make sure the kids get variety, as well as good, solid meals.

We're a small company, but a strong one. And we're growing by leaps and bounds. Our sales numbers blossom each month. In our fourth quarter, we actually begin turning a profit. An amazing feat for a company just out of the gate.

Carlton and I celebrate by leaving the office before midnight, drinking champagne straight from the bottle—we didn't have time to muddle around with glasses—and having hot, steamy sex on Carlton's awful bear rug. In front of the fireplace. The henna tattoo of the Organics 4 Kids logo was still visible across my tailbone. And Carlton licked the tattoo with his tongue back and forth. Very saucy stuff.

The workload is exhausting and exhilarating. I drink buckets of coffee each day, and become thin and pale from lack of exercise. Sometimes Carlton and I play tennis on Sunday mornings, but afterward, we head straight to the office.

Our week is seven days long, with late nights, too.

Yet, even as I struggle at my computer, field hundreds of e-mails from customers, suppliers, distributors, local school boards, the press, and even some school kids, I feel alive. An idea I've created on paper has finally become reality.

It's trial by fire. Every day. All day.

I interview candidates for my staff and have the brilliant idea to set up an internship program. "Free labor!" I declare. "We'll set up a great program where the students get college credit and where they really learn the nuts and bolts of the business."

Carlton agrees it's a great idea. I spend three months developing and marketing the intern program at local colleges. I speak to college professors, campus advisors, and finally to the students themselves. I hire five interns, get them desks and computers, and start them on a program so that their work benefits them as well as the company. Everyone agrees it's a win-win situation.

Twice a month, Carlton and I treat the interns to dinner and drinks. They love it. Everything is going splendidly.

Carlton spends time traveling to Denver, Los Angeles, and New York trying to attract new investors and generate new customers. I run the home office. Fifteen full-time employees. Five interns. At times, I've got phones on each ear. And two lines holding. I'm triaging my e-mails. I'm slammed. But I manage. The ship sails in a nice, straight line.

Chapter 29

Michael, that little snitch, called my brother about the carbon monoxide thing. So now, I've got Ronnie up in arms over the whole deal. He's calling me every five minutes. Probably to check whether I'm still breathing.

"Yoga," my brother will say.

"Boring," I'll reply.

"Church."

"They revoked my membership."

"Why don't you learn how to scuba dive, Maddy?"

"Sharks."

Finally, he relents.

My brother tells me he knows a guy who knows a guy.

"I think he does light jobs—you know, like when people don't pay their drug debts," Ronnie says.

I clutch the phone tightly in my hand. "He breaks their legs?" I ask, and I shudder a little bit at the thought.

"I think he just scares people. Maybe punches 'em a few times in a dark alley, tells 'em to pay up or else."

"Okay, but that's it. There's nothing else. No broken fingers? No baseball bats? No knives?"

My brother sighs into the phone. He's smoking a cigarette and blowing it away from the receiver. "I don't know, Maddy. I'm not an expert at hiring thugs. Look, why don't you come over so I can talk you out of this."

I stretch my arm over my head and glance around my lonely kitchen. My empty townhouse. "Want me to bring you a burger?"

"It's 9:00 a.m."

"Oh."

I hop in my car and cruise over to Ronnie's bachelor pad.

My brother calls it his "low-key" flat for a "low-key kind of guy." It's nothing fancy. Just your basic garden-style apartment with a balcony overlooking the communal pool.

I knock on the door and hear him say, "Maddy-go-laddy!" Stepping inside, I see my brother is going overboard with his plants again. Mr. Greenthumb buys exotic flowering plants from Brazil and Africa. Stuff that's hard to keep alive. Like the teenagers he counsels, he likes the challenge.

"It's a jungle in here," I say, parting my way through two large potted ferns.

"Isn't it great? I'm really getting this gardening shit down," Ronnie says.

I step over a stack of self-help books piled high on the floor. Ronnie doesn't have a TV. Instead he's got a couch facing the windows and tons and tons of books. He calls it his "library."

"Step into my library," Ronnie says, motioning to a leather recliner. "Take a load off, Maddy. You look beat."

I see my brother is wearing his weekend uniform. A Longhorns T-shirt and jeans. He's got a Longhorns baseball cap perched crooked on his head, so he looks like a white rapper.

I plop down in the recliner, push down the wooden lever, and pop back with my feet up. Behind me, a plant brushes up against my head. I push the dangling leaves out of the way.

"Hey, take it easy," Ronnie says. He strolls over to a table filled with drug paraphernalia. His "temptation table" as he calls it. There's a bong for smoking marijuana, a crack pipe, a mirror and razor blade for cutting cocaine, and some other things I can't even identify.

My brother has turned the bong into a French Press.

He holds it up in the air and says, "coffee?"

"Sure."

I watch as he carefully upturns the bong and pours a steaming cup of mud-black coffee. He hands me the mug.

I take a sip, gingerly. "This is delicious," I say, because it really is.

"It's the beans," he says. "I got them from this Columbian guy I know."

"Funny," I say.

My brother smiles coyly and lights a cigarette. He sits on the couch's edge, slides the balcony door open and blows the smoke outside.

"Why do you keep all this stuff?" I ask, motioning around the table at all of the drug paraphernalia.

He stares out the window a long moment. Takes a sip of coffee. A drag from his cigarette. And exhales the smoke slowly.

"It reminds me of what I overcame," he says. "Like when Jesus was in the desert fasting forty days and forty nights. And Satan approached him and told him to turn stones into bread. And Jesus was starving but he told Satan to essentially go fuck himself. When I look at this stuff every day, Maddy, these implements of destruction, I tell them to go fuck themselves," he says. "And it works."

"I thought they told you in AA classes to keep all this stuff out of sight and out of mind."

"I'd prefer to face my demons head-on," Ronnie says. He stabs his cigarette into a tray and then holds up the butt. "This is the worst fucker of 'em all, but I can't seem to kick this bad boy." He looks down at me, resting in the recliner. "You know what today is, don't you?" he asks, and his voice is suddenly soft. Almost child-like.

My brother and I don't talk about our parents. It's a subject we just don't bring up. We keep photographs hidden away and if we're really in the mood to torture ourselves, sometimes we'll sort through them on Christmas and cry and cry.

But of course I know today is the day they died.

I nod my head.

"I'm gonna go to five o'clock mass tonight and light a candle for them," Ronnie says.

"That's . . . good," I say.

We sit a few minutes and both stare out the window. It's nice and quiet in my brother's place. I can hear a few kids out at the pool. Splashing around and calling out, "Marco Polo."

My brother breaks out into a grin. He pivots around and stares at me with his flashy green eyes. "So you want to hire a hit man to take out Carlton," he says, shaking his head. "And I thought I was the hot-blooded Italian."

"I know it sounds crazy, but I think it's the only sane thing to do."

"Will this give you closure?"

"How else am I going to get even with Mr. Perfect? What am I going to do, Ronnie? Hex him and hope he falls over on his bike and scrapes a knee?"

"Why get even?"

I pop up in the recliner. "He's ruined my life! I just want to ruin a single day for him. One Single Day. Of his Perfect Life. Is that too much to ask?"

My brother hesitates. Then reaches into his pocket and flashes a slip of paper in front of my eyes.

"Memorize this number quickly," he says.

"Why?

My brother pulls out his lighter and sets the paper on fire.

"Before I change my mind about giving it to you."

"Thanks, little brother."

"For the record, Maddy, I have to tell you that I'm totally against you doing this. The only reason I'm giving you this guy's name is because I owe you my life. But I'd prefer if you'd let it go. Haven't you heard the saying, 'Let go, Let God'?"

"Yes, but I like the saying: *Hire hit man, Laugh hard*."

My brother kisses the gold cross on his neck. "Do you know the story of Jesus? How he turned the other cheek? It's a powerful story. There's power in forgiveness. Lead a good life, Maddy. Become a huge success. You should start your own marketing and P.R. firm and become more successful than Carlton ever imagined. That's the best revenge. Why let this guy get to you?"

"You don't have all the facts," I say, abruptly.

"You're my sister, Maddy. Trust me. I wanna kill the guy. I can only imagine what he did to you because I've never, ever, in my entire life, seen you look this miserable. It's as if he's stolen the light from your eyes, and the goodness from your heart."

I pause for a moment.

"Wow, that's deep," I say. My brother tends to speak in the language of "rehab ministry." He's been to so many self-help and addiction classes, he could write a book on the subject.

"C'mon, Maddy. Pray with me," Ronnie says. He makes the sign of the cross. "In the name of the Father, the Son, and the Holy Spirit," he says, kissing his fingers at the end.

I stand there, watching him.

"You're being dramatic," I say, crossing my arms over my chest. "I'm not talking about cement boots, here. I'm talking about a more subtle type of revenge."

"Fine. I'll pray for you," he says.

"Great. I can use all the help I can get."

I turn and walk toward Ronnie's refrigerator. It's covered in magnets that say things like, "Seal of Approval," and "You can do it!" and "I love mornings!" My brother has covered his fridge in positive affirmations.

"What do you have to eat in here?" I ask, swinging open the door.

"Nothing, nada, zip."

My brother's refrigerator contains a jar of peanut butter and a carton of milk. I close the door and look at him.

"How about the International House of Pancakes?" I suggest. "My treat."

I don't really care for pancakes but my brother is a pancake freak. Plus, he loves all the different flavors of syrup.

"You know I can't pass up that syrup," Ronnie says, rubbing his belly. "Their boysenberry kicks ass," he informs me.

See what I mean?

My brother grabs his house keys and wallet and stuffs them in the pocket of his jeans. He follows me out of the apartment and down the steps.

"Oh, and Maddy," Ronnie says.

I swing around.

"Be careful with that number I gave you. You know hiring a hit man is a federal offense punishable by a long, long time in the pokey."

"I'll take my chances," I say, as if I'm a stud.

Ronnie opens the car door for me, and gracefully pushes me into the passenger seat. "No matter what happens, Maddy," he says, "I know you'll do the right thing."

Chapter 30

In the midst of what Carlton and I call our "Crazy Season," Carlton decides to have a Boys' Night Out. It's a Saturday night, and I don't mind. But as each Saturday rolls around and Carlton does it over and over, I begin to get frustrated.

"We're spending every waking moment together, Maddy," he complains.

"It's not quality time," I reply.

I swivel around in my office chair. Carlton is standing at the door, hands on his waist like a drill sergeant. "C'mon, sweetie. You're cooler than that," he says. And I really want to be cool, so I drop it.

Carlton, sometimes, really knows how to pull my strings.

So, despite our hectic workweek and the fact that I stay late at the office on Saturday nights alone, Carlton decides he needs time with the boys. Saturday Night Out with the Guys becomes an institution to which Carlton remains strictly faithful. Even if something important comes up, he reschedules around Boys' Night Out.

Our relationship is fine, for two people who work so much, but we're definitely not the same moony-eyed Romeo and Juliet lovers we used to be. It's all ebb and flow. So I decide not to stress. Better to just roll with it.

One night, when Carlton isn't home by 3:00 a.m., I call his cell phone, but hang up when I get the answering recorder. I feel silly for doing it. As if I've become the jealous type. The type of woman I've never respected. These women always seemed weak, in my opinion. If a woman had to keep her man on a tight leash, she lacked self-esteem, I figured. I always thought the man should be concerned about me, not the other way around. But I was beginning to get concerned.

Even when I felt I knew Carlton down to his inner core— that there were no secrets this man held . . . he was still removed. A sly detachment that wasn't betrayed in his smile or in the way he whispered, "I love you, Maddy," before he rolled over and went to sleep each night.

No, the detachment was in a subtle, but dangerous flicker in his eye. I'd noticed it just a few times in our entire relationship. And most recently, when I told him I didn't like the way he stayed out so late with the guys.

I wait up in bed, one Saturday night, reading through customer e-mails. The front door slams and I hear Carlton whistling softly in the hall. He must see the bedroom light on because he stops whistling.

"Knock, knock," he says, walking zigzag into the bedroom. He flops down onto the edge of the bed and kicks his shoes off. He reeks of smoke and alcohol, and even pot.

"I thought you and David were coming home after the concert," I say. I rub my eyes and check the alarm clock.

"It's 4:00 a.m. Carlton!"

He shrugs his shoulders. "We ended up at the after-party."

"Why didn't you call? I waited up," I say, and my voice sounds weak. Pleading.

Carlton spins around on the bed and stares at me. "You

shouldn't have," he snaps. And that's when I spot the flicker. He stands and heads over to the closet, shooting me a wary, cautious look—the kind of look a wild animal gives to someone trying to capture it. As if I'd just leapt on the floor, grabbed his ankles, and tried to restrain him by locking him up in a ball and chain.

"Look, babe. I'm not meaning to bust your balls or anything, but a relationship is about give and take," I say, quietly, under my breath.

I watch as Carlton undresses. And he knows I'm watching him. He turns around slowly and I see the muscles rippling down his stomach. He lifts weights in his office when no one's looking, so he's still got a killer physique.

Carlton strolls over to the bed, completely naked. He loops his arms around me and pulls me against his chest. "Oh, I'm about to *give* you something all right," he says, and poof! Like that, the flicker is gone and we're back.

I smell sour gin on his breath, and it stinks, but even in his intoxicated state, he takes me hard that night. In the way that only the most experienced of lovers can take a woman. And I, Madeline Jane Piatro, love every moment of it.

We start on the bed first and then Carlton drags me into the living room. It's cold without a fire, but he takes me on the bear rug. Like in the movies. Hard and fast. The fur scratches my butt. Leaving small welts.

Afterward, he says, "I love you, Maddy," and stares at me with those rakish eyes that make my knees weak.

I don't reply.

I love you more, I think.

Chapter 31

I unfold the crinkled napkin from the International House of Pancakes. Flatten out the edges. I stare at it. Debating.

When my brother wasn't watching, I wrote down the number. So I wouldn't forget it.

The phone number he showed me in one split second before he set it on fire.

There is no name. Just the number. I don't recognize the area code. I bet it's difficult to trace.

I pick up the phone. Dial the number. It's a beeper. Damn. I hang up.

Ronnie told me I wouldn't be able to use a pay phone and now I see why. So I'm calling the meathead-for-hire on my cell.

I redial the number, punch in my digits followed by the pound sign for the beeper, and wait.

A minute ticks by, or maybe an eternity, I can't tell. But my phone rings, suddenly.

I stare at my phone. It rings and rings until I snatch it off my coffee table.

"Hello?" I say.

"You just paged me," a voice replies. It's a man's voice, of course. A deep, sexy man's voice.

My goodness.

"Uh . . . I was interested in discussing your services," I stutter.

Am I really doing this? I wonder. I hear that voice in my head again, this time saying, *What are you doing, Maddy?* But I press on.

"How did you get this number?" the voice asks.

"Friend of a friend."

"Not good enough, lady. Try again."

"A friend of Snoop Santino's."

"Snoop's got a lot of friends."

I pause and consider hanging up the phone. I certainly don't want to bring my brother into this.

"A former business associate of Snoop Santino's gave me your number," I say.

A moment passes. And I wait.

"I don't discuss anything over the phone," the voice says. "But we can arrange a meeting."

"Uh . . . okey dokey," I say. And then I cringe because I can't believe I just said "okey dokey!"

"You pick the time and place, lady," the voice says.

I have a sudden urge to hang up. I stare at the cell phone in my hand. And I'm about to click it shut when I hear the voice go, "Hullo? You still there?"

"Uh, how about the Starbucks on 3rd Street. You know where that is?"

"Yes."

"Tomorrow afternoon. Let's say four o'clock?" I'm apparently scheduling teatime with my very own hit man. Perhaps we'll enjoy a plate of scones.

"I'll be wearing a leather coat," the voice says.

"I'll be wearing—" my voice falters and drops off. What on earth am I going to wear? For my big meeting? A disguise would probably be best. But a disguise seems so cloak and dagger. Plus, I've always looked ridiculous in a wig.

"I'll be wearing an Organics 4 Kids T-shirt," I say quickly. And I don't know why I say this. But it seems appropriate.

"Those are good-looking shirts," the voice says. I hear a click and a dial tone as he hangs up the phone.

I put the phone down and I can't help myself. I smile like a cat.

Chapter 32

Carlton goes to a bachelor party on Saturday night. And while he's hooting it up at some titty bar, our Chief Financial Officer decides to quit.

I'm in my office working late when Steven Schultz taps on my door.

"Hey Steve," I chirp, and I immediately know something's wrong. His face is ash-gray.

Steve holds up a spreadsheet. "I've got something to tell you, Maddy. And it's not easy to say," he begins.

Usually, I'd try to multitask. Like sending out e-mails or something, but Steve's eyes look dead-serious. He's even sweating.

I turn and face him, my hands folded on my lap. "Shoot," I say.

Steve takes his glasses off and wipes the lenses on his shirt. "Carlton is dicking around with the numbers," he says. "It's bordering on fraud. Actually, it's not bordering on it—it is fraud."

"What?"

He shoves the spreadsheets in my lap. "Look for yourself. I've highlighted all the relevant portions."

I glance down and see Steve has prepared two sets of balance sheets. I recognize one set, but the numbers on the other set are unfamiliar.

"Look, Maddy. He didn't tell me he was doing this. So I'm signing off on this stuff and he's turning around and changing it behind my back. I'm not interested in having the federal prosecutor up my ass," he says.

"I'm sure there's a perfectly reasonable explanation—"

Steve shakes his head vigorously back and forth. "No, Madeline!" he nearly shouts.

I pause and sit back in my chair, with the paperwork in my lap.

"I knew you wouldn't believe me. Being his girlfriend and all . . ." Steve mutters.

"Carlton hasn't said a word to me about this," I say. "And let me assure you, we tell each other everything when it comes to this company."

"The CFO always goes to jail, Madeline! Look at Enron!" Steve shouts. "Now, I'm not going to sit here and justify why these numbers don't add up while you turn a blind eye!"

Steve bursts out of his chair and storms out the door.

He returns a minute later and apologizes. "Sorry, I lost my head," he says. "I just feel taken advantage of. Working all these weekend hours."

I sift through the papers on my lap.

"What do you want to do, Steve?" I ask, because I already know what he wants.

"I've already taken a new job, Maddy. Sorry for the late notice but I know Carlton won't cut me a severance check."

"You'll get three months' salary," I say, quietly. "And I wish you the best of luck. Thank you for bringing this to my attention. You're an earnest guy, and a good employee, but I need time to crunch these numbers—so I'll know what's really going on."

Steve looks at me and says, "Carlton is a real schmuck."

I say, "You're fired, Steve."

He breaks out into a nervous smile. And we both laugh.

Later that night, I ask Carlton about the spreadsheets.

"Steve is too conservative," Carlton shrugs. "He's not a good fit for the company. We need someone more aggressive. More willing to take risks."

"Steve went to Wharton and is a CPA!" I counter. "He treats expenses as expenses, not as assets."

"That's exactly his problem, Maddy. He has no understanding of our business."

I frown and press my hand against my hips. "You're just trying to impress your dad with inflated numbers," I say.

Carlton raises his hand. "That's unfair, Maddy. Steve has always felt underpaid and overworked. I'm glad he quit because he just wants a piece of the company. Plain and simple. But I'm not willing to give him any of my shares. Are you?"

"I don't have any shares!" I say. And it's official. I'm suddenly yelling.

"Please, Maddy. Not that subject again. You'll have half my shares as soon as we get married," Carlton says. "And let me tell you, my dad isn't going to be happy about that. He's had plenty of women taking half of everything."

"Jesus, Carlton. What does he expect? He never picks a woman of intelligence. A woman of substance. Someone who's going to stand on her own two feet. He's the king of cocktail waitresses."

Carlton raises his hand. "Hey! You're out of line," he says sharply. "My father is the guy who made this company happen. He didn't need to invest millions of dollars in our little pipe dream."

I stare into Carlton's eyes. And his pupils look mean and piercing. Like small black needles. For a moment, he reminds me exactly of Forest Connors.

I catch my breath. Take two steps backward in the kitchen.

"Unlike your stepmother, HOLLY, I'm working for my shares in Organics 4 Kids," I say, my voice rising. "And I'm working my TAIL off."

Carlton takes a deep breath. "I know, sweetie. We both are," he says, and his voice is suddenly soft. He steps toward me and encircles me in his arms. He's back. My good ol' Carlton.

I smell the scent of his cologne and it reminds me of the woods—as always. A log cabin with a fire. I nuzzle my head into his chest. He strokes my hair like he always used to. And for a moment, I feel like Juliet again.

So I decide to drop it. Against my better judgment, I let Steve Schultz walk. Maybe Steve was too conservative for our small, start-up company.

I take Carlton's word for it.

Chapter 33

So, what to wear, what to wear. What to wear for my meeting with my very own hit man. Well, he's not really a hit man. He's more of a punch-and-kick man, I think. A bruiser. The type of guy who grunts when he moves. The type of guy whose biceps are so large, he can't bring his arms to his sides. So he walks like a penguin. This is what I'm expecting. A Guido. A Goombah.

I wear all black, of course. Black pants, black T-shirt, and then I don a baseball cap and sunglasses. Miss Incognito. Like I'm a famous movie star lunching with my famous movie star friend.

I decide not to wear the Organics 4 Kids T-shirt because with my luck, I'd have a bunch of kids running up to me in Starbucks, asking me where they could buy one. Certainly Mr. Goombah will recognize a fellow partner in crime.

I stroll to the coffee shop because it's within walking distance from my apartment. I don't want you-know-who to see my car. In fact, I don't want him to know anything about me at all. And I think, though I can't be sure, he feels the same way.

It's a beautiful day, but I skip the outdoor tables and take a table inside. A corner table— far from the coffee counter and any window.

I wait. With a copy of *Love in the Time of Cholera* on the table. A book doesn't seem suspicious, I think. So I brought a book.

My middle name is Jane, my mother's name. I decide to use it to meet my hit man. I don't want him to know my first name. So, instead of Madeline Piatro, I'll be Jane. Just Jane.

I'm clever that way. Like a CIA agent. Dressed in black, using my middle name. Gosh, who would ever recognize me?

I'm expecting a big, meaty, bald guy. Or maybe some greasy motorcycle guy in a leather jacket. With a tattoo of an eagle across the back of his neck.

I'm certainly not expecting a young Richard Gere look-alike. A hottie in a tailored leather jacket.

My, my. An officer and a gentleman.

I stand up and wave. Richard Gere comes toward the table and I notice he moves lightning fast.

I surge forward and offer my hand. He looks down, shakes it, and I see a glimmer of a smile shimmer across his lips.

"Hi, I'm Jane," I say.

"Dick," he says.

Great, so we're Dick and Jane. And we've got a little dog named Spot. See Spot Run. Run, Spot, Run.

This is too much. It really is.

"Do you ever go by Richard?" I ask.

"Call me Dick," he says, sitting across from me. He's wearing sunglasses, too. He raises them breezily onto his head and I notice his eyes. Crisp, dark, beautiful eyes. Eyes the color of dark African coffee.

My, my. My hit man is hot.

Don't mind if I do . . .

"I usually don't meet my clients face-to-face," Dick says, "But Snoop is a good buddy of mine, and he said your brother was trustworthy."

"My brother?" I ask, and I instantly regret it.

"You don't got a brother named Ronnie?" Dick shifts in his seat, as if he's about to stand up.

"My brother keeps his friends close to his vest," I say, quickly. And I realize now that Ronnie called Snoop Santino after all.

Dick looks uncomfortable.

"Can I get you anything? A cappuccino, maybe?" I ask my hit man.

"Coffee. Black," he says. "Oh, and a chocolate chip cookie."

O. Kay.

"Sure, no problem," I say. I stand and hustle to the counter. I don't know whether to be a little scared or bemused. Here I am. Ordering my hit man a cookie. But I guess everyone likes a cookie, right? Even trained killers.

I walk back to the table with a tray of snacks. Dick is staring at me.

"You got a real nice way about ya, lady. You don't seem the type," he says, as I sit back down. I take a sip of my latte and break off a piece of cinnamon scone.

"You mean, the type to want revenge in the form of bruised and bloody?"

"Yeah. Most broads I know. Most broads don't have the balls for it. I got this one lady, though—she hired me to facilitate a little accident with her husband. He'd been cheating on her all these years and one day she just got tired of it. So she called me. Mostly I do threat jobs. You know, low-level shit. If a guy don't pay his dealer or his bookie, he deserves me on his back, don'cha think? I mean, two men made a deal. And the way I see it. A deal's a deal. You don't go runnin' out on a handshake. It ain't right."

I nod. "What 'r ya gonna do," I say, shrugging and raising my hands in the air, palms up. I've suddenly become really, really Italian. Like super Italian.

Dick picks up his cookie. It's the size of his hand, but he bites the entire thing in half. "I see myself as an equalizer," he says, his mouth full of cookie goo. "Bringing a little justice to an unjust world."

"That's poetic," I say. I realize my American Gigolo is not so suave when it comes to table manners.

"So, first things first," Dick says, his lips covered in cookie crumbs.

I pass him a napkin across the table. He takes it and mops his brow. Then uses the back of his hand to wipe crumbs off his mouth.

"First, I gotta know where you live," he says. "In case I get burned, or in case you're some female detective, then I'm gonna send someone for you."

"Eek. Scary," I say.

"Insurance policy. That's all," Dick shrugs. "Nothin' to worry about unless you got somethin' to worry about, capiche?"

"Well, what if *you're* a cop?" I say.

Dick laughs out loud and I can see his teeth are bone-white. As if he's recently had them capped.

"I ain't no cop, lady," he says, crossing his arms over his chest. "And I think you know that."

"Now that we've got that out of the way," I say. I slide a picture of Carlton across the table. "This is my target."

I actually say these exact words—*This is my target*.

Dick fingers the top of his coffee cup. "I'll do what you want, Jane. But first," he picks up the photo and taps at Carlton's picture, "You gotta tell me what happened between you and the dude."

"Why?"

"Cause I never do a job unless I know it's the right thing. I mean, if he's just some innocent prick who broke your heart, well, I'm sorry. I won't do the job. I got principles."

"Okay, but I warn you. It may take a while."

Dick smiles at me, a wan smile. He sits back in his chair and puts his hands behind his head, elbows-out, like he's a big-shot wheeler and dealer.

"I got all afternoon," he says.

Chapter 34

I start interviewing other candidates to replace Steve Schultz. And I finally narrow it down to two people. Nathalie is a recent University of Houston graduate. She's got an accounting degree, but no real business experience.

"There's no one else who will work for such a low salary," I tell Carlton.

Carlton glances at her resume. "Who else," he asks, flippantly.

I pass him the resume of my star candidate. "Priscilla is forty-two years old. She's worked in accounting at a large company for the last fifteen years."

"What's the catch?"

"She's a single mom. So she can only work part-time."

Carlton sighs. "Great. So my options are a college graduate with no experience and a single mom who can only be here thirty hours a week."

"You're the one who wanted to get rid of Steve," I say, and I immediately regret it.

Carlton shoots me an eat-shit-and-die look.

"Bring them in for an interview," he says, sharply. I suddenly feel as if I'm his secretary, instead of his partner, his fiancée, his right-hand man.

"You got it, babe," I say. I lean forward and kiss him on the cheek.

"Remember our pact," Carlton says.

I nod. Before we started working together, Carlton and I talked about our relationship in the office. We would be strict colleagues during office hours, nothing more. It was the only way it could work, we decided. Sometimes I broke our pact and sent him little e-mail messages.

"Let's make love tonight after everyone leaves," I'd write.

"Okay, but this doesn't mean you're getting a promotion," he'd write back.

Sometimes we'd lock the office door and have sex under the desk. Or if we were really feeling frisky, right on top of it. Carlton usually liked to stand up and bend me over the office furniture—taking me from behind. I joke about him being in love with the back of my head. Carlton thinks this joke is hugely funny.

A few days later, we interview both candidates. Priscilla is professional, courteous, and a terrific candidate. She's dressed in a conservative navy suit, panty hose, and flats. She wears small gold earrings and I notice a gold cross around her neck.

Nathalie is young, bright, and blonde. What she lacks in experience she makes up for in eagerness. She's bouncy and sweet as a summer breeze. I notice Carlton smiling and nodding his head as she speaks. She's got a 22-inch Pamela Anderson waist and breasts the size of cantaloupes.

"She's great," Carlton says, after Nathalie leaves. "Good job finding her."

"Yes, but I think Priscilla is a better candidate."

"Why? Because she's black? Because she's a single mom and she really needs the money?" Carlton shakes his head back and forth. Crosses his arms over his chest. "I knew it. I knew you were gonna say Priscilla. You've got that whole Save the Whales mentality," he says.

I roll my eyes. "Since when was hiring a qualified black woman akin to saving a whale, Carlton?"

Carlton puts both his hands out, palms up. Like he's pleading for his life. "We need someone full-time. Nathalie said it herself—she's willing to work long hours." He shakes his head. Pinches the bridge of his nose. "Priscilla is a liability. A single mom has too many responsibilities. I mean, what if her kid gets sick? We can't afford to have someone miss work. We need a warm body!"

I suddenly imagine Nathalie's warm body. Chipper and bouncy. Dressed in tight, dipping blouses. Sure, she was a bright girl, I give her that. She was no dummy. But still.

I chew the edge of my lip. Put my hands on my hips. Stand military style. Like an Army General. "I don't know about Nathalie," I say, firmly.

"C'mon, Maddy. Don't let jealousy get in the way of clear thinking. I know you're not the type of woman who's threatened by the younger version—it's beneath you," Carlton says.

"Younger version!" I almost spit. "Jesus, Carlton!"

"Easy there, wildcat. You know what I mean." He throws his arm around my waist and pulls me close to him.

"You're breaking our pact," I say. I try to struggle from his grip but he holds me tight.

"Fuck it," he says, planting a long, wet kiss on my lips.

I'm at a loss for words. I can't argue on Priscilla's behalf without looking insecure. And I don't want Carlton to think Nathalie got to me. Nathalie and her warm, bouncy body.

I wave my hand airily. Not a care in the world. "Look, if it's Nathalie you want, it's Nathalie you get," I say. "But don't come bitching to me when she makes a mistake."

"That's my girl," Carlton says. He stares down into my eyes, and I feel my knees weaken.

After we have sex, I trudge back to my office. Call Priscilla with the bad news.

"I knew it probably wouldn't work out," she says, calmly.

I sigh. And then dial Nathalie. I have to cover the phone with my hand when she squeals. "Ohmygaaah, this is so incredibly awesome! Thank you so much, Miss Piatro. You're awesome!"

"Please," I say. "Call me Maddy."

Chapter 35

"Let's cut to the chase, here. What do you want, lady? You want him in the hospital? Broken legs, what?" Dick leans over the table and stares at me.

I press my hand against my chest, all prim and lady-like. "Oh no. Nothing violent."

"Got it. So you want me to threaten his life. Scare the b'jesus out of him. Tell him I'll cut his balls off if he bothers you?"

I cringe. But then, I imagine Carlton hearing a man with the darkest black eyes he's ever seen threaten to cut off his crown jewels and as much as I hate to admit it, the thought kind of tickles me. I wouldn't mind if this guy scared the crap out of Carlton. Got his blood pumping. It might be good to take Mr. Perfect down a notch.

But that's not really my style.

"Actually, I was thinking of something a bit out of the ordinary," I say.

Dick leans back in his chair and cracks his knuckles. "After what that asshole did to you, he ain't gonna need a band-aid. He's gonna need a priest," he says.

I stare at Dick a moment and wonder if he's jerking my chain.

I mean, the guy is one gorgeous piece of ass, and he really looks like a softie. Except for those black, black eyes.

"You know, Dick. Maybe you should think about going into personal security. Instead of hurting people," I say, because suddenly I've morphed into Dr. Phil.

Dick shakes his head, vigorously.

"Oh, c'mon. I bet Madonna could use another guy like you," I say.

"Nah. She got it covered," he says. "Plus, I already tried doin' the personal security gig. Didn't work out."

"Really?"

"Sure. Did you ever see that movie with Whitney Houston and Kevin Costner?" he asks.

"*The Bodyguard.* Of course," I nod. "It's a classic."

"Well, it ain't like that, guardin' people. I had this gig guardin' some big-time drug traffickers in Columbia, Guatemala, Mexico—all over down there," he says. "And it was terrible. Talk about a bunch of spoiled brats. It was like I was their servant, or somethin'. One guy made me wax his Ferrari."

I throw my arms up in the air, dramatically. "Jeez, Dick! You can't let a couple of rich South American drug dealers get you down," I say, shaking my head. "They're the worst kind of brats. *Everyone* knows that."

"You think so?" he asks, raising a thick, dark eyebrow.

"I know so," I say, confidently. "Those cartel guys make Elizabeth Taylor look low maintenance."

Dick chuckles, leans back in his chair, tucks his hands behind his head like an executive. "You're pretty funny for a broad," he says.

"I try," I say.

And I wonder what this is. Exactly. Witty repartee? Flirting? What? Am I actually trying to seduce my hired gun? I mean, sure. It's been an Ice Age since I had sex, but still—

"Trust me," Dick says. "Guardin' ain't for me. And plus the money's no good. I'm much better doin' what I do. That way, I get to work for myself. I'm like, my own boss, ya know?"

"Well, there's certainly a lot of business out there," I say.

"Yeah, trouble is, I'm havin' problems gettin' the word out about my services. I mean, it's like, I know there're a lot of broads out there—broads like you—who had some guy dump on 'em, and they want a little revenge, you know. Sometimes not a lot. Just a little. And it'll make 'em feel better. But they don't know how to get in touch with me."

"I see," I say, stroking my chin. I sit in silence for a few minutes and think about Dick. I picture him as one of my clients. My juices start flowing, suddenly, and I go into "Maddy Marketing Mode."

"The problem here is not clients, Dick. You've got plenty of potential clients, like you said. Your problem is marketing. It's all about marketing."

I lean forward in my chair and stare him in the eye, like I've done a hundred times before when I worked for Henry.

"You need a slogan," I advise. "Something that really nails it home. Because your services are up in the air. I wasn't even sure what you did. In advertising and marketing, the key is—Specifics. Be specific. Nail it. Bring it home. I mean, you definitely need business cards. And maybe some fliers."

I'm talking fast now, moving my hands in the air, like I'm juggling balls. "You can't just sit back and wait for clients to come to you," I say, pointing in the air. "Because that's not steady business. You've got to reach out and touch someone," I say. I lean forward across the table and grab Dick by his leather jacket lapels. "Get it?"

"If anyone other than you had just grabbed my jacket like that, I would've broken their fingers," he says, winking at me.

"Yikes," I shudder. I let go of the jacket. Give Dick his space.

He's nodding as I grab a notepad from my messenger bag and scrawl out a brief marketing plan.

"What are we looking at here? You want to expand your customer base to women. Am I right? Well, there's something you should know about women, Dick. We're not big on blood and guts. You've probably got some male clients who get off on hearing about broken ribs and hacked-off limbs. And that can't be helped. Boys will be boys. But women are different. We're a little queasy when it comes to that stuff. I mean, for example. I bet Scarface is your favorite movie, right?"

"Love Pacino," Dick says.

"Exactly. Well, women hate that movie. Especially the part with the chainsaw. We cover our eyes and turn our heads. But it's not because we're weak. We simply prefer our revenge to be more subtle. More clever, if you will. We're more like spiders."

Dick sits up in his chair and smacks the table with both his palms. "Black widduhs, right?"

I point at him. "Exactly." I look Dick straight in the eye. "You're going to market yourself as the Black Widow's Best Friend—you, my dear Sir, are *The Web*."

"I'm the web?" Dick says.

"That's right. You're the web."

"So let's practice," I say. "You're going to market yourself to me. Really sell me on your services. Pretend that I'm a female client."

"But you are a female client."

I take a deep, patient breath. "Let's pretend I'm *another* female client. Someone brand new. I've seen your brochure."

"I'm doin' a brochure?" Dick asks, incredulously.

I raise an eyebrow. "How're you planning to get clients if you don't advertise?"

"Word of mouth?"

"Guess again," I say.

Dick looks stumped.

"We want to tell people about your skills," I say. "I'm imagining something along the lines of"—at this point, I put my palms up in the air to emphasize my banner headline— "Safe, discreet, street-savvy. Man-for-hire. To do your dirty work."

I pause for a moment. And then I nail it. "They say Hell hath no fury like a woman scorned. But Heaven is in the Sweet Revenge."

Dick sits back in his chair, awestruck.

"Awesome," he whispers. His eyes are distant. As if he's envisioning himself as the CEO of Revenge, Incorporated.

"So pretend I'm a new female customer, Dick. I've seen your brochure and my interests are piqued. I've taken a small bite of the hors d'oeuvre that you've dangled in front of me."

Dick's face gets serious. He bites his lip and rocks back and forth in his chair. I can tell he's really concentrating.

"Okay. For example," I say. "I come here and tell you some guy has left me at the altar. He says the reason he can't marry me is because I'm fat. I tell you I want revenge." I snap my fingers. "Quick. What do you recommend?"

"I'll take a crowbar and jam it up his ass!" Dick offers.

"Wrong! Your goal here, Dick, is to tailor the punishment to fit the crime. And remember the heeby-jeeby factor."

"I offer to break in the guy's house, and steal his TV." Dick smiles broadly. Obviously pleased with his answer.

I shake my head. "This asshole will just buy another TV. Doesn't solve anything. And besides, he left me at the altar and called me fat. I think he deserves much worse."

Dick peers at me. "What if the lady is a real porker? Then the guy was just tellin' the troof, right?"

I wag my finger back and forth. "A man who leaves a woman at an altar needs a better excuse than her weight. That's sleazy and abusive."

"Good point," Dick says.

"First, ask the woman if there's something this guy loves. Something he truly cherishes. Like, let's say he loves his job. And his boss thinks he's terrific. So, you can offer to embarrass the guy in front of his boss. Or you send a fax to the guy's boss saying that the guy is laundering money—clever, you see."

Dick grins.

"Or you could always call the IRS," I say.

"Why?"

"Because there's nothing more excruciating than an audit, Dick."

"I've heard this."

"So, you can call the IRS and tell them the guy's been hiding bundles of cash in his attic."

"Can't the broad do that herself?"

"When you call the IRS, they make you wait on hold," I explain.

Dick nods. "It's a good service and it won't get me busted," he says. "I need to get away from the violent stuff."

"Exactly!" I smack the table with my palm and Dick reacts to the noise. I see him reach quickly inside his leather jacket. As if he's about to pull a gun. And my heart almost stops.

Dick relaxes a bit and then grins at me. "Sorry. Creature of habit."

"Are you . . . carrying?" I ask.

He pats his jacket on the bulge where the gun is located. "I never leave home without my Marlon Brando."

"You've nicknamed your gun "Marlon Brando?" I ask.

"What? Too obvious?" Dick is looking at me in a way that makes me think he really wants my opinion.

"Are you a Godfather fanatic?" I ask.

"I loved the Don," Dick says. And then, to my huge surprise, he puffs out his cheeks and does a Marlon Brando impression. Right there in Starbucks.

"If I do you a favor, you do me a favor," he says, in that hoarse, throaty, half unintelligible Godfather voice. He's not bad, really. He's even got the accent down.

"Pretty darn good," I say, and I nod my head approvingly. Like a schoolteacher trying to boost the confidence of the slow kid.

Dick beams at me. He taps his finger at Carlton's photograph. "I can't wait to see what you've got up your sleeve for this bozo," he says.

"I need a week to come up with a plan," I say.

Chapter 36

I work like a dog until midnight. When I walk past Carlton's office, I see his light is still on. Part of our pact involves business independence. Carlton and I drive to the office in separate cars. We never have lunch together and we never ask the other person what time they're going home. We don't want to become one of those couples who's always trying to schedule their day together. It's exhausting and it spoils the spontaneity. Sometimes I love it when Carlton gets home late from work. And he loves it when I get home late. We surprise each other that way. It keeps things interesting. In a four-year relationship where we work together, play together, and live together, we've got to take active steps to keep the romance alive.

I stop outside his door but I don't knock. He must think I've gone home. I'm usually home by this hour, and so is he.

He's on the phone with his father. I can hear his dad's voice loud and clear over the speakerphone.

Carlton says, "Maddy wanted me to hire this woman, Priscilla. She's got great experience but she's a single mom so she can only work part-time. Oh, and she's black," Carlton adds, to my surprise.

"Well that's just terrific, Carlton. Next thing you know, Maddy'll wanna hire a goddamn AIDS patient."

"Dad, please."

"Tell Florence Nightingale we're in business to make some goddamned money. Not to give away the farm, you hear? You need a full-time accounting person. Period. Hire the college graduate. I don't care what she looks like. She could be a supermodel or Miss America for all I care."

"It's distracting, Dad. She's a D-cup," I hear Carlton say. I feel my face get hot. It's not that I didn't expect Carlton to notice Nathalie's huge melon tits—we even joked about it—Carlton and I. After Nathalie left, he'd said, "Do you think those were real?" And we both burst out laughing. But now he was telling his dad about it.

Not good.

Carlton's dad chuckles. "Makes going to the office a damn pleasure. Not a chore."

"I know, Dad. It's just, Maddy's been great. If this girl Nathalie makes her uncomfortable—"

Carlton's dad whistles over the phone. A low whistle. Like a death march.

"Sounds like your girlfriend is stirrin' up a hornet's nest over there," he says. "Just remember what I told you, son."

"I know, Dad. And you're right. I'm gonna do something about it," Carlton says.

"Better sooner than later," his dad says. "No room for broken hearts in this business."

I hear Carlton replace the phone in the receiver. My heart is beating quickly so I tiptoe out of the office. My car is parked in back, thank God. I gun the engine and race from the parking lot.

I'm gonna do something about it, Carlton had said. Something about what? Our office arrangement? That must be it. Carlton wants me to work from home. The office thing is hurting our relationship.

I get home and I don't want to be mad. But I'm steaming. When Carlton comes in the door, I lay it on him.

"You didn't hire Priscilla because she's black," I say. "And you're afraid your dad wouldn't approve."

"Please," Carlton says. "Spare me your PC bullshit. My dad hires more black people than anyone in East Texas."

"I think you're uncomfortable having a black woman in the office," I say.

"I think you're uncomfortable having an attractive, young woman in the office," he snaps.

"You're right, Carlton. You've figured it out. I'm jealous of a squealing, twenty-two-year-old with fake tits the size of Rhode Island. Not to mention, she's got zero, ZERO experience." I'm fuming. I can even feel sweat pooling under my arms.

"Look, sweetie. Priscilla was better qualified. Hands Down. But Nathalie had huge bazoombas," Carlton says.

"Don't be sarcastic."

Carlton puts his hands in front of his chest, like he's cupping a huge pair of breasts. "Get a load of these cannonballs!" he says. He struts across the room, swinging his hips side-to-side, walking like a girl.

He's rarely goofy like this. And I can't help myself. So I laugh.

Carlton grabs me and hoists me over his shoulder.

He hustles me into the bedroom and throws me down. "That's it. You're mine," he says, crawling on top of me.

That night, I let him do whatever he wants.

At breakfast the next morning, Carlton tells me he thinks it best if I work from home. "Look, babe, this office thing is putting a damper on our sex life," he says.

"It didn't seem to put a damper on it last night," I say, smiling at him. Pouring more coffee in his mug. Tussling his hair.

"I'll get you everything you need. High-speed Internet, phone, fax, printer, scanner. You name it. Plus, you can still have your office."

"Gee thanks, boss."

"Maybe you could spend a few days at the office, a few days at home. Mix it up."

"Oh. I see. I run the company for the past two years during the hardest part while you're traveling around. And you come back, things are steady. On the upswing. I get everything off the ground. And now you want me working a few days at home?"

"Don't take it personally, Maddy. You've been phenomenal. It's just that—what couple in their right mind spends all day and all night together? It's stifling." He smiles up at me and flutters his eyelashes in a funny way. "And besides, absence makes the heart grow fonder."

I know Carlton's problem. He feels like I'm running the show. The employees, the interns, school officials, and even the customers have gotten accustomed to calling me. It's not that they don't like Carlton, it's just that I've been the go-to guy for so long, they're familiar with me. Plus, I've got a knack for thinking on my feet. Problem solving. Carlton, on the other hand, tends to dilly-dally. He's a huge procrastinator, and I've had complaints from customers about him not returning their calls or e-mails. It's bad for business. Carlton knows it's not his strong point.

"My job is to find new money. Grow our investor pool," he says. "The nuts and bolts of the day-to-day operations don't interest me."

The other day, Carlton took a call from one of our largest distributors, but the distributor asked to speak with me. This threw Carlton for a loop. He was in a surly mood all day.

"I'm the goddamned CEO!" he kept saying. It was bad.

So I'm not surprised he wants me to work from home. He

feels threatened. "I won't be effective working from home," I say. "I have to be in the mix."

Carlton carries his cereal bowl to the kitchen sink. "You're probably right," he mutters.

I walk over to him and put my arms around his waist. He turns around and pecks me on the forehead. A quick peck.

"We'll make it work," he says.

That night, Carlton takes me out to dinner. He orders an expensive Italian wine, a Brunello. It's so delicious, we end up keeping the label from the bottle.

Carlton raises his glass, and we toast our relationship, our company, and our future.

Chapter 37

"If you don't want me to slam his balls in a vice, why'd you call me?" Dick asks. He chomps half of his chocolate chip cookie and I notice his eyes roll back. Kind of like a Great White shark.

We're back at Starbucks. Sitting at the same table. Drinking the same coffee.

"You're a professional, Dick. You know how to find people and be discreet," I say.

I pull out my notebook from my messenger bag. The revenge plan I've outlined is detailed inside. I've spent a week devising the best ways to get back at Carlton in nonviolent retribution.

"I need you to do three jobs for me, Dick. Three different jobs. Each one is going to hurt Carlton in a different way. But not, I repeat, NOT in a physical way."

Dick scowls so I know he's disappointed.

"Promise me you won't cross the line on this," I say, shooting him a stern look.

"You're the boss, Jane," he says, shrugging. He wipes crumbs off his mouth with the back of his hand again. Swigs some coffee. Burps.

"Okay, there's an awards ceremony tomorrow night at the Marriott. In the Grand Ballroom. Carlton will be receiving an award for best young CEO. There'll be a lot of customers, employees, public officials, and, most importantly, press at this event."

"How do you know?"

"Because I set it up that way. It took me six months to get this event off the ground. The worst thing Carlton could imagine would be bad press. Losing face in public. So, when he gets up to accept the award—"

"You want me to rush the stage with a baseball bat and beat the crap out of him?"

I hold my hand in the air, like a stop sign.

"As fun as that sounds, Dick, this'll be much worse. Trust me. That guy could use a little public humiliation. A pimple on his perfect image."

"I don't want no one to take my picture," Dick says. "Not in my line of work."

"No one will take your picture. You're going to blend in."

"Like a lizard?"

"Yes, Dick."

"Hey, Jane. What are those lizards called? With the skin that changes color?"

"Chameleons."

Dick sits back in his chair and nods his head, appreciatively. "So, I'm the chameleon," he says.

I sit for a moment and imagine Dick inside the Grand Ballroom of the Marriott. Wearing his leather jacket and black motorcycle boots.

"Do you own a suit?" I ask.

"Does a cat have an ass?" Dick replies.

"There will be hundreds of people at this awards banquet. So if you wear a suit, you'll blend in just fine."

"I got it, Jane. What's next?"

"Okay. When Carlton accepts the award, he'll give a speech

about the future of the company—I wrote this speech and he's given it a zillion times. That's when it's time to pounce."

I pull a sheath of papers from my bag and plop them on the table. "I want you to leave copies of these on all the tables."

"What is it?"

"Copies of last quarter's balance sheet. I've circled a few discrepancies which Carlton's investors and the business journalists may find interesting. A miniature version of Enron."

"Jeez, you don't pull no punches, do you, lady?"

I smile. "During his speech, I want you to start circulating these to different tables. In fact, make sure they fall into a lot of people's laps. Then I want you to leave. And leave quickly. Like within a minute or two."

"Won't he know it's you? Who came up with this?"

"He'll never in a million years think it was me," I say. "This guy tends to fire his employees on a regular basis—especially accountants and financial geeks who don't agree with his numbers. Carlton's got more than a few enemies out there. He was even getting death threats from an employee once. Plus, he never thought I understood the numbers. Because we never talked about it. I learned about this from an employee who used to work for us. A guy I trusted."

"Here's your entrance ticket," I say, handing Dick an envelope. "This event is pretty fancy, but I know you already own a terrific suit."

Dick looks at me and the light dances in his otherwise jet black eyes. If I didn't know better, I'd think he was pleased.

"Okay, so that sounds easy. What's the next project?" he asks.

"One at a time," I say. "One at a time."

"I still wish I could set his hair on fire," Dick says.

"Dick, Dick, Dick," I say, shaking my head. "Physical pain is only temporary. But emotional pain lasts a lifetime."

Chapter 38

I'd been having unprotected sex with Carlton for four years, and yet, the week I was late, I never expected to be pregnant.

In the morning, I woke up and felt nauseous, so I knew something was up. I felt my body changing, slightly. My stomach felt hard as a brick. My breasts were tender and sore. But I didn't have time to pay attention to this.

Carlton was heading for an important breakfast called "Breakfast with the Mayor," where he was about to receive an award from the mayor himself. The **Sensitive Young CEO** award. I'd arranged the whole shebang. It took me four months to lobby the mayor's office, another month of sending out press releases, and getting the editor of the *Business Journal* to write a front-page piece on Carlton—including photographs of him and the Organic School Kids logo. I ordered dozens of golf shirts. Carlton was even wearing one to the ceremony. He wanted to wear an Italian suit but I encouraged him to wear a golf shirt tucked into a pair of freshly pressed khaki pants.

"You want to be instantly recognizable—and approachable," I say, pulling his pants from a dry-cleaning bag.

I prep him for the awards ceremony. "Be sure to thank the mayor and his staff—especially Doug Matthews, his economic development guru. Doug is the guy behind the guy. And he never gets recognized in public. You'll score miles of points," I wink.

Carlton says, "I thought his name was Paul Matthews."

"Everyone calls him 'Doug,'" I reply. "He hates the name 'Paul.'"

"How do you know?"

"I saw him on TV," I say. "Channel 7 did a segment on him."

Carlton smiles at me in the way that makes my knees weak. "My little tiger," he says, tweaking my chin.

I smell the scent of his cologne.

"Go get 'em," I say, kissing him on the lips.

He wipes his mouth with the back of his hand.

"Can't have lipstick on me today," he says.

"I'm not wearing lipstick," I say. I'm expecting Carlton to say, "In that case—" and lay a huge, wet one on me, but he doesn't.

"Gotta jet," he says. "I'm running late."

I smile. Lately, Carlton has taken to saying phrases like, "Gotta jet," or "It's time to bounce," when he's ready to leave. I don't know where he's come up with these. It's almost as if he's been watching late-night VH1.

I want to correct him. To tell him he's much too mature to talk like this. And besides, he should be more careful with his image. Especially as a budding young CEO. It would be a public relations nightmare for a reporter to print something along the lines of . . . "I was in a bar when I overheard Carlton Connors, the CEO of the largest growing organic foods company say, "I gotta blow this joint."

As soon as Carlton walks out the door, I feel my stomach do a cartwheel. I rush to the toilet and vomit. On a hunch, I speed to Walgreen's and buy a pregnancy test. I hold my breath as I pee, but it isn't necessary. The two pink lines show up immediately. I read the instruction manual. The EPT test has a 97 percent accuracy rate. This means there's a good 3 percent chance I'm in the clear. It's not great odds, but I'll take what I can get. I race back to the store, cursing myself for not buying more tests. I buy one of each brand. Even the generic Walgreen's brand.

Two lines. Two lines. Two lines. Two lines.

The news doesn't hit me for a while. I throw the tests away. Make some chamomile tea. Watch a Seinfeld re-run. I think I even laugh. It's the one where Elaine asks whether a guy is "sponge-worthy."

I call into work and tell everyone I'm sick. My employees are surprised because it's the first time I've taken a sick day. Ever. In the history of Organics 4 Kids.

I regard the stack of pregnancy tests in the trash. It's not the right time for a baby, I know that. But Carlton and I are both in our thirties. We've lived together four years, and we're basically engaged. I twirl the Juliet ring around on my finger. I never imagined myself as a shotgun wedding type of gal. But hey! Maybe this is fate.

I'm excited about the possibility of Carlton and I starting our family. I walk into the study. Plenty of space for a nursery, I think, imagining a baby bed tucked neatly in the corner.

I know I shouldn't bother Carlton in the middle of his coffee with the mayor, but this news can't wait. I punch the numbers to his cell phone.

"What's up?" he says, automatically.

"Are you still with the mayor."

"Just left," he says.

"How did it go?" I venture.

"Awesome," he says. "And I owe it all to you," he chuckles.

"Well, I've got something big I need to tell you."

"Shoot."

"I'm pregnant," I say, because there's no reason to beat around the bush.

Carlton doesn't speak.

"Hello?" I say. "Still there?"

"I . . . I don't know what to say, Maddy. How did this happen?"

"Well, I think you know how it happened."

"No—I mean, are you sure?"

"Unless seven pregnancy tests are wrong," I say.

"Jesus," he says. And I notice his voice has dropped to a low, unrecognizable tone.

"When are you coming home?" I ask.

He sighs. One of those weight-of-the-world sighs. I imagine him pinching the bridge of his nose.

"Ah, Maddy. C'mon. I'm booked solid this afternoon. Meetings, meetings, and more meetings. Then I'm playing racquetball with David Myers. I'd hate to cancel. He's a potential investor if we need to do another round of financing."

"Don't cancel," I say, in a strong voice. "We can talk about this tonight. When it's convenient."

"Great," he says, as if he's ending a conference call.

I'm a little taken aback but then I catch myself. He's nervous, I think.

"Well, good-bye, Romeo."

"Bye," he says, and hangs up.

I mope around the apartment. Then call Cheryl. My ob-gyn. Better to have a doctor tell me I'm pregnant. Just in case.

Cheryl agrees to fit me in.

"It's an emergency," I say.

"Herpes outbreak?" she asks.

"Baby," I reply.

She's silent a moment. "Come in for a blood test," she says, firmly.

Cheryl is a really good doctor. She actually talks to her patients on the phone. Can you believe that?

An hour later, I've got my feet in the stirrups again and I'm staring up at the awful cat poster. The cat dangling upside down from a tree with the tagline "Hang in there!" It's awful. It really is.

Cheryl presses my abdomen in different spots, reads the lab results from my blood and urine samples, and confirms the pregnancy.

"Are you SURE, sure?" I ask.

"I'm positive, Madeline. We can schedule a vaginal ultrasound if you want to see it," she says.

"Uh, what are my options?" I ask. And I realize this is a stupid, stupid question.

Cheryl walks to the sink and washes her hands. "I don't do terminations here in this office," she says. "But I work at Planned Parenthood on Tuesdays."

"I wasn't thinking about uh . . . um, termination," I say. "I'm thinking of having the baby," I say.

Cheryl says, "That's your choice, of course. I thought you were asking me about termination services. Since you're single."

Before I can tell Cheryl I'm in a long-term monogamous relationship, and that I live with my fiancé, she walks briskly out the door.

She's a fast cookie, Cheryl.

Chapter 39

Dick and I agree not to have contact by phone or e-mail. We'll exchange messages on the message board at Starbucks. So instead of the usual lost dog, and babysitter needed, I'll tack up a secret missive to my favorite hired gun. It will say, *To D. From J. Wednesday. 4:00.*

Yep. This is how Dick and Jane have decided to communicate. It's simple. Easy. Convenient. Not a lot of bells and whistles. There won't be any messages waiting for me in my morning newspaper. Like in the movies. No carrier pigeons or anything like that. There will just be a note tacked up on a corkboard at good ol' Starbucks.

The next night I go to my tennis lesson. Deepak introduces me to the new guy. The new *very cute* guy. Apparently, he will be my hitting partner during the lesson.

"This is Nicholas," Deepak says.

"Nick," the guy corrects him.

Wow. First Dick. Now Nick. I never saw the storm cloud coming, but apparently it's raining men.

Nicholas, or Nick, strolls over and I see he's wearing all black. Not a tennis purist like me, but still. He's six feet tall, with wavy blond hair, and the nicest smile I've seen in a long time. Nick has cute dimples when he smiles and sharp blue eyes.

"I'm Jane—I mean, Madeline," I say, shaking his hand.

I hold my breath and check his hand for a wedding ring.

Nada. Nothing. Zippo.

He probably has a live-in girlfriend, though. Or maybe he's gay. "Nice to meet you Jane Madeline."

"It's just Madeline. But everyone calls me Maddy," I say. I smile at him and flutter my eyelashes a little. I realize I'm nervous. My palms are even sweaty.

Jeez, Maddy. Get a grip!

Deepak tells us to "pair up" so Nick and I move to opposite ends of the court and begin warming up.

I lob the ball over easily because I don't know Nick's level of play. I'm pleasantly surprised when he expertly hits the ball low and fast back across the net.

I return the ball hard down the line. Nick races for it and I watch his body move as he whacks it back. This guy is certainly graceful on the court. And quick as lightning. I'm glad for the competition.

We hit back and forth for a while. Nick plays well. In fact, he's the best man I've ever played against, besides my father.

I think he's impressed with me, too, because he walks up to the net and says, "Where did you learn to hit like that?" I notice he's out of breath. And I'm just warming up.

"My dad enrolled me in tennis camp when I was still in a stroller," I say.

Nick smiles and I notice his nice, straight teeth.

"Smart guy," he says.

"Yes, he was. He passed away a few years ago, but every time I'm on a tennis court, I think of him."

Whoa, Maddy. Hold your horses.

I'm suddenly sharing personal information with this guy and I've known him a whole two seconds.

Nick shuffles his feet a little. And taps his racquet against his shoe. First one shoe, then the other.

"Yeah, my dad died of cancer last year. He was a big tennis buff, too," he says. "We even went to Wimbledon."

"Oh my gosh! I bet that was incredible," I say.

Nick looks up and our eyes meet. We kind of stare at each other for a second too long. And then we both look down at our shoes. There's suddenly so much chemistry between us, I think I'm going to be electrocuted. Of course, it could all be in my head.

Deepak is watching us from the sidelines and he says, "Back to work, lazy people!" Then he decides to ignore us and circulate around the other couples in the class.

I lean against the net. "So why are you taking lessons, Nick? I mean, you don't seem like you need them."

"I can use a little help on my swing," he says. "But how about you? I mean, you've got this tennis thing down to a science. You definitely don't need to be here."

I refrain from telling Nick that I'm a lonely, pathetic woman. Because I figure it might end up sounding lonely and pathetic. So I say, "My serve isn't what it used to be."

He says, "Tell me about it."

We go back to our individual sides of the court and have a vigorous hour of play.

Afterward, Deepak congratulates us on a game well played.

Nick sits on the bench with a water bottle. He turns to me and says, "Hey, do you want to get a smoothie or something?"

I zip my racquet up inside my tennis bag, stand and brush my hands off against my tennis skirt.

"Absolutely," I say, flashing him my most winning smile.

I follow Nick's car to Jamba Juice. And I'm wondering what on earth is going on. I haven't dated anyone since Carlton the Terrible. So it's been, like, forever. I wonder if this guy is actually interested in little ol' me? Or does he just want company? *Maybe he's bored*, I think. I decide that he's bored.

Nick gets out of his car and escorts me into the juice bar. "After you," he says, holding the door open for me.

"Thank you so much," I coo, and I realize I sound like Heather.

I order a strawberry, banana, and peach. Nick goes with a protein shake. We sit outside at a table and slurp at our straws.

So, tell me about you," Nick says. He's looking at me with those blue eyes and smiling with those dimples. And honestly, it throws me a little off balance.

"I went to the University of Texas for both my undergraduate and graduate degree," I say. "They say that people who come to Austin never leave, and I guess I was one of them."

Nick laughs. "It's a great school. I went to Vandy, myself. But, unlike you, I couldn't wait to leave Nashville. I guess I'm an East Coast guy at heart," he says.

"Oh yeah? Where are you from?"

"Boston originally. But my family moved around a lot."

"Witness protection program?" I ask, and Nick laughs.

"My dad was in the Air Force," he says. "So tell me more about you. Any siblings?"

"A younger brother. He's great. Ronnie," I say. And I realize I'm smiling like a proud sister.

Nick chews on his straw a minute and stares down at the table.

"What's wrong?"

"Huh? Oh nothing. I'm an only child. I always wished I had a brother, though."

"I don't know what I'd do without Ronnie," I say. I finish my smoothie, crumple the cup and lob it into the trash can from a good distance.

"Two points," Nick says.

"Well, thanks for the great tennis match," I say. I suddenly feel sweaty, tired, and a little grungy. I wonder if Nick thinks I look gross. I'm second-guessing myself because it's been so long. Plus, I wish this juice joint were a tad darker. The sidewalk tables are lit up like a Christmas tree. Nick can probably see every dirty pore on my face.

"Same time next week?" I ask, and I immediately regret leaving so suddenly. Nick looks like he was just about to ask me for my phone number.

Oh well.

I'm on a mission. And this guy probably wouldn't think it was very attractive if he found out I'd hired a mercenary to get back at my ex-fiancé.

He'd probably think I was nuts. In fact, I'm beginning to think I'm nuts.

But that's what happens with women in love. They do some crazy shit, sometimes.

Nick says, "I'd like that." He stands and we shake hands, awkwardly. We stroll back through the parking lot.

I look up at the sky. "Nice night. Lots of stars."

Nick takes a moment to look up at the sky, too. Then he looks straight at me.

"Beautiful," he says.

An hour later, after I've showered and brushed my teeth, I'm sitting in my bathrobe with my feet propped up. Leafing through the various business journals. That's when I spot the article. On the front page, no less. The *City Business Journal* shows a picture of Carlton at the awards dinner. The headline reads, YOUNG CEO AWARD'S DINNER INTERRUPTED BY HECKLER.

Heckler! I sit up straight on my couch.

> Carlton Connors, recipient of the Young Giants Award, was called a fraud last night, by an angry heckler. The unidentified man threw a sheaf of paper in the air, which turned out to be a secret balance sheet from the company that did not

match the balance sheet sent out to the public. When asked to explain the discrepancy in the numbers, Mr. Connors was at a loss for words. "Certain forces have been against me the entire time," he said. "It's too bad my competitors had to falsify a document and stoop to this level."

Oh. My. God. I clap my hand to my mouth. I feel a momentary pang of guilt. But then, I can't help myself. I begin to laugh. And I can't stop. I imagine Dick jumping out of his seat, calling Carlton a fraud, throwing the papers in the air, and rushing from the ballroom.

Ready for round two, I think.

Chapter 40

I wasn't overjoyed about the pregnancy, but I wasn't sad about it, either. Deep down, in some odd way, I thought the experience could possibly bond Carlton and me. And make us closer as lovers and companions. I knew there were many couples that decided, for one reason or another, it wasn't the right time. A baby would be welcome at a later date, but not today. And I believed that day would come for us. Even if a baby seemed wrong now. At least we knew it was possible. Some couples had to turn to artificial insemination. But our love had created a natural pregnancy. And that was a beautiful thing. Our love would conquer all, I thought.

If Carlton thought having a baby was too much pressure, too much expense, too much everything—I didn't have to agree with him. Deep down, in my heart, I really wanted this baby.

Later that afternoon, Carlton shoots me an e-mail out of the blue. I'm expecting something sweet like: *It's all gonna be okay, my Juliet. Don't worry about a thing*. But instead, his message is weird. Formal.

I suddenly panic.

Maddy,
 What I want to tell you is difficult, so I thought it best to

e-mail you. That way, you have an opportunity to read what
I have to say and really think about it. I love you, but I'm
starting to think it would be best if I expanded my horizons.
Especially in light of the news from today. I think I need to be
honest. That is only fair to you.

I sit for a moment. Read the e-mail in silence.

Expand his horizons? What does that mean?

Oh, I get it. He doesn't want the baby. He wants room. Space.
Freedom from the responsibilities of fatherhood. And this is his
way of telling me. Expanding his horizons—makes sense. He
wants to travel freely, play golf, go hunting, hang out with the
guys on Saturday nights. He doesn't want a crying baby around.
A wife who keeps him tied up. A ball and chain on each leg.

I understand, Carlton. I understand, I think.

My dearest Romeo,
    Please don't freak out. I agree this isn't the best time for a
baby, but is it ever? I'm willing to discuss options.
    I love you!

Your Juliet

I sit by my laptop and wait. Five minutes later, Carlton sends
his reply.

Maddy,
    When I said I wanted to expand my horizons, I meant it. I
think it would be best if you and I re-evaluated.

Re-evaluated? Re-EVALUATED!

Hmm. I read about this once. In one of those "men are from a
different planet" books. Sometimes men like to retreat into a cave.
And women aren't supposed to chase them. We're supposed to

let them go into their caves and they'll come out and love us and want to be with us more than when they went into their cave.

Carlton,
   If you need some space, take it. I understand.

                                     M.

I get an instant response this time.

Maddy,
   The type of space I need, sweetie, may be permanent.

                                    Carlton

My body feels cold all of a sudden, and I shiver involuntarily. I stare at my laptop. Let the e-mail sink in.

Is Carlton breaking up with me on the day I tell him I'm pregnant?

I take the Juliet ring off my finger and read the engraving inside. *Forever, my Juliet.* But now Forever wants Permanent Space?

This doesn't jibe.

Before I can think about what I'm doing, I log into Carlton's hotmail account. I type "carltonconnors@hotmail.com."

Hmm. Password, password? I'm frantic. Is it another woman? What? I know I shouldn't be spying, but I want answers.

I try typing a few passwords, but get an instant message: *The password you typed is incorrect. Please try again.*

Damn!

I type in the word "Organic."

Nope.

"Organic 4 Kids"

No.

I type my own name.

Of course not.

Think!

I suddenly remember Carlton's dream boat. A 50-foot Bene-teau.

"What will you call it?" I remember asking him, one Sunday, as I glanced over his shoulder. He was surfing the Internet for sailing yachts. His favorite pastime.

"The Heretic," he replied. "I've always wanted to name my boat The Heretic."

I hold my breath. And type in the word "heretic."

The screen changes. I'm in! God, I should be in the CIA. Put my talents to use.

I scroll through Carlton's messages. I can feel my face burning bright red. I know what I'm doing is wrong. I've never doubted Carlton. Not once. Sure, I've caught him looking at other women. But what guy doesn't? Still. Something's not right. I feel it in my gut.

I see a message from his friend, David.

"Vegas, baby. Vegas." It reads.

A few months ago, Carlton went on a weekend trip for David's bachelor party. Carlton told me he hired a few strippers to come to the suite. The girls went a little crazy and had a sex show. Complete with toys. Right in front of them. Boys will be boys, I figured, at the time.

My fingers shake. I click open the *Vegas, baby. Vegas* e-mail. And scroll down the message.

Man, don't be an idiot and write this shit down, Carlton warns.

My heart starts beating. I know what's about to come. But I don't believe it.

His friend David writes, *Carlton, who was that hottie you took back to your room? You paid extra, didn't you, you sonof-abitch?*

I feel my heart stop. Maddy Piatro. Found dead in front of computer. Reading fiancé's e-mails.

I race through the other messages in Carlton's in-box.

Another from David.

How's the homefront with you know who? he asks.

Carlton replies. *The bomber has its target in sight.*

The bomber has its target in sight! Gee whiz. Apparently, Carlton's the Enola Gay and I'm Hiroshima.

My heart is pounding hard in my chest and that's when I hear the front door slam. Carlton! I quickly close out of the e-mail, stand up, and wipe my hair back from my face.

Carlton cruises into the room, a dark look on his face. "I don't feel the same as I did when we first started dating," he says, out of the blue.

I look at him. My heart is really going to town, now. My voice is shaky, but I try to sound calm. "Isn't that normal, babe? Doesn't every relationship have some ebb and flow? Ups and downs? I didn't even realize we were in a slump."

Carlton looks at me. Shrugs.

"Things have gotten so trivial," he says. "I mean, you told me what goddamn shirt to wear today."

"I'm your publicist!"

"Still," he says. "It's not sexy."

"Life is not a movie, Carlton. Don't you think I miss the flowers you used to bring me? All the love notes? Don't you think I miss that, too?"

"I can't bring flowers if I'm not feeling it," he mutters.

I want to tell him I know about his e-mails. But I can't. It'll be the straw that breaks the camel's back. He'll never forgive me.

"You cheated on me in Las Vegas, didn't you?" I demand, pointing at him.

"Does it really matter, Maddy? At this point?"

"Yes!"

"As a matter of fact, no. I thought about it. Some girl even came up to my room. Knocked on the door. One of the strippers. But I told her to get lost."

"And you expect me to believe that?"

"Believe what you want," he says, sounding fatigued.

I stare down at the floor.

"What if I tell you I'm having this baby?" I say. I want my voice to sound strong, but it's weak. Shaky and weak. A pathetic attempt at strength.

"Then you'll be alone," he says, simply.

At that moment, I feel as if I've been stabbed. Now I know how a stabbing feels. It hurts. Hurts in the gut. Not a quick jabbing pain. But a dull, sharp one. The kind of searing pain that never goes away.

I rush into Carlton's arms in a ball of tears. I'm crying so hard, my shirt is sopping wet.

"Please don't tell me you're breaking up with me! I thought you loved me!" I say, and I feel my shoulders hopping up and down. Uncontrollably.

"I do love you, Maddy," Carlton says. He holds me for a while and I completely crumble in his arms.

Carlton hustles me into the bedroom. "Don't cry. Don't cry," he says, over and over.

He hands me a box of Kleenex and I blow my nose. Hard.

"Look, Maddy. We've been together four years, we live together, and nothing's going to happen overnight. Let's just take a breather," he says.

"I'm pregnant, Carlton!" I almost scream. I hold my ring finger in the air. "I thought we were engaged!"

"I'll be there for you when you have the abortion," he says, quietly.

Chapter 41

I meet Dick at the coffee shop. Same table. Same coffee. Same big cookie.

He grins at me and tucks his thumbs underneath the lapels of his leather jacket. "I was good, wasn't I?" he asks, right away.

"You did great!" I chirp. I lean forward to pat him on the shoulder, but then I remember what he said about broken fingers. Dick likes his space, apparently.

"So whatcha got next? What does the female Don have for me?"

"It's time to hit Carlton where it really hurts," I say.

"In the balls?"

"In the pocketbook."

"I know. I was just kiddin' around," Dick says. He bites off half the cookie. Munches it down. Wipes crumbs from his lips. Takes a swig from his coffee.

Dick motions for me to come closer. Like he wants to tell me a secret. "Wanna know somethin'?" he asks, and I'm not sure I do. Because he could confess to murdering someone and then I'd be stuck knowing about the crime. Better to be ignorant, I figure. But I hear myself say, "Sure! Tell me."

"I drink my coffee black because it's part of the look—you

know—you can't be a tough guy and ask for a latte. But honestly, I prefer my coffee with honey. You mind puddin' some honey in my coffee?" he asks, holding his cup up. "I can't have anyone see me do it."

"Sure, Dick." I stand and walk over to the counter where there's nonfat milk, cream, cinnamon, napkins, and coffee stirrers. Sure enough, there's a small honey bear. I turn it and squeeze honey into my tough guy's coffee.

I walk back to the table, set the cup down.

"Just like my mom used to make," Dick says. He takes a sip and actually sighs, "Ahhhh." Just like they do in the commercials.

"Been a long time since I had it with honey," he says, and he looks pleased.

I feel someone tap me on the shoulder so I spin around. It's Nick. The new guy from the tennis court.

He looks terrific. In smart-looking dress pants, and a pressed navy shirt. "Hey there," he says. "I see you found my favorite Starbucks."

He smiles at me with those gorgeous dimples and, I may be dreaming, but the electricity is back.

I glance quickly across the table. Dick is shifting around in his chair, looking annoyed and uncomfortable. His black eyes flash and I suddenly remember who I'm dealing with. A real hired gun. Someone who's been in the trenches. Someone who carries a concealed weapon that he calls his Marlon Brando

Nick is looking across the table at Dick, and I guess he expects an introduction. So I say, "Nick, this is Dick."

I like to keep it simple.

Dick scowls at me but rises up halfway in his seat and shakes Nick's outstretched hand.

"Nice ta meet ya," Dick says. He stands up abruptly and says,

"Excuse me a sec, Jane. I gotta use the can." I watch as he strides into the bathroom.

Nick looks at me and says the inevitable. "Jane?"

"Sometimes I go by my middle name," I say, and I feel my face turning pink.

Of all the Starbucks on the planet, you had to walk into mine, I think.

"Sorry, am I interrupting a date?" Nick asks and he's peering at me with those clear, clear blue eyes.

"No, it's nothing like that," I say. "This is just. . ." *Just what, Maddy?* I take a deep breath. "This is just business."

Nick says, "Oh."

And I can tell he wants to know about the business. I mean, what kind of business could I be doing with a guy like Dick?

I don't want to lie because that's no way to start a relationship—so I say, "I'm doing some freelance marketing for Dick."

Nick smiles down at me. "Well, in that case, I was wondering if you wanted to grab dinner or something later."

Yes.

"No."

Nick looks a little taken aback.

"I mean, I would really love to, but I'm kind of busy tonight. Can I take a rain check?"

He smiles. "Sure. How do I get in touch with you?"

I pull my notebook out of my bag and jot down my cell number, along with my full name, *Madeline Jane Piatro*, and a smiley face. Then I cover the paper with my hand and write, "for a good time in bed, please call me." I fold the paper in two and hand it to him. I expect him to put it in his pocket but he opens it right up and looks at it.

"Funny," he says.

"I thought you'd like that," I say.

He smiles at me with those killer dimples and I feel the electricity buzzing and I wonder if he feels it, too.

"I'll call you later," he says, winking at me. My goodness. A man who actually winks.

"I look forward to it," I say, cool as a cucumber.

Dick watches Nick leave as he walks back to the table. "Who the hell was that?" he demands, and I see that he's pissed.

"Just some guy. I barely know him. He's in my tennis class," I say.

"Well, what did Mr. Banana Republic want?"

"My phone number."

"Hmph. Figures."

I watch Dick take another massive bite of his cookie. He's frowning and munching and he looks like a big dumb kid. I'm really starting to like Dick.

"So back to business," I say. "Carlton stole something important from me. So I want to steal something from him."

"What do I look like, Jane, some kind of smash and grab guy? Some junkie off the street? You don't need me, you need a street thug. A fifty-cent guy. I'm more of a fifty-thousand-dollar man."

"Fifty. Thousand. Dollars," I say, slowly.

"You heard me," Dick says.

This is the first time he's broached the money subject.

I swallow my coffee and it goes down hard. "I don't have that kind of money."

"I take credit," Dick says.

"Really?"

"No."

"Well I guess this meeting is adjourned."

"Hey, now. We can work something out," Dick says. He smiles at me with his white, white teeth. "I'm sure you've got something I *want*," he says.

Oh dear Lord.

"I actually brought you a present," I say. I reach down into my messenger bag and pull out a bag.

"What is it?" Dick asks. He's rubbing his palms together, back and forth.

"Books," I say.

Dick frowns.

"On tape," I add. "So that means you can listen to them." I show Dick the books on tape—*The Beginner's Guide for Self-Promotion, Advertising 101,* and my all-time favorite, *Marketing for Dummies*.

Then I pull out my marketing notebook. I've spent a few hours working up a detailed marketing plan for Dick. Complete with spreadsheet data. Brochures. I've even had business cards made up. There's a black widow spider in the corner. And Dick's pager number. The card reads, PERSONALIZED, DISCRETE, MUSCLE SERVICES FOR HIRE. FOR THE HOTHEAD IN YOU . . .

Dick loves the cards. I've had two hundred of them made. He slips five of them in his money clip, slides a few in the pockets of his leather jacket. I hand him the bag with everything in it.

"Consider this part of your fee," I say.

Dick waves his hand airily. Or at least, airily for him. "Fee, schmee," he says. "You're doin' me a good favor—helpin' me promote my services to the female persuasion."

He leans back in his chair, hands behind his head, and that's when I spot the gun again. Hidden in a holster under his black leather jacket.

"Are you *carrying again*?" I ask, and my voice is suddenly small. Meek.

"Yeah," Dick says, abruptly. "Wha'd you think? That I did this kinda work with my bare hands."

"Have you ever shot—" Shut up, Maddy!

"A real man never shoots and tells," Dick says. He casts an eerie smile and I feel goose bumps prickle the back of my neck. As if a cold hand just swept over me.

Dick must see my face drain its color because he says, "Don't worry, Jane. I like you."

Which is sort of a relief. I guess.

Chapter 42

Cheryl tells me that the pregnancy is Ectopic. That women in my age range—thirty-five to forty-four—are at the highest risk of this type of abnormality. That I will have to abort because the egg is not attached to the right place.

"It's not a major surgery, but if you allow the pregnancy to continue, it could be fatal," Cheryl says.

"For the baby?" I ask.

"For you," she says.

So, I do the deed. Have the surgery. And afterward, as I lay in the recovery room, a nurse hands me a Ziploc bag filled with animal cookies and a juice box. As if I were a kid myself.

Carlton had a conference call with some big investor, so he didn't come pick me up.

"Don't worry about it," I told him because I didn't want him to see me as a victim. A weak-willed woman. I would be strong. And I'd do this on my own. I bet a lot of women did. But, when I walked into the clinic, I was surprised to see quite a few men. Men of all races and ethnicities. Holding their women tight. Protecting them.

"You've got to have someone drive you home," the nurse told me at the front desk. "We can't release you otherwise."

I called Carlton.

"I'm swamped, sweetie," he said, in a muffled voice. "Can't you call Heather?"

"I haven't told anyone!" I said.

"I can be there in an hour," he replied. "Maybe two. If things get crazy."

"Forget it. I'll call a cab," I said, and I was surprised when he agreed.

"Good idea. You're only ten minutes from the house," he said.

I snuck out of the hospital, feeling guilty about everything.

That night, when Carlton got home, he brought me a chocolate milkshake and a small teddy bear. He sat next to me on the couch, put his arm over my shoulders, and we watched a re-run of *Survivor*.

I hugged the bear to my chest, and let the tears stream down my face. Why was everyone giving me things that reminded me of children? I wondered.

"It was the right thing to do," he said, finally, his voice like gravel. "Don't give it a second thought."

I stared at him. "Easy for you to say."

"It's a worse crime to bring an unwanted child into the world," he said, staring at the TV. "And plus, it could've killed you," he adds.

We went to bed early that night, but when I woke up the next morning, I found Carlton asleep on the couch. The separation had already begun.

Chapter 43

I study my hit man. "Carlton has a road bike that he rides home from work every Thursday," I say.

Dick takes a sip of his coffee. "I'm a hundred percent on hit and runs," he says.

"No. I want you to steal the bike."

"Look, you don't need me to steal some guy's friggin' bike. You can hire a midwife for five hundred bucks to do that."

"It's no ordinary bike. It belonged to Lance Armstrong."

"The Tour duh France dude?"

"That's right. Carlton bought Lance Armstrong's training bike at some benefit auction. He used company profits to buy the bike and then rode it himself in an amateur race. He calls the bike his "sure thing." And when he's riding it, he thinks he's as good as Lance Armstrong. The bike gives him some kind of power trip. And, because it was Lance's training bike, it's worth a whole lot more than an ordinary bike. So he keeps it inside his house, under tight lock and key."

"I'll take my good buddies along with me," Dick informs me. "Mr. Crowbar, Mr. Pliers, and Mr. Wire-cutter."

"That's why you're the professional," I say.

Dick smiles with his white, capped teeth.

"But I need you to steal something else, too. Something that's really hard to take. It's a watch. A wristwatch. Problem is, Carlton never takes it off."

"Now we're talkin'," Dick says. "You want me to cut off his hand?"

"Not exactly."

"Okay. No limbs. That's right," Dick pounds his head. "I keep forgettin' no limbs," he says. "So, I'll threaten him. Hold my Marlon Brando to his head." Dick pats his jacket, on the bulge where his pistol's packed.

He puffs out his cheeks and does another Godfather impression. Right there in Starbucks.

"I'm uh gonna make him an offer he can't refuse," he says, in that hoarse, throaty, half unintelligible Godfather voice.

I nod my head approvingly. Take a deep breath. And opt for patience.

Dick bites into his chocolate chip cookie, looking pleased with himself. "So what is it? Some kind uh Rolex?"

"It's a Patek Phillipe, circa 1952. Trust me, you've never seen anything like it. It's a rare watch. One-of-a-kind, actually. The face of the watch is decorated with an English galleon."

"A wha?"

"A ship. A great sailing ship. From the old days. Think Russell Crowe in that movie *Master and Commander*. Carlton is a sailing nut. He loves every boat that doesn't come with a motor." I motion to my crotch area. And blush slightly. "He even refers to his thingie as Captain Hook," I say, quietly.

Dick waves his hand. "Too much information," he says.

"Sorry."

"Okay, so you want me to steal a watch from Mr. Pirates of the Penz-Ants."

"Yes. The problem is, Carlton never takes the watch off."

"I could beat him unconscious and then take it off."

"Nothing physical, remember?"

"I could hold a gun to his head and make him take it off."

"Sounds frightening," I say.

"You don't think Captain Hook can handle the heat?"

I ignore this comment by Dick. "Carlton takes off the watch when he sleeps and puts it on the bedside table," I say. "Here's the challenging part. You'd have to sneak into his room while he's asleep."

Dick breaks into a huge smile and bucks out his chest. "I may have bricks for arms, Jane," he says, "But I got feathers for feet."

He stands up from the table and taps each of his black motor-cycle boots. First one, then the other.

I notice that Dick actually has small feet for a guy his size.

"Carlton goes out drinking on Saturday nights. It's what he calls his "vacation night," I say, "so he'll be passed out by 3:00 a.m. It'll be easier to get the watch while he's passed out. So, I want you to do it on Saturday."

"No problemo," Dick says.

"Oh, and one more thing," I say.

He pivots on his motorcycle boots and I see he's light and agile, like a ballerina.

"Leave Mr. Brando at home. I don't want you to be tempted."

"Aw. C'mon. Jane. You're spoilin' all the fun," Dick says. He glides out the door. My feather-footed hit man.

Chapter 44

The week after the abortion, it's suddenly raining babies. I see babies everywhere. Peeking out the window of my townhouse, I spy young mothers with baby strollers. Mothers who are a lot younger and more youthful than me. In similarly small townhouses. Okay, so maybe they're not running a start-up company, and maybe they're married—unlike Carlton and me— but still.

I walk to the public tennis courts to get some fresh air. A pregnant woman is on the sidelines, watching her husband play. She claps her hands when he aces his opponent. Dainty little claps—clap, clap, clap. Her husband smiles at her, blows her a kiss. They've got a young boy with them. A blond-headed toddler dressed adorably in tennis whites. He holds a little kid racquet, sees a ball on the ground, runs over and whacks it. He swats the ball. Over and over. Like he's trying to kill a bug.

His dad strolls over and says, "Easy there, cowboy," and ruffles his hair.

The scene is so picture-perfect, it's enough to make me cry. I watch TV all day for the first time in years, and see commercials for diapers and baby food. The tipping point comes when Heather calls me and announces she's pregnant. She and Michael are having a baby. I'm happy for her and we both squeal on the phone, but afterward, I burst into tears. I want to tell her about Carlton and me, about the baby, everything. But I'm weak, ashamed, and emotionally spent.

I read a pamphlet from the clinic. It says I may suffer from severe depression due to the rapid drop in hormones after the loss of my pregnancy.

No shit, Sherlock.

Carlton, bless his heart, sends me a formal e-mail from the office that reads:

Maddy,
    I'm sending a moving company for my things. I've also sent your key by FedEx.

He's so polite, Carlton. And he's not wasting time. Another e-mail arrives later that afternoon from Prince Charming that reads . . .

Maddy,
    We need to discuss your exit strategy from Organics 4 Kids, pronto.

My exit strategy? Wow. He's really in a hurry to screw me. I didn't see any of this coming, of course, but hey, you've got to roll with the punches, right?

I feel myself crumbling on my couch. Melting like the wicked witch.

The day turns into night. But I don't shower. I don't eat. I don't even move.

Chapter 45

When he was sixteen, my brother drove a carload of marijuana across the Texas–Mexican border. With his boyish good looks and affable smile, the border patrol agents didn't bother checking the car, figuring he was just another high school student on a fandango. Drinking and club hopping.

After that, Ronald Piatro became a regular driver for one of the largest, most powerful drug gangs in South Texas. He spent his weekends in Matamoras, became fluent in Spanish, and funded his cocaine habit by making Sunday afternoon drug runs in a dusty, beat-up Jeep. When he was busted, at age nineteen, he spent a year in jail for trafficking. I hired Michael Wasserstein to get him out, and because of a technicality with an eager-beaver patrol agent forgetting to advise my teenage brother on his right to counsel, Michael succeeded.

That was how Michael and Heather met. Heather came with me to the courthouse for moral support, and she and Michael hit it off. It was "love at first trial," as Michael calls it.

That was ten years ago, and Heather and Michael have been together ever since.

I'm at the Wasserstein home because it's the day of Heather's baby shower and I've promised to come over early and help decorate.

Heather tells me that the Jews consider it bad luck to have a baby shower before the baby is actually born.

"It's not technically a baby shower," she says, fluttering around her kitchen. "It's more like a house party," she says, as we both tack up powder blue baby decorations everywhere.

Heather points to the tray of miniature cupcakes that she's baked—complete with little plastic toy storks poking out of them.

"Some house party," I say, and Heather slaps me on the arm and giggles.

"How's Ronnie?" Michael asks. "Still counseling troubled youth?"

"Ronnie refers to them as 'challenged,'" I reply. "They're not troubled, they're 'challenged.'"

"I'm always behind on the lingo," Michael says. He comes up behind Heather, wraps her up in his arms and presses his hand to her belly. "Well, if this little guy ever becomes 'challenged,' he's gonna see the short end of my temper stick," Michael says.

"This is your unborn son you're talking about," Heather says. "And you're already grounding him for bad behavior. Taking away his car keys."

"Gotta lay down the ground rules while they're still in the womb," Michael jokes, his eyes flashing in amusement.

Heather titters around the kitchen in a beautiful floral dress that would look like a curtain on me.

Michael sneaks a cube of cheese from a tray, and Heather slaps his hand away. "These *hors d' oeuvres* are for the ladies," she says.

Michael says, "Well, you gotta feed the poor sucker who paid for all this stuff." He opens his mouth wide and sticks his tongue out. Heather giggles and places a cheese cube on it.

Michael swallows, rubs his hand over his stomach, and says, "Well, I guess I'm outta here. You ladies seem to have everything under control."

He points at me and says, "Take care of my gal."

I bow my head, clasp my hands together as if I'm praying, and curtsey like a Geisha girl. "As the Master wishes," I say.

Michael says, "Thadda girl."

Heather and I watch as Michael slings a dry cleaning bag over his shoulder and strolls out the door with a lot of fanfare.

We carry the trays of hors d'oeuvres into the living room, light pretty candles, and arrange the flowers and baby decorations for Heather's "open house" party.

I'm nervous for Heather. She's invited Michael's cousins, and some of his friends' wives. Heather tells me that I will be the only non-Jew, because, apparently, my prom queen girlfriend is now a Jew. I don't know which Rabbi performed the conversion; I can only assume Michael slipped him a winning lotto ticket.

"Don't worry, everyone will love having a Chick-sa goddess like you to join us," she jokes.

"Shiksa. With an S," I say.

"Whatever," she replies, sighing. "I can't wait to have this baby, Maddy."

"You and Michael are going to be terrific parents," I say. "The best."

"As long as he's got Michael's brains, I'll be happy," she says.

"Hey! Don't sell yourself short in the brains department," I say.

The women arrive in groups. I become the official greeter. I answer the door each time and say, "Welcome!"

After thirty minutes, Heather fetches me from the front door. "Everyone's here," she says, "Let me introduce you." She swishes me into the living room.

Heather claps her hands. "Oy! Everyone—everyone—this is

my best friend, Madeline," she announces to the roomful of Jewish women.

"Maddy is a good Munch," she adds.

I jab Heather with my elbow and whisper in her ear. "Mensch!" I whisper. "M-e-n-s-c-h. Not munch."

The women smile, politely.

I hoist up a tray of champagne and swirl around the room. The women raise their glasses. "Mazeltov," they say.

Heather smiles and raises her Diet Coke. "Yes, Muzzle-top," she says.

I notice a few women exchanging glances, but no one says anything. They all know Heather is doing her best.

She sits down and opens her "house party" gifts. It's the usual baby stuff. But there's also some red lingerie, and even a book called *The Sexy New Mom in You*.

I bring Heather a huge gift. One of those baby strollers she can jog with.

When Heather opens the huge box, she squeals and claps her hands to her mouth like the sorority girl she is.

I try not to flinch.

"Ohmigaaah, Maddy! It's exactly what I wanted!" she says, grabbing me in a hug and swinging me side-to-side.

My goodness.

I hug her back and see the women in the room smiling very, very politely.

After that, Heather begins a long journey across a landmine of faux pas.

One of Michael's cousins says, "We sent Nathan to St. Paul's." And Heather pipes up, "Why would you send your Jewish child to Catholic school?"

The woman just looks at her.

I give Heather the secret signal by slashing my hand back and forth under my neck. But Heather bulldozes ahead.

"I mean, why not send your child to a Jewish—"

I squeeze Heather's knee and pipe up, "Excellent choice! St. Paul's is the best private school in New England."

And everyone smiles. So the disaster is momentarily averted.

But then one of the women from the baby shower says, "Those private schools are so expensive, it's like you have to sacrifice your first born to pay the tuition. Oy Vay . . . don't get me started."

And Heather says, "Started on what?"

The women glance around at each other.

I say, "Heather, isn't there another tray in the kitchen?"

Heather stands, smiles, flutters into the kitchen. She has no idea.

The women all smile at me and I smile back. I hoist a champagne bottle and a pitcher of orange juice and proceed to pour a round of Mimosas for everyone.

"Drink up, ladies!" I say, figuring that if everyone gets sloshed, they won't remember Heather's little mistakes.

Just then, Heather bursts out of the kitchen. "And for the next course, ladies," she squeals. "Bagels and lockets!"

Oh. My. God.

Chapter 46

I put on my pinstriped power suit. "Be strong," I tell myself, but my heart is like a policeman pounding on my front door. I'm afraid Carlton will hear it beating loud and hard. This is my final day at Organics 4 Kids. I'm headed to the office for one reason only. To clean up my workspace. I've accidentally slit my finger on scissors as I taped up packing boxes. I stick a band-aid on my bleeding thumb, hoist the boxes into my car, and drive up Barton Creek Road in total silence.

Carlton and I haven't spoken in nine days. But we've exchanged e-mails. Mine were pleading. Emotional.

Why are you doing this? I don't understand, was the general tone.

His were formal.

At this time, I think it's best for you to halt all future employment with Organics 4 Kids.

Ten minutes later, I roll into the Organics 4 Kids parking lot. I flip the visor down, and check the mirror. I've been crying for weeks, so I look exhausted. Beaten down. Crumpled. Saggy.

I trudge up the stairs to the office, balancing the boxes in front of my face. Inside my office, a guy with curly red hair is behind my desk. He swivels around and jumps up.

"Can I help you?" he asks.

Cool and calm, I tell myself. Cool and calm. "You can help me with these boxes," I say.

"Oh. Of course. Sorry." He takes the boxes from my arms, awkwardly, and sets them on my desk.

I look around the office. But it isn't my office anymore. The guy with the red hair has pictures of his family on my desk.

"Where's my stuff?" I say, suddenly. I reach for the desk and rip open one of the drawers. "All my stuff! Where is it?" I say, my voice rising.

He holds both his hands up in the air, as if I'm robbing him.

"Look. I don't know who you are. But I just started this job yesterday. Carlton told me to use this office."

"He did, did he?" I say. "And who might you be?"

He sticks his hand out. "Chris Jackson. V.P. of Marketing."

"V.P. OF MARKETING!" I roar.

Chris Jackson looks scared. As if I'm carrying a butcher knife.

I turn and storm toward Carlton's office. Burst through the door.

Carlton looks up from his phone, startled. "I'll call you right back," he says, slamming the phone down.

I notice immediately he's taken our photograph off his desk. The one from our ski trip.

"Where's the picture of us?" I say, pointing at the empty space on his desk. He stands up, closes the door behind me.

"Sit down," he says. "Please." His eyes are looking at me differently now. As if I'm the enemy. A disgruntled employee waving a pistol.

"I don't want to sit down!" I say. My voice is no longer cool and calm, but feverish. Frantic.

"Please, Maddy. Don't make this harder than it has to be."

"Where's our picture?" I demand.

He slides open his bottom desk drawer. Tosses me the picture. It hits my knee and falls to the floor. "Take it if you want it," he says, coldly.

I scoop it off the floor. Set it on my lap. Look down at it. Suddenly, I feel as if I've been drugged. My movements are slow. Like a sleepwalker.

Carlton takes a deep breath. He clasps his hands together on his desk like I imagine his father does when he fires people.

"I told the cleaning people to clear out your office, Maddy, and leave your things in boxes. I thought it would be easier for everyone involved. You, especially. But there was some miscommunication. They didn't understand my English."

He sighs. Rubs his temples. "Long story, short. They threw everything in the dumpster."

I look up at him. Stare into his eyes. "What?" I say, my voice cracking.

"It was an honest mistake," he shrugs. "An accident."

"I had everything in my desk, Carlton! Why would you . . ." my voice trails off. I choke back tears.

"OhmyGod, my portfolios! What about my portfolios? I—I can't interview for another job without my portfolios."

"I was thinking Henry could hire you back," Carlton says, matter-of-fact.

My head droops. I feel myself caving in—a snail retreating into its shell.

"Look. You had a lot of stuff saved on the computer. I copied your hard drive," he says. He stands from his desk, walks around it, and thrusts a zip drive into my hands.

"You're unbelievable," I snap. "Do you have any feelings *at all*? Did you ever?"

"Let's not do this here, Maddy. Not at the office."

"The office I helped build! This company was MY IDEA."

Carlton stares at the floor. "It's not like you didn't get paid," he says, quietly.

I jump from the chair. I want to scream, shout, throw things. But I don't. For some reason, I stand and breathe quickly. In and out. In and out.

"Thanks Romeo. For the ring. For Forever." I say. I rip the Juliet ring off my finger and slam it down on the desk.

Carlton doesn't say a word. I turn and rush out the door.

Later, in my car, I'm a wreck. I'm crying so hard. I can't drive. I can't breathe. I swerve over onto the side of the road, fling open my car door, and throw up on the concrete.

Chapter 47

I'm at Starbucks squeezing honey into Dick's coffee. When I walk back to the table, he smiles up at me and says, "I want one uh them apple strudel things."

"Sure," I say. I go to the counter and get Dick an apple strudel *and* a big chocolate chip cookie. So he can have double the fun.

Dick's eyes light up, as much as it's possible for dark black eyes to light up, at the sight of all the sweets.

He rubs his palms together back and forth, bites into half the strudel.

"Captain Hook sleeps like a baby," he says, revealing a mouth full of apple goo. "I got the wheels and the watch, and I was considerin' taking Mr. Big Shot's money clip, as a little bonus, but I restrained myself," he says.

"Where is the stuff?" I ask.

"The bike is in my Hummer."

"You drive a Hummer?" I ask Dick.

He takes a sip of coffee and says, "Only the best for yours truly."

"What about the watch?"

Dick reaches into his jacket pocket and slides a brown paper deli bag across the table.

I peek inside. Pull the watch out of the bag. Turn it over in my hands. I remember the time when I had tried to surprise Carlton . . .

Last year, on Carlton's birthday, I'd taken the watch to a jeweler to have it professionally cleaned. Carlton was furious. "Don't ever, ever touch my watch," he'd warned. And I was taken aback by the ferocity in his voice.

"I . . . I thought you'd like it," I stammered.

"Why!" he'd nearly shouted.

"The watch was scratched, Carlton, and the jeweler was able to polish it. Doesn't it look nice?" I'd said.

He'd grabbed the watch from my hand. "That's not the point, Maddy. I mean, what if you'd lost it?"

"I wouldn't lose it!" I said.

"Lose it, drop it, accidentally break it. Who knows what could've happened. Christ! The jeweler could've stolen it."

"Mr. Richardson has been in business thirty years, Carlton! He was a friend of my mother's!"

Carlton held his hand up in the air to shut me up. "This watch is worth thirty grand," he'd said.

So that was it.

Carlton treasured the watch because it was valuable. Not because it was a gift from his father. And not because it was rare. But simply because it was expensive. It was like cash on his wrist. A status symbol. Carlton wore the watch to assert his status. That's why he always flashed it around. Mentioned it at parties.

"My father gave me this watch. He got it at a Sotheby's auction," he'd say, explaining the history of Patek Phillipe watches. How in 1868 Patek Phillipe made the first wristwatch in history. And pocket watches before that. How Albert Einstein owned a Patek Phillipe . . . .and blah, blah, blah.

I set the watch carefully back down into the bag and pass it over to Dick.

"Do you have anyone who could fence this stuff?" I ask, and I actually use the word "fence." It's the only criminal lingo I know.

"I gotta guy. How much you want for it?"

"Twenty thousand."

"Twenty G's, huh?" Dick wipes his mouth with the back of his hand.

"For the watch and the bike," I say.

Dick crosses his arms over his chest. "I don't know, Jane. This guy don't really pay top dollar."

"That's how much you need to get," I say. Dick looks doubtful.

"Tell your friend the price is twenty thousand flat—or no deal," I say. "He can easily get twice this amount if he sells it right."

"You're one tough broad," Dick says, grinning at me. "You sure you don't know Snoop Santino? Cause you're exactly the kind uh gal he'd want to hire."

I hesitate. Should I admit my ignorance to Dick? Or pretend to know more than I do? I opt for ignorance.

"I know Snoop Santino is some drug kingpin you used to work for. The big dog on the block. And I know my brother used to work for him, too."

"Pretty good, Lady Sherlock."

"Well, the answer is no. I don't know Snoop. I've never met Snoop. And I'm certainly not interested in working for Snoop."

Dick shrugs. "Suit yourself. I just thought you might like an introduction."

"No."

"Okay, so le'ss say I get you your fifteen G's. What're you gon-na do, Jane? Go to Disneyworld?" Dick says. And apparently, he thinks this is hugely funny. Because he chuckles so hard his eyes tear up. He grabs his belly and goes, "Disneyworld! Get it?"

"I'm not keeping the money," I say.

"You wha?"

"I'm giving it away."

"C'mon, Jane. You ain't no Mother Theresa."

"Trust me, Dick. It's for a good cause."

Chapter 48

At 7:00 a.m., Carlton sends me an e-mail titled "Urgent!" I open it and read the following missive from my former fiancé.

> M:
>   We need to discuss your exit strategy from Organics 4 Kids, ASAP. I have papers I need you to sign.
>   C

I type back a single sentence:

I'll be at the office with a U-haul trailer by nine a.m.

Carlton replies immediately.

What do you need a U-haul for?

I shut my laptop and begin to get dressed. Instead of a business suit, I pull on a pair of jeans and a sweatshirt. My Saturday clothes. Because today, I'm going to haul my desk down a flight of stairs and into a U-Haul trailer and I know Carlton won't lift a finger to help me.

I'm stunned by the fact that Carlton instructed a cleaning crew to clear out my office. And that they accidentally threw everything away. Including all of my portfolios. All of my files. Everything I'd done for Organics 4 Kids in the past several years. I'm also stung that Carlton hired a guy to replace me within nine days of our break-up. And before I'd even officially quit.

So I figure the least Carlton can do is give me my office furniture.

During our first few months at Organics 4 Kids, Carlton spent ten thousand dollars of company money to buy himself a mammoth-sized desk. He was a fan of heavy, traditional furniture. Mahogany, walnut, and solid oak. Despite me urging him to take it easy on expenses, he went wild in the furniture store. He then spent another ten thousand on the matching credenza, file drawers, and an executive chair of fine, burgundy-colored leather.

"I've got to look like a CEO, because image is everything," he'd said.

I preferred the sleek, black-and-tan lines of Charles Eames or Le Corbusier. The theme for my office was "minimalism-with warmth." Since Carlton had spent all the available company funds to outfit his own office suite, I searched the newspaper for "moving sales," spent several weekends browsing thrift stores, and ended up buying my furniture with an advance on my first paycheck.

So, I figure the furniture belongs to me.

I drive to the office with the trailer bouncing behind my car. I wonder what papers Carlton needs me to sign. What could they possibly be?

I roll into the parking lot and the gravel crunches underneath my tires. I take a deep breath, flip down the visor and regard myself in the mirror.

It's the eyes that worry me. There's something missing from my eyes. I mean, sure. They look tired and bloodshot. Like eyes that have spilled a lot of tears and haven't gotten much sleep. But there's something else, too. It's almost as if my eyes are missing a certain brightness. They seem dull. Dead, even.

"C'mon. Buck up, Maddy," I tell myself. But my words mean nothing. I feel empty as I trudge up the stairs to the office. I can't bear to face Carlton again.

I pause outside the office door and peer at the Organics 4 Kids logo.

Then I open the office door and step inside.

Nathalie sees me first. She's bustling toward the copy machine carrying a stack of papers. When she sees me, she stops in her tracks. Stares down at her high heels.

"Hello, Maddy," she says, in a low voice. As if she's embarrassed by my appearance.

"Nice to see you, Nathalie," I say. I smile at her, a friendly smile. I notice she's wearing a low-cut dress that shows off her enormous, cantaloupe-sized breasts.

"That's a lovely dress," I say. "Where did you get it?"

"Saks," she says. "They were having a sale."

"I love Saks," I say, shooting Nathalie a warm, parting smile. I walk toward Carlton's office. My heart beats rapidly as I stop outside Carlton's closed door. I take a deep breath and barge right in.

Carlton looks up from his desk. "Have you heard of knocking?" he says, and his voice is biting and sharp.

"The furniture in my office—I paid for it," I say, my voice trembling. "I didn't use company money."

"What? Are we arguing over a chair, now? A rickety desk?" Carlton snaps. "I checked the records. You paid for that stuff with an advance on your paycheck. An advance you never paid back."

"I guess all those weekends I spent working for nothing, no overtime, don't count?"

Carlton stares at me from behind his massive desk. He pulls out a sheet of paper and passes it across the desk. "I need you to sign this. My dad's lawyers drew it up. In exchange, you'll receive nine months' severance pay."

I look down at the contract.

"This is a noncompete agreement," I say, and I'm feeling numb.

Carlton nods.

"How can I get another job if I sign this?"

"You're a savvy person, Madeline," Carlton says. And I'm momentarily shocked. I can't remember the last time Carlton used my full name. Instead of Maddy, Sweetie, or Babe. I feel a lump in my throat; I'm choking on grief.

"A week ago you were calling me 'Juliet' and now I'm Madeline?"

Carlton's face doesn't move an inch. He stares at me, a hard stare, as if he's looking at a bear he just shot.

"You can have the desk," he says. Then he flicks his finger in the air. "But only the desk."

Chapter 49

The phone rings and surprise, surprise. It's Nick.

"Hey there," he says. "It's Nick."

"Nick who?" I ask, because I feel like a tease.

"I'm the really good-looking guy in your tennis class," he says, in a funny, deep, sexy voice.

My goodness. I like this guy's sense of humor already.

"I'm sorry, but I don't remember you," I say, in my sweetest little-girl voice.

"I was driving a Ferrari," he continues. "Fire-engine red with black leather interior."

"It looked an awful lot like a Volvo," I say.

"So *you do* remember me," he says, and we both laugh. (Definitely a good start.)

"I was wondering . . ." he says. "After tennis tonight, would you like to get a proper dinner? Something a little more filling than a smoothie?"

"You betchya!" I say.

Just kidding. I don't say this.

I say, "That sounds nice," in my cool, calm voice.

"Great, I'll see you on the courts," Nick says.

"Okay."

"Oh, and Maddy?"

"Yes?"

"I'm bringing my A-game. So don't think I'm going to let you win again."

"Bring the Ferrari, too," I say, and Nick laughs.

A few hours later, I'm rushing around my house trying to get ready for the tennis lesson. I pull on my white tennis skirt—the fancy one with little pleats—and a thin, white workout top. I sweep my hair back in a ponytail, paint my fingernails a shade called "candy rose" and put mascara on. I even wear tiny gold stud earrings in my ears. When I'm finished I look at myself in the mirror, and I don't look half-bad. My skin even looks clean, thanks to my huge vat of Noxzema.

In fact, I look like I'm ready to go lunching with the ladies— instead of playing an hour of vigorous tennis. That's the problem with "exercise dates." You've got to try to look good *after* the workout. Which is kind of a pain. I feel like one of those women who put on eye makeup to go to the gym.

I drive out to the courts and see that Nick is already there, warming up. He's practicing his serve. I watch him. He throws the ball high in the air, arches his body and hits a perfect strong serve over the net.

"Bravo," I say, clapping.

Nick turns and smiles slightly. "People compare me to Agassi," he says.

I see he's wearing black shorts again. And a black Addidas top with a white stripe down the side.

I'm wearing all-white, so we look like the opposite sides in a chess game.

I jog over to my side of the court, stretch a wee bit, crouch down into a tennis stance, and say, "Ready when you are, pretty boy."

Nick throws up another serve and whacks it into the net.

"You're making me nervous," he says. I smile and act cool but that's exactly how I feel. I'm nervous. My palms are even sweaty. So the Slazenger feels loose in my hands.

Nick looks at me and catches my eye. I feel the electricity again. And I think he feels it, too, because he looks down at his tennis shoes. Yes, the chemistry between us is almost palpable.

"Second serve," I say.

Nick bounces the ball, throws it up, and whacks it low and hard over the net.

I swing and miss. Which is something I rarely do.

"Nice serve," I say, smiling at him, because Nick just aced me fair and square.

"It was a fluke," Nick says, sheepishly. "I never ace anyone."

I think back to Carlton. If Carlton had just served me an ace, he'd be shouting, "ACE! ACE! Who's Your Daddy, Now!"

I'm suddenly very glad to be playing tennis with Nick.

Nick and I hit the ball back and forth for a while. And then Deepak and the other members of the class show up. The lesson seems to drag on forever. When it's finally over, Nick has beaten me. Six games to four. He motions for me to meet him at the net. I walk up and say, "Good game."

I hold my hand out to shake. Nick takes my hand in his and brings it up to his lips. I hold my breath as he kisses the top of my hand like I'm a princess or something, and says, "Nice game, Madeline."

I gaze into Nick's eyes and realize I haven't felt this good in a long, long time.

We walk out to the parking lot, together. Deepak is loading his tennis gear into the back of a gold Suburban. "My family," he says, motioning toward the car. "They wait for me." I see a beautiful, thin, Indian woman behind the wheel. And Deepak's two smiling daughters waving from the backseat.

Nick and I wave good-bye to Deepak, and then Nick turns

to me and whispers, "Quick! Let's get out of here before we're invaded by picture-perfect families!"

Gee whiz. I really like this guy.

"Shall I follow you?" I ask, but Nick opens the door to his Volvo and says, "Hop in."

So I hop in.

"I was thinking of Le Bistro," Nick says—which happens to be one of my favorite restaurants.

It's a quaint little French bistro with a casual dining atmosphere and great wines by the glass.

"Excellent choice," I say.

In the car, on the way to the restaurant, Nick slides a Rolling Stones CD into the player. Mick Jagger crooning, "I Can't Get No . . . Satisfactiooon."

"This was my mother's favorite album," I say, absently. I don't want to bring up my parents, but I can't help it. This music reminds me of her.

Nick says, "Tell me more."

"They died in a car accident. Drunk driver," I say, quickly. "My brother was fifteen. So it affected him the most," I say.

Nick is unusually quiet. I'm afraid I've said the wrong thing again. Here I am, talking about my dead parents, when I'm two seconds into a first date.

"Sorry," I say. "It's been a while since I've been on a . . ." I hesitate to say the word "date." But Nick rescues me.

"Date?" he asks.

"Yes."

"That's hard to believe," Nick says. "I imagine a woman like you has tons of guys beating down the door."

He looks at me and suddenly the electricity between us is positively zinging. I feel my face blush slightly. Nick turns the CD player off, grits his teeth a little, and taps his hands against the steering wheel. I notice that he's a good driver. Not sloppy. He's one of those guys who just seems like he's in command.

"Here we are," he says, softly.

We pull into the parking lot of Le Bistro. Nick runs around to my side of the car, opens my door for me, and actually takes my hand and leads me out of the car. We're both still in our tennis clothes, but it doesn't matter. Nick asks for a table outside and I watch him, closely. He's poised. In control.

He leans over toward my ear—so close—that his lips brush against my face.

"I'm glad you decided to come," he says, simply. Just like that.

I feel something stirring inside of me. It's the weak-knee thing. Sometimes, it just happens and you can't help it. It's that gushy feeling.

Within five minutes, Nick has scored a prime table outside on the patio.

There's a candle flickering in the center of the table. The light bounces off Nick's face and he looks handsome and rugged. He doesn't have Carlton's fine, model-like features, but where Carlton was "pretty," Nick is truly "handsome." Nick seems more of a guy's guy. The type of guy who could fix his own car and who knows the difference between the Fighting Irish and the Crimson Tide.

The waiter swirls around with menus.

I order a glass of Bordeaux. Nick orders a Pellegrino, to my surprise.

"You're not drinking?" I ask. And I'm wondering if Nick is an AA guy, like my brother.

"I'm on the job," he says, in a serious tone.

I giggle and cover my mouth, a la Heather.

We both order steak frites, because, after all, this place is

French. Nick leans over the table, cups his hands under his chin. I can smell the scent of him, sweet and raw from the tennis game. It's a good smell. Manly.

He clinks his water glass against my wine. "So tell me more about you, Maddy. You say you have a brother? Does he live around here?"

I nod. "He's a rehab counselor, so he spends most of his time at work. He's got an apartment about a mile from here," I say.

"Do you guys spend time together?"

"Sure," I say. "We see each other once a week, sometimes twice. Ronnie's really involved with his work."

"What line of work is your brother in, Maddy?"

I pause a moment.

"I just told you he was a rehab counselor," I say, quietly.

Nick chews on his lip and he seems to be thinking about something. I decide to take this moment of silence to blabber on.

"He's really a saint, my brother."

Nick raises an eyebrow and says, "Really?" as if he doesn't believe me.

I nod. "If there's a heaven," I say, "Ronnie's got a front row ticket."

Nick is quiet. He seems contemplative, like he's concentrating on something. It's disconcerting, but I decide not to ask him what's what.

The waiter brings our plates and I'm careful not to eat too quickly. Nick, I'm pleased to see, likes food as much as I do. He cuts into his steak, stabs a French fry with his fork and pops the whole thing into his mouth.

"This place cooks a mean steak," he says, grinning at me between bites.

"Thank you for bringing me here," I say. "It's just what the doctor ordered."

Good one, Maddy. Real sexy.

Nick says, "When I saw you at Starbucks with that big guy, I thought you might be dating him. Dick was his name, right?"

Suddenly a red flag goes up in my head. I'm surprised Nick remembers Dick's name. But then again, it's not hard. Nick, Dick. I'm probably being paranoid.

I shake my head. "That was business," I say. "I'm designing a marketing campaign for his company."

"Interesting," Nick says. "What business is Dick in?"

Without hesitation, I reply, "He's an entrepreneur. That's why he needs a marketing plan."

I try to be informative and evasive to move beyond the subject.

"How did you two meet?" Nick asks. And I suddenly feel like I'm being probed. I want Nick to drop the subject but he seems really interested in finding out all about *moi*.

"My brother put us in touch," I say, quickly.

Nick smiles at me with those killer dimples of his, but I see a slight shadow cross his face. Maybe it's all in my head. *Get a grip, Maddy!*

I really need to learn how to start dating.

After dinner, Nick drives me back to my car, and I think he wants to kiss me but he doesn't. He says, "I'm going out of town for business, but I'll call you in a few days."

I say, "Sounds great."

He leans over a moment and looks straight into my eyes, like he's searching for something.

I decide to go for it.

I kiss Nick full on the mouth. It's a long, slow kiss, and he almost seems shocked by it at first.

I'm shocked, too. Because it's perfect.

Nick pulls away first.

"Uh, sorry. I wasn't expecting . . ." he starts in.

I notice him blushing slightly. A man like this, blushing.

"It's okay," I say, quietly. I unclip my seatbelt, and step out of the passenger side.

"Have a good business trip," I say.

"I'll see you at tennis," Nick replies.

As I drive away, I realize that I talked about myself the entire dinner. In fact, I know nothing about Nick. I don't even know his last name.

Chapter 50

I am not a furniture mover. In fact, I suck at moving furniture. And so, after the building maintenance man helped me lug the desk down three flights of stairs and load it into the trailer hitched to the back of my car, I forgot one small detail. To close the trailer door.

I don't realize there's a problem until I enter the on ramp of the highway. I hear a huge thump and crack noise. The kind of noise that spells trouble. In my rearview, I see the desk fly out onto the road. Before I can even pull over, an eighteen-wheeler slams into it, and the desk explodes into a million tiny wood chips. The big rig is undamaged and—as they say—just keeps on truckin'. The driver even toots his horn as he passes me by. Toot toot.

I see the desk carcass on the highway, and it's a mess. I pop open my phone and call the police department to report it.

The guy on the phone goes, "The interstate is not your personal office, ma'am."

Everyone's a comedian.

I guess it's somewhat poetic. The smashing of the desk. But still, the tears come easily. I could flood the place.

I speed over to Michael's law office. Even with the windows

rolled down and the nice, cool breeze hitting my face, I still can't shake this funk. I'm a sniveling, drooling, wet-eyed funk of a person. A sad-sack. A washed-up has-been. I check my face in the rearview. My mascara is smeared under my eyes. If I were Heather, it would look like heroin chic. On me, it looks like Maddy the Racoon has come crawling back to town.

Waterproof my ass, I think. I wipe my eyes and manage to smear the mascara further down onto my cheek and hand.

Carlton's noncompete agreement is sitting on the passenger seat next to me. I look down at it and consider tossing it out the window.

Bastard!

I'm so riled up Carlton has me speaking in tongues.

I screech into the parking lot, my tires crunching gravel. Michael's got his own law practice. "I'm a one-man army," he likes to say. The office is in an old renovated house. Complete with white shingles and a sign hanging above the door that says, "Michael Wasserstein, Attorney-at-Law." I grab the offensive contract, and bang into Michael's office. His receptionist is probably on a lunch break so I march right into Michael's office.

Michael looks up from his desk. He's on the phone but he says, "I'll call you back in fifteen," and hangs up.

"You look like shee-it," he says, generously.

I glance down at my wrinkled, day-old clothes. I haven't washed my hair or brushed my teeth in as long as I can remember. And I'm pretty sure I smell.

"Thanks for noticing," I say.

"Hard not to," Michael says, motioning to a chair in front of his desk.

"Take a seat. You want a tissue or somethin'?" he asks, handing me a box of Kleenex.

"Thanks," I mumble. I pluck a Kleenex and try to wipe underneath my eyes. The tissue is streaked with black. I ball it up. Michael holds up a trash can.

I shoot and miss, of course. The tissue bounces off the side of the can.

Michael rolls his eyes. "Women," he says, picking the tissue off the floor.

I look around the room. I've never been to Michael's office before, and I don't know what I was expecting, but this certainly isn't it.

Instead of a bookcase filled with hardbound legal books, like you see in the commercials, and heavy, wooden furniture, Michael's office instead looks quaint. Homey, even. He's got potted plants, a small leather couch with a few throw pillows, and framed pictures of Heather everywhere. The furniture is all light, blond wood. And behind his desk, instead of diplomas, he's hung a painting. A framed print of Andy Warhol's Marilyn Monroe.

"I love your office," I say.

"I like to make my clients feel at home," he says. He opens a mini fridge next to his desk and says, "Care for a Coke? Or Perrier?"

I notice Michael doesn't pronounce it the French way, like "Perri-A." Instead, he does that Southern drawl thing and says it like this: Pear-eee-air.

I lean forward and shove the noncompete agreement across Michael's desk. "Get a load of this B.S.," I say.

Michael raises an eyebrow. "I expect a year of free babysittin' in exchange for any legal advice," he says.

"Of course," I say. I lean back in the chair and rest my head. It's the middle of the afternoon, but for some reason, I feel beat.

Michael regards the contract in front of him. He scrunches his face up, rubs his hand over his head, and chews anxiously on his lower lip.

"What he's proposing is to pay you nine months' salary in exchange for a promise not to work for any competing business for a period of three years. Sounds like extortion. But unfortunately, the laws of this great state allow for this kind uh' crap." He folds the contract into a neat paper airplane and sends it zinging in my direction. "You didn't have any other type of employment contract, right? Like when you first started with the company?"

I drop my head like a scolded dog. "No," I say, softly. And I suddenly feel like the dumbest woman in the world.

"If you take the money—and you sign this thang—then you're stuck."

"So I can't work for another company in this industry—unless I don't take the severance pay."

"Correct," Michael says. He rests his elbows on the desk, fingers laced, chin on his hands. "How important is the severance? Do you have any savings?"

I think of the rainy day check from Henry.

"Very little. I'm plowing through it."

"I didn't even know Carlton had competitors," Michael says. "I thought this Organics 4 Kids was a one and only. A first in the field."

"There's one," I say. "And it's not really a competitor. It's more of a giant. Carlton was hoping to sell out—to cash in his millions. He wanted to sell Organics 4 Kids to Giganto Foods. See, Carlton has a strong regional foothold in the South—Texas, Oklahoma, Georgia, Alabama, Mississippi. So, Giganto would rather buy Carlton's company and roll out Organics 4 Kids across the entire U.S. Often times, a company would rather buy a smaller company that already has a strong market niche rather than develop its own product line. Sometimes it's easier to buy a smaller company and roll the product line out nationally rather than start from scratch," I say.

Michael waves his hand breezily and says, "I get it. Go on."

"The problem is, Giganto Foods was wanting to develop something like this way before Carlton and I ever came on the scene. I think they tabled it because they wanted to see if it would work. So, our company—I mean, Carlton's company, was like a guinea pig."

"So now Carlton's afraid you'll jump over to Giganto," Michael says.

"Exactly," I say. "And with their unlimited budget, Giganto can either buy out Organics 4 Kids, or stomp all over it."

"I guess you better line up an interview," Michael says. "Tell Carlton to keep his lousy severance package and stick this non-compete up his very small asshole."

"Yeah, it's great in theory. But there's one small problem."

"C'mon, Maddy. Giganto Foods will hire you in a heartbeat."

I shake my head. "You don't understand, Michael. Carlton told the janitors to clean out my desk. They accidentally threw out all of my portfolios. All of my work product. Everything I'd been working on at Organics 4 Kids."

Michael holds up his hand and says, "Repeat that."

"The janitors don't speak English and Carlton told them to box up everything from my desk, but they misunderstood him and trashed everything."

Michael crosses his arms over his chest and peers down his nose at me. "Sounds like there's a fox in the henhouse."

"How do you mean?"

"I mean, it doesn't add up, Maddy. You still trust this guy. Even now."

I stare at Michael.

"Ask yourself this question," he says. "Who had more incentive to lose your files, other than Carlton?"

Chapter 51

The only thing worse than running into an ex-fiancé is running into an ex-fiancé when he's on a date. And so, imagine my surprise . . .

I'm at the Congress Cafe, a trendy Austin hot spot, sitting at the bar with Heather. We're discussing baby names over a plate of fried calamari. She's drinking a Diet Coke. I'm having a vodka tonic with no tonic. And that's when I spot him. His movie star hair is unmistakable and he's got a prime table by the window, of course. Our old table.

Carlton!

My entire body tenses up. Heather swings around on her barstool, sees Carlton, and says immediately, "Let's get out of here."

I say in a solid voice, "We're not leaving. This is one of my favorite restaurants. Carlton didn't even know this place existed until I brought him here."

I lean past Heather and spy on Carlton. He's sitting at a table, ordering the same bottle of wine we always used to order, the same shrimp appetizer, and lo and behold, guess who's with him? It's his new accounting whiz kid. The brilliant Miss Nathalie. Looking absolutely divine in a sheer white dress—a V-shaped, low-cut neckline exposing cleavage that would make Pamela Anderson jealous. Nathalie, with her huge, Double-D cantaloupe knockers. This is no business dinner, I can assure you.

I watch as Carlton pours Nathalie a glass of wine. I don't know how it happens, but I guess Carlton feels my presence. Because, suddenly, he looks straight at me.

Our eyes meet for a split second, and a world of emotions is exchanged, and then Carlton does the unthinkable. He brushes the side of Nathalie's cheek with the back of his hand, leans in closely to her face, and probably says something impossibly romantic—and impossibly full of donkey doo doo in her ear.

I throw back the rest of my vodka. And, in the spirit of drinkyland, I decide what the heck? Time to spoil all the fun. I stand abruptly from my barstool.

Heather says, "What are you doing, Maddy? No, don't!" But my dear, sweet girlfriend is too little, too late.

I march toward Carlton's table. Arms a swingin'. I storm, really.

Carlton sees me heading his way. He doesn't stand up, that piece of shit.

"Hello, Madeline," he says, taking a sip of his wine. Mr. Cool. Speaking to me in that ridiculous formal tone.

"Hi, Romeo," I snap. "I see you've chosen a great bottle of wine. Let me guess. The Brunello?"

Nathalie is staring up at me—her former boss—with her eyes open wide, looking a little scared.

She knows she's busted, so she stands up quickly and her chair squeaks against the floor. "I . . . I have to use the Ladies," she stutters. I watch as she races across the restaurant, nearly knocking over a waiter balancing a full tray of plates.

Graceful, I think.

Carlton says, "What the hell do you think you're doing?" His voice is sharp and he's looking up at me with defiant, angry eyes.

He's still sitting, his arms crossed over his chest, but he's sliding around in his chair. Like a rattlesnake on a leash.

I look down at Mr. High and Mighty and glance at his wine glass. A part of me wants to dump it on his head. But I resist. No need to cause a big scene. Get the whole restaurant involved.

I point my finger at his chest. "Saving her *from you*," I say, pointedly. And with that, I march straight toward the ladies room.

I push open the door. Nathalie is in a stall. I can hear her sniveling and blowing her nose and it sounds like she's crying.

I tap on the stall door. Gently.

"Nathalie, it's me," I say.

"Leave me alone!" she cries out. It's a little melodramatic but that's what you get with young women in their twenties. Even if they've been around the block, they still haven't been around the fucking block. *Wait ten years, girlfriend. Then see if you're hiding in a stall,* I think to myself. If Nathalie were thirty-something, she'd be in front of the sink, doing what any smart woman would do. Trying to get the skinny about Carlton. A thirty-something girl would use this as an opportunity to bleed me for information. And I'd gladly talk because all's fair in love and war, right?

"Nathalie, I think you're a bright woman with a great future ahead of you," I say. "I also know that you care for Carlton because, on the outside, he's got a lot of great qualities."

She surprises me by swinging open the stall door with some force. She's standing there, clutching a wad of toilet paper in her hand, black mascara tears running down her cheeks. When she speaks, I'm a tad offended by her ferocity.

"You don't care about Carlton and me! You just care about yourself! You don't want Carlton to move on and find happiness with someone else!"

I give her a pointed look. "It's true," I say. "I'm angry with Carlton for many reasons he probably hasn't told you."

"Yeah, like you got dumped and you can't handle it!"

Well, now she's getting personal.

"Nathalie, my parents died in a car accident when I was nineteen. Let me assure you, getting dumped is not the worst thing that can happen to a person. It happens to everyone. It's . . . part of the life cycle," I say, in a calm, counseling tone. I've suddenly become my brother.

Nathalie pushes past me and rushes to the mirror. She turns the sink on and wipes frantically under her eyes.

I walk up and hand her a paper towel.

"Look, I shouldn't have interrupted your romantic dinner, but I think you've got great potential to become a female CFO at a major corporation. You've chosen a career field that doesn't have many women. I admire that. And I believe you'll succeed. Because you're a good financial analyst."

Nathalie looks at me in the mirror.

"Why are you telling me this?"

"Sometimes, women need to stick up for one another," I say. I want to tell Nathalie about Abigail Adams but I'm afraid I'll lose her. Plus I've already followed her into a bathroom. If I mention the line about "all men being tyrants if they could," she might think I'm nuts.

"I'm not here to poison you against Carlton, Nathalie. Because trust me, if he's not dating you, he'll be dating someone else. And I can't go chasing off all his new girlfriends, right?"

"I think he's already dating someone else," she sniffles. She swings around and stares at me with her pretty, wide blue eyes. "I counted the condoms in this box he has in his bathroom and two were missing . . ." she trails off.

I wince. Nathalie realizes she's cutting close to the bone.

"Sorry," she mumbles.

"It's okay," I say, quietly. "I'm glad you're using condoms because Carlton has genital herpes. And he hates to wear them, but you're a young woman and you definitely shouldn't compromise on that point," I say.

She nods. I've got her full attention now.

"At first, I thought Carlton hired you because you're attractive and fresh out of school. Sometimes it's easier to have a young employee who's willing to put in extra overtime. Not some middle-aged woman who won't take any crap," I say. "You're more moldable," I say.

Nathalie twists the paper towel in her hand. Wringing it back and forth. A nervous habit, I guess. I can smell a hint of flowery perfume, but it's not overwhelming. Nathalie probably did the thing where you spritz the perfume in the air and then walk through the cloud.

I take a deep breath. Pause. Find the right words. "At first, I was a little jealous, Nathalie. Which is hard to admit. But I realized you were bright and would do a good job."

"Thanks," Nathalie says. She's looking at me, and I can see she's earnest as apple pie. Maybe she's from the Midwest, bless her heart.

"Anyway, Carlton is a pretty cunning person. You're a smart woman and you'll figure that out soon," I say. "So it took me a while to realize he hired you for another reason."

Nathalie looks down at her chest.

"I knew no one would take me seriously with these!" she says, motioning to her breasts. "When I was young, the guys used to call me 'Flat Nat,' and it really hurt! I mean, I never even put on a bathing suit until I was twenty. So I begged my mom to get me new breasts for Christmas a few years ago."

I'm struck by Nathalie's honesty. I really like this girl all of a sudden.

"You can be a sexy woman *and* a successful woman," I say. "And that's not the reason Carlton hired you. He hired you, Nathalie, because he's cooking the books. And you're too young and inexperienced to figure it out. The problem is, if he sinks, you'll sink with him. Or, even worse, he'll say it was your fault and he had no knowledge. What he's doing is committing securities fraud. Now, I love Organics 4 Kids. It used to be my baby. My concept. So it gives me no pleasure to see the company burn. But you should definitely take precautions to protect yourself. I know what Carlton's paying you, and it's not enough to ruin your future career."

Nathalie stares at me and I can tell she's weighing things in her mind.

"What should I do?" she asks, finally.

"You're a bright woman and you'll figure it out," I say. "But don't let good sex with your first boss blind you to reality."

I can see the good sex part really hits home. Nathalie's face seems to redden a little.

"Carlton's gonna ask what we were talking about," Nathalie says.

"Just tell him I was yelling at you. I was irrational. He'll appreciate that."

"Oh, and one more thing." I reach into my purse and hand her a business card. "This man has a terrific company. His name is Henry Wrona, and he's an honest, brilliant guy. He gave me my first start when I was still in school. He's always looking for good people. Especially finance people. If you need a new job, this is your man. And he pays a lot more in salary than Carlton," I say.

Nathalie looks at me one last time. She slips the business card in her purse. And then, unbelievably, she gives me a quick hug and rushes out the door.

Just then, Heather pushes the door open and peeks inside.

"I'm afraid to ask," she says.

"Has Carlton left?"

"He just paid the check."

"Terrific. I scared him away."

Heather giggles and covers her mouth. "I can't wait to tell Michael," she says.

"Just another day at the office," I say.

Chapter 52

My brother is what you'd call an "idea man." An innovator. Six months ago, he came up with an idea to provide free rehab services to disadvantaged youth. Particularly black and Mexican kids from the east side of town.

"Not everyone can afford rehab," Ronnie told me, over one of our cheeseburger dinners. "It can cost thirty grand a month at a good place," he'd said.

His plan was to provide drug counseling sessions and a distinguished speakers series for troubled teens. And he'd do this at zero cost to the family.

His only problem—and it was a doozy—was lack of funding. Free drug rehab is good in theory, but not so good when someone's got to pay the bills.

Ronnie figured he'd deal with the money issue later. "I'll go knocking on doors if I have to," he'd said. He recruited me to help him devise a new slogan.

"I want something new. Something fresh. Something that'll stick, Maddy," he instructed, as we munched our juicy cheeseburgers. My brother rarely asked for a favor, so I knew it was important to him. He even sprung for the burgers. And so, because of this, I brainstormed for a full month.

The "Just Say Yes!" to Sobriety Campaign was the slogan I came up with. My brother wanted a slogan with "staying power." Something that would attract private donations and help advertise the new program. I did a glossy color brochure and got my old graphic designer from Organics 4 Kids to help design it. I even dipped into my emergency money from Henry to help pay for the set-up.

I go see my little brother at the rehab center.

His office door is decorated with a new poster. It's a cheesy poster—a family of dolphins swimming underwater. A daddy dolphin, mommy dolphin, and baby dolphin. "Every day is a miracle," it reads.

Ronnie knows I'm coming because the security guard has buzzed me through. My brother opens the door wide. "You're never going to believe this," he says, smiling broadly.

I know what he's about to say.

"We got the money!" he says, grabbing me in a bear hug. He lifts me off the ground and swings me in a circle. He's that happy.

"The money?" I ask, as if I don't know what he's talking about.

"For the 'Just Say Yes!' campaign," Ronnie says. And I see his face is beaming. "An anonymous donation, Maddy!—Twenty thousand bucks!—enough to pay for everything! Books, materials, advertising—the whole works! We've rented out the community center—and we're starting classes in two weeks!"

My brother sighs and shakes his head back and forth. As if he can't believe the enormity of it all. He drops into his swivel office chair. "Finally," my brother says, lifting a finger in the air. "These teenagers can 'Just Say Yes!' to sobriety."

"That's terrific, Ronnie."

"Can you believe it, Maddy? An anonymous donor. I bet it's a former addict. Somebody famous. Maybe an actor, or musician," my brother muses.

Move over Bono, I think. I've got Carlton Connors. My new secret weapon in the war on drugs.

As I anticipated, Dick was able to sell Carlton's bike and wristwatch in a jiffy. And after taking a percentage for himself for what Dick referred to as his "carrying costs," I had my favorite hired gun direct the rest of the money to my brother's "Just Say Yes!" Donor Fund.

"I can't believe it," my brother says. He looks up at the crucifix on the wall of his office and crosses himself. "God heard my prayers," he says.

I think of Carlton. Of the way he loved the Lance Armstrong training bike. And that obscenely expensive watch. I think of how he'd roll up in the driveway with the bike, take off his helmet, and say something ridiculous like, "I'm invincible." I think of the way he always flashed the watch in meetings, and when he met a new woman whom he found attractive or a man whom he found threatening, he flashed the watch as if it were a Swiss bank account.

So, I think of the bike and the watch and the twenty thousand dollars I've secretly donated to my brother's drug abuse crusade, and for some reason, I smile. I don't know why—maybe it's the devil in me—but I can't help myself. I wish I were the type of person to forgive and forget. But apparently, I'm not.

Carlton will buy himself another bike and another wristwatch, pronto. So, as much as I'd like to think I've delivered a mortal wound, it's just a bee sting.

"Come to the first meeting, Maddy," my brother says. He grabs his cigarettes and offers the pack to me as a joke. I reach for a cigarette, another joke. My brother snatches the pack away. (We do this a lot.) He shakes a cigarette out, lights one up.

"Come on, Maddy-go-laddy. I want you to see a miracle in action," he says, his eyes wet with tears. My teenage drug crusader for a brother. My tough brother. Smoking a cigarette and crying tears of joy.

"I'd love to," I say. And I really would.

Chapter 53

I meet Heather at The Tavern for a quick drink after work. *Her work*—not mine. Heather does a part-time gig at the Neiman Marcus outlet store. She's seven months pregnant and still manages to pad around the store and sell cute designer blouses. Meanwhile, I'm gainfully unemployed and I'm not even carrying baby cargo.

I'm too embarrassed to go crawling back to Henry, so I've been spending my days toiling away at Kinko's. Trying to recreate my portfolios. My plan is . . . not to have a plan. I'll start interviewing when the money runs out.

Heather and I slide onto barstools.

"What are you ladies drinking?" the bartender asks.

"Diet Coke," Heather says.

"Vodka. Neat," I say.

The bartender raises an eyebrow. "So you've decided to join the party people," he says.

"Make it a double," I say.

Heather looks at me, her face serious. She tugs at the diamond stud in her ear, an anniversary gift from Michael.

"There's something I think you should see," she says, under her breath.

I throw back the vodka. Straight up. Like I'm from Moscow or something. No cranberry juice, no ice. Nothing to take the sting away. Yep, I'm onto the hard stuff now.

Heather pulls a magazine from her messenger bag and slaps it on the bar. It's a copy of *Young Entrepreneur*.

My heart jumps.

Carlton.

On the fucking cover.

His arms crossed. And . . .

I gasp.

He's wearing the T-shirt with my Discount Lunch card program logo.

My organics school kids are smiling in the background. Precocious. Cute as buttons. And dressed in the T-shirts with the new logo.

"Why CEO Carlton Connors Does the Right Thing— " the title screams.

I cup my hand to my mouth. Suddenly I feel nauseous. The vodka is sticky in my throat.

The pages tremble in my hand as I flip through the magazine. More photos of Carlton. And I know what's coming next. But when I see the words, I can't believe it.

> Five years ago, CEO Carlton Connors started an enterprising company selling boxed organic school lunches for kids. So why did this successful entrepreneur suddenly decide to create a discount lunch program for Single Mothers?
>
> **REPORTER:** "How did you come up with this novel idea, Carlton?"
> **CARLTON:** "The fat content and preservatives of the typical school lunch program has gotten a lot of press in the past few years. I decided to do something about it because

parents deserve more for their children. Child obesity in
the United States is becoming a major health epidemic.
I saw a fundamental need in our society—a need for
healthy and delicious school lunches—and I tackled it."

REPORTER: "How do you respond to critics who say your
school lunches are too expensive for the average working family? That only wealthy parents can afford them?"

CARLTON: "As you know, organic food is more expensive
to produce and bring fresh to market. However, I've
created a new lunch card program for single, welfare
mothers and other parents with limited resources. I call
it the Discount Lunchcard Program."

"OHMYGOD!" I shout. The magazine drops from my hands
and falls to the floor with a thwap!

Heather jumps in her chair and accidentally knocks her glass
over. It spills across the bar.

"Maddy! What is it?" she says, mopping the soda with a hand-
ful of cocktail napkins.

"He told me they'd thrown out all my files! The housekeepers. On accident. And I believed him!" I cry out.

"I don't understand," Heather says. She's looking at me now
and chewing on her lip.

"He stole my marketing files out of my desk! With all my
ideas. And my portfolio books!"

"What do you mean, Maddy?"

"The discount lunch card program—I never TOLD Carlton
about it! I'd just come up with idea before we broke up. I was
still working on the proposal . . . running all the numbers . . . It
was in my desk. He said the housekeepers threw everything out
by accident!"

Heather shakes her head back and forth. "You should sue
him."

"I don't have any proof. It would be his word against mine. I don't have any documents, any backup files, nothing . . ." my voice trails off.

I turn and stare at Heather. I can feel my face burning hot red. My eye is twitching uncontrollably.

Heather rubs my shoulder and shoots me The Look. The dead dog look.

"I'm so sorry, Maddy," she murmurs.

Chapter 54

My mind twists and turns like a criminal's. Late at night, I do a drive-by. Carlton's new townhouse is in the posh Heights neighborhood. His car is parked outside. Well, well. Mr. Big Time CEO has traded in his old Honda for a slick, black 7-series BMW. I know the new car is his because I see his stupid sunglasses hanging from a clip on the visor. He's got a vanity license plate that reads "CEO." And a bumper sticker with the organics food logo on it, of course.

Hmm. Bumper stickers. Another idea from *moi.*

I park my car two blocks down the street. My heart is beating wildly, as I get out. I don't think about what I'm doing. I just move. With the stealth of a ninja. The night is my friend. The darkness hides me. I'm a foot soldier. A mercenary. Waging my own private war.

I sneak down the street toward the BMW. The windows of the townhouse are dark. I guess Mr. Big Time is fast asleep. He always did need a solid nine hours.

"Romeo's beauty sleep," I used to call it.

I reach the car, and check up and down the street, slyly. It's three in the morning. No one is around.

I consider breaking a window, but the alarm will surely go off. Inside the BMW, I see a flashing red light on the dashboard.

Who cares about a broken window, anyway? What kind of revenge is that? A broken window is a two-hundred-dollar repair. A nuisance, sure. But not much else.

I suddenly wish I knew more about cars. Like Angelina Jolie in *Gone in Sixty Seconds*.

If I knew more about cars, I'd cut the brakes. Like they do in the movies. Of course, knowing Carlton, he'd slide right into a prime parking space, instead of into a tree.

Bananas in the tailpipe? I don't have any bananas.

Sugar in the gas tank? I don't have any sugar.

In fact, I don't have any tool whatsoever. What the heck am I doing?

I turn and hurry back to my car. Deflated. Dejected. The wily coyote unable to catch that wascaly wabbit.

But suddenly I remember something. One thing I do have. I smile, turn on my heel, and shoot back to the BMW.

I remove the stickpin from my hair, and let my hair fall around my shoulders. It's the stickpin Carlton gave me when we first started dating. A cheap rhinestone thingie.

I bend down toward the tire.

Reaching my arm back, I jerk it forward, hard. Stabbing the tire with the pin.

The tire doesn't budge, but the pin snaps in two. I look down at my hand, at the two pieces of hairpin lying side by side.

How apropos, I think.

I consider leaving the two pieces of hairpin next to the tire—a little note from yours truly. A symbolic gesture.

Of course, Carlton would probably just run over the damn thing. Or if he did notice the two broken pieces of stickpin—I mean, *really* notice, I still don't think he'd get the point.

I jog back to my car. My hands are covered in black soot from the tire. I dust them off and flick the pieces of hairpin in someone's trash.

After jumping into my car, I drive cautiously down the street. I realize I'm tired. I'm tired of this. Tired of trying to win a battle I've already lost. I should just give up. Tell Dick it's all over.

I glance in my rearview one last time and see Carlton's new BMW parked at the curb. The "CEO" license plate.

Suddenly I see Carlton. Walking out to his car. And . . . he's not alone.

My heart drops into my stomach. I pull over to the curb and turn off my lights.

Through the darkness, I watch as Carlton opens his trunk. He's with a woman, and when she pivots to the side, I can tell from the melon-sized breasts, it's definitely Nathalie.

I hear the sounds of yelling. A man's yell.

Carlton.

Nathalie looks like she's crying up a storm. She's pacing around Carlton, her arms crossed over her chest.

I watch as Carlton pulls a small overnight bag from his trunk and points down the street toward my car. I duck down and consider speeding off, but then I realize he doesn't see me. He's pointing at another car. A taxi rolls down the street past me.

Carlton waves his arms over his head and the cab pulls over. Nathalie opens the back door, and Carlton, gentlemen that he is, drops her overnight bag on the ground. He stalks back into the house.

Nathalie grabs the bag in a huff and disappears into the backseat of the taxi.

Thoughts of Carlton drop away, and I'm suddenly worried for Nathalie. She doesn't deserve this. No woman does.

I decide to call Henry tomorrow on her behalf because I know Carlton just fired her.

All men would be tyrants if they could—

"It's time to do something big," I say, gunning the accelerator.

Chapter 55

I spend day and night working at my computer. Developing my models. Working up charts and graphs. Getting prepared for the only thing I know that will save my career.

When I'm finally finished, I look down at my Marketing and P.R. portfolio book. I've had it professionally copied onto thick color paper, and bound by the best printing company in town. All in all, I have to say, it looks pretty good. But in this competitive market, good won't cut it. It's gotta be great.

I pick the portfolio off the table, check my interview suit in the mirror, and cross my fingers.

"You can do it, Maddy," I say, giving myself the ultimate pep talk. I've got butterflies in my stomach. Today's the day. The day that will determine whether I, Maddy Piatro, have what it takes to make a comeback.

As I'm hurrying out the door, my phone rings. I dash back into the kitchen and reach for the phone.

"Hello?" I say.

A familiar voice comes on the line.

"How's my FAVE-rite gal?"

Good ol' Henry.

I smile broadly. "Thanks for calling me back," I say, immediately.

"Of course, kiddo. And let me start by saying *thank you* for sending me the brilliant Miss Nathalie. She already found two accounting errors that could've been expensive mistakes. I'm telling you, Maddy, she's a knockout with numbers."

"She's a knockout in more ways than one," I say.

Henry chuckles into the phone. In the background, I can hear him splashing what I imagine to be Jack Daniels into his coffee.

He takes an audible sip and sighs into the phone. "That body of hers could certainly sink a navy ship," he says. "I've already had to protect the poor gal from a few of our more aggressive male clients."

"I think Nathalie is in good hands," I say.

"Ahh. If I were only twenty years younger . . ." Henry muses. "And not happily married to my dear Eva."

"Try thirty years younger," I say, and he chuckles again.

"Never sass a crusty old Polak," Henry warns.

I feel my shoulders relax. A warm feeling washes over me.

We're back. Henry and me. And it took no time at all.

"So I assume you need a recommendation for your big interview?" he asks.

"Yes, I listed you on my resume, because I couldn't list Carlton. Is that all right?"

"The H.R. woman from Giganto Foods already called, kiddo. I gave her a dazzling review of your work performance."

"Thanks, Henry. How can I ever . . ." I pause. Because I'm at a loss for words.

"You can let me take you to lunch next week," Henry says. "My treat."

"Enchiladas at Manny's Mexican?" I ask.

"Now you're talkin'," he says.

Henry is quiet a moment. I expect him to say something along the lines of "*I told you so,*" but he doesn't.

"Did you hear the one about the Polish kamikaze pilot?" he asks.

I pause a moment.

"He flew forty-eight successful missions!"

I don't want to remind Henry that I've heard this joke about forty-eight times myself.

He chuckles at him own joke and says, "Break a leg, kiddo."

"I'll try."

I cross the lawn and slide into my car. Driving slowly through my neighborhood and onto the expressway, I rehearse what I'll say in the interview.

The Giganto Foods corporate office is housed in one of the larger and more impressive skyscrapers downtown. It's a towering, sheer glass structure with a needle on top. The building is shaped like a triangle and vaguely resembles a space ship. People in town jokingly call it "The Death Star." Probably because there are so many law offices on the bottom floors.

I reach the building and park in the garage underneath. Then I take the elevators up to the top suites. Only the best for Giganto. As I step into the reception area, I see that the view over Town Lake and the Texas hill country is breathtaking. I could get used to this view, I think.

I never pictured myself as the corporate type. Trying to rise up through the ranks. But then again, I would love an opportunity working for the top dog in the industry.

A smiling woman greets me at the reception desk.

"Ms. Piatro?" she asks.

"Yes."

"They're expecting you in the conference room. Can I get you some coffee?"

"I'm fine. Thank you."

She smiles and leads me through a wide, airy hallway and into a beautiful room filled with floor-to-ceiling windows. Two women and two men are sitting around a large conference table. We shake hands all around and I pass a woman named Gretta my portfolio.

"We were impressed with your resume, Madeline," she says, motioning for me to take a seat at the table.

"Thank you." I sit down. I'm dressed in my sharpest interview suit, but I see that everyone else in the room is wearing smart-casual. Which is nice to see, especially on a Monday. There's a plate of breakfast pastries on a side table, along with coffee and tea.

Everyone goes around the table and tells me about themselves. About how they started in the industry. They seem friendly and welcoming. And they're all foodies. They love to talk food. In fact, before the interview, they invite me to enjoy some of Giganto's low-fat croissants and muffins.

We gather at the side table, and Gretta hands me a small plate. I point to the muffin tray and say, "If these are low-fat, I'll take two of everything."

This gets a good chuckle all around. So I start to feel more comfortable.

A few minutes later, one of the men kicks off the interview. "So tell us, Madeline, what is your vision about the logistics involved in rolling out an organic lunch program for kids nationwide?"

I open a folder and pull out copies of all my data. My spreadsheets, my marketing proposals, my cost/benefit analysis. Everything I've worked up for the interview. I pass the sheets around, and then spend the morning discussing the pros and cons of the organic niche market for children. Things I've learned while working at Organics 4 Kids. Things you can't read in a book. I go into every detail, big and small. I really get into the nitty-gritty.

When I'm finished, my interviewers sit back in their chairs. "That was very thorough," Gretta says. "You answered all my questions. It's obvious you have a firm grasp of the market-place."

The other interviewers nod in agreement. They tell me they'll be in touch soon.

Gretta offers me a tour of the building, and the office where I would be working if I got the job. The office is gorgeous. With more floor-to-ceiling windows, and, I notice, a terrific, modern-looking desk. The whole place is sleek black and tan, not cluttered with the usual clunky brown office furniture.

Gretta tells me that the position I'm interviewing for—V.P. of the new Organics For Children Division—comes fully staffed with a secretary, and several staff assistants.

She wishes me luck and says I've been the best candidate so far.

"Have there been a lot of other candidates?" I ask.

"You're the first," she says. And we both laugh.

Gretta, I'm pleased to find out, has a sense of humor after all.

Chapter 56

I post a message to Dick on the Starbucks corkboard. It's short and sweet and reads:

> *To: D.*
> *Meet me for final project. 4:00. Thursday.*
> *Hugs and cookies,*
>   *J.*

I grab a cappuccino in a to-go cup. As I'm breezing out the door, I run smack dab into Nick.

"Hey there, stranger. I thought I might run into you, here," he says, grinning. I see he's wearing jeans and a short sleeve polo shirt. He looks incredible, really. I'm suddenly glad that I decided to wear makeup this morning.

"Are you following me?" I tease.

Nick's face changes and he takes a small step backward.

"I'm kidding," I say.

He breaks out into a relieved smile and motions for me to sit at one of the outdoor tables. So I sit and sip my cappuccino. Like the dainty little butterfly that I am.

"I missed you at tennis the other night," he says, sliding into the chair across from me.

I nod, quietly. I don't want to tell Nick about why I missed the lesson. About my run-in with Carlton at the restaurant.

But he persists. "Why were you a no-show? You better have a good excuse," he says, in a playful tone.

"I was working late," I say. "I just had an interview with Giganto Foods that I'm pretty excited about."

"How'd it go?"

I flash my sexiest kitty cat smile. "I think I nailed it," I say.

I realize that I may sound overconfident, but some guys appreciate that kind of bravado in a woman. Especially guys like Nick.

"So now that you know everything about me, Nick, why don't you tell me something about yourself? I mean, the other night at dinner, I didn't even catch your last name."

"You're going to laugh when I tell you," he says.

"Why?"

"My last name is Nolte."

"You're Nick Nolte?"

"In the flesh."

"You're kidding."

Nick flashes me a grin. "I wish I were."

I laugh and say, "Will you autograph my coffee cup?" I pull a pen from my bag and toss it toward Nick. He snatches the Styrofoam cup from my hand, scrawls something in large, bold letters across the side, and passes it back across the table.

For a good time in bed, please call Nick.
P.S. No refunds or exchanges.

"Clever," I say. "But that's *my* line."

"Imitation is the highest form of flattery," Nick informs me.

He grins and I look into his clear blue eyes. The electricity is zinging between us again, and I know he feels it, too, because I see him blush slightly.

"I never asked what you did for a living," I say.

And poof! Just like that, the electricity is gone.

Good one, Maddy.

I'm—apparently—about as sexy as a blackout.

Nick stiffens in his chair and then gives me one of those lopsided smiles. Like a person trying really hard to smile.

"I'm a hit man," he says, with complete seriousness.

I stare down at the table. And feel my face burning hot red.

Okay, Maddy. Get a grip, here.

When I look back up at Nick, he winks at me and laughs.

"I bet you've never met a hit man, have you?" he asks.

I wonder, suddenly, if Nick knows something about me. Or am I being paranoid?

"You're creeping me out," I say.

Nick shrugs and says "Sorry."

So I decide to write it off. I'm being paranoid after all.

Nick stands up abruptly and says, "Excuse me a sec while I get my daily caffeine fix."

He swings through the door of Starbucks and heads to the counter. I lean back and sip my coffee. Nick still hasn't told me anything about himself, except for the fact that his last name is Nolte. Which I'm not sure whether I believe. I should ask to see his driver's license.

Yep, that's exactly what I'll do.

A few minutes later, Nick returns with a coffee for himself and two slices of lemon pound cake. (Yum. My favorite decadent dessert.) He passes a slice across the table along with a napkin. "I thought you might enjoy a sugar boost," he says, smiling at me. God, those dimples. They really do get in the way of logic and reason.

"Thank you." I pinch off a bite of pound cake and pop it in my mouth. "I'd like to see your driver's license to confirm your last name," I say. And I'm kind of teasing, and kind of not.

Nick looks closely at me. He says, "I left my license at home."

"Mysteriously," I say.

"I walked here," he explains. "And I don't like to carry a big fat wallet when I'm walking. Just my money clip."

"I see. Well, in that case, why don't we walk back to your place and get it?"

I'm really going balls to the wall with this one. And I'm not sure Nick likes it. But I don't care.

"Are you trying to sleep with me, Maddy?" he asks, shooting me a mischievous grin.

"Yes."

"Okay, okay. You got me. My last name isn't Nolte. It's Montana," he says. "Nicholas Montana."

"Thank you." I shake my head back and forth. "I almost believed the Nick Nolte story. Which shows you what a sap I am."

Nick stares at me a moment. A long, hard stare. And then he says, out of the blue, "Are you really a sap, Maddy? Could someone pull the wool over your eyes? And get you involved with something you really didn't want to be involved with? Because I'd really like to believe that."

I glance down at the table, and then look up into Nick Montana's clear blue eyes. He's staring at me in a really intense way. I'm not sure about his question, but I suddenly feel uncomfortable. My stomach does a little flip flop.

I check my watch and say, "Oh my gosh! Look at the time. I've got to run."

Nick stands from the table and I stand up, too. We do this awkward handshake thing, and I say, "Thanks for the cake. It's been . . . entertaining."

Nick's face suddenly seems dark and solemn. He isn't smiling anymore. He says, "Can I give you a lift?"

I stare at him. "That would be great, Nick. But you walked here, REMEMBER?" I pivot around and am surprised when he grabs my arm.

His grip is firm. A little too firm.

"It's not what you think," he says, his eyes crinkling at the edges. "I'm not some kind of weirdo."

I jerk my arm away.

"Right," I say.

I turn and literally race out of the coffee shop and down the block.

"Maddy, wait!" I hear him shout out. But I'm already rounding the corner.

Chapter 57

Heather and I are having a super fabulous afternoon at the Neiman Marcus outlet store. We're strolling through the maternity clothes section, and I'm helping Heather pick out some great outfits. I'm saying brilliant stuff like: "The blue in this shirt totally matches your eyes."

Actually, that's not true. Heather's picking out her own outfits while I mill around aimlessly. As she digs through the racks, I regale her with a History of Nick Montana and Maddy Piatro. The abbreviated version.

It goes something like this . . .

Tennis with Nick
Smoothie with Nick
Dinner with Nick
Coffee and pound cake with Nick
Psycho Nick
Maddy fleeing Nick—which, I admit to Heather, was possibly overdramatic.

"So, in conclusion . . . ." I say, waving my hands in the air. "Another one bites the dust."

She turns and gives me a supportive pat on the shoulder. "That's a shame, Maddy," she coos in a soft, baby doll voice that only Heather can get away with.

"I NEVER should've tried to date someone new," I sigh.

"Nonsense," Heather says. "What happened to my 'Leap Before You Look' best friend?"

"I'm actually feeling better than I've felt in a long time," I say.

Heather looks at me, but this time, it's not the wounded dog look. It's not the look of pity that I've become accustomed to.

This time, my girlfriend is looking at me with pride.

"You seem conf lent, lately. More bouncy," she says, simply.

She pulls a hanger from off the rack and holds up a pair of mud-brown overalls in front of her bulging belly.

"Too blah?" she asks.

"On me, it would look like someone rolled me in a pile of cow dung," I say. "On you, it'll look like maternity runway couture."

"I'm going to try it on," Heather announces. We walk to the back of the store and I hold her purse while she zips inside one of the dressing rooms.

"So tennis boy turned out to be Ted Bundy?" she calls out, from behind the door.

"Not quite. I mean, he was nice at first. We went on an official date."

"I remember," Heather says. "He took you to Le Bistro."

"Right. Well, I thought we had tons of chemistry but then things went south."

"How so?"

"He's been completely mysterious. He hasn't told me anything about himself, including where he works. And then he tells me his last name is Nolte."

"Nick Nolte?"

"And I believed him."

"Maddy," Heather says, in a tone that makes me feel like a gullible idiot. If my dear, sweet girlfriend realizes that Nick was pulling my leg—and Heather's not all that street savvy—then I'm definitely slow on the uptake.

"His last name is actually Montana, which is a nice name, but it was strange the way he told me. As if he didn't want to tell me. The conversation just got weirder after that."

"Maybe he's an undercover agent," Heather comments.

"Yeah, like an undercover serial killer?"

Heather giggles from behind the door.

"Nick Dahmer," she says.

"Nick Rifkin," I say.

"Son of Sam, Nick Berkowitz," she says.

"Nick Manson."

We go back and forth for a few minutes until we run out of serial killer names.

After what feels like a year and a half, Heather swings out of the dressing room and says, "Ta-da! What do you think?"

She looks like a million dollars, of course. Like a pregnant supermodel Heidi Klum. The brown overalls hide her pregnant belly so, from the front, you can't even tell she's pregnant.

"It's a keeper," I say. "You look like you should be on the cover of *Maternity Magazine*."

"Oh, stop."

Heather steps back into the dressing room and reappears a few minutes later with the overalls folded neatly over her arm.

"These are only thirty dollars and they're designer, can you believe it?"

I say, "The price of clothes these days. Oy Vay. Don't get me started."

Heather shoots me a funny look and says, "Started on what?" And we both burst out laughing.

Chapter 58

I walk quickly to Starbucks, a crisp, white envelope in my hand. I'm wearing sunglasses and my hair is tucked up inside a baseball cap. Not a sophisticated disguise, but still. I hope I don't run into Nick Montana.

The bell on the door tinkles as I swing it open. I turn toward my usual table and stop in my tracks.

Dick is already sitting at our table. Two coffees. One for him. And one, presumably, for me. There are also two big chocolate chip cookies on two separate napkins. But I think both of the cookies are for Dick.

"You're early," I say, scooting out my chair.

"Surprise," he says.

"Is this for me?" I ask, holding up the coffee cup.

"Least I could do was buy ya a cup o' Joe," Dick says, smiling sheepishly.

"Oh yeah. Why is that?"

He leans back in his chair and stretches his thick arms behind his head. I check to see if he's carrying his gun, and am pleasantly surprised to see that Marlon Brando has left the building.

"You're one killer business chic," he says. "I did what you said with the business cards and the brochures, and already, I got too many lady clients to count."

Glad to hear it," I say. I imagine swarms of women, all wanting to hire Dick to plot some kind of pranks on their cheating husbands, boyfriends, whatever.

Dick says, "I never knew there were so many angry broads out there."

"Remember what I said about the violent stuff," I say, wagging my finger back and forth.

Dick nods and pats the spot on his jacket where his gun used to be. He even opens his coat and shows me that he's sans weapon. "I'm hanging all that up, Jane," he says, proudly. "Life's too short, ya know?"

I smile and say, "Is this what they call 'personal growth?'"

Dick chuckles and takes a big swig from his coffee cup. "Ouch. Careful, Jane. I just burned my tongue on this bad boy."

I take a small sip from my coffee. I was expecting plain, black coffee. But Dick has sprung for the expensive stuff. I taste the froth from the cappuccino and realize that he even remembered to ask for low-fat milk.

"Want me to put some honey in your coffee?" I ask my favorite hit man.

Dick grins at me and flashes his white, white teeth. "I did it myself this time, Jane. I mean, I figure if a guy wants honey, he should have honey."

Dick chugs back more coffee and says, "Ahhh. Honey bee does me right." Then he looks at me across the table and gets down to business.

"So, what does my favorite female Don have in store for me next? You gotta tell me, Jane. I'm dyin' ta know."

I slide a plain, white envelope over to Dick.

"What's this?" he asks.

"Your last assignment," I say.

He turns the envelope over in his hand. Shakes it. Holds it up to the light.

"It's not sealed. Go ahead. Take a look," I say.

He opens the envelope cautiously, as if he's worried about letter bombs. A single business card falls onto the table. Dick picks it up, reads it quietly to himself. His lips move as he reads.

"You're one tough broad," he says, smiling at me. "So I guess you want me to deliver this to Wonder Boy?"

"Please do. Oh, and make him sign for it," I say. "You know. Pretend you're a delivery guy with a clipboard."

"No problem," Dick says. "So, is it real? Did you really score this job or what?"

I nod. "I can't believe it myself," I say.

"If anyone deserves it, you do," Dick says. He looks at the card again and shakes his head. "*Madeline Jane Piatro. Executive Managing Director, Organic Children's Division, Giganto Foods,*" Dick reads. "I guess Wonder Boy is gonna shit his pants when he sees this."

"He's going to be even more surprised when he finds out that *I created* this new division for Giganto Foods."

"Let me guess. Organic lunches for kids."

I smile. "You know, you're pretty smart for a tough guy," I say.

"Watch it," Dick says, pointing his finger in my face. He shoves the card back into the envelope and licks the seal shut.

"Why don't you jus' mail this sucker," he says, tapping the envelope on the table.

"Carlton gets tons of junk mail. I don't want it to get lost in the heap," I say. "And besides, I like the idea of having him sign for it. That way, he'll open it right away."

"So, this is it?" Dick asks. "A business card?"

"That's it," I say.

"So you still don't want me to break his bones," Dick says, but I think he's joking.

"This is going to be more painful. Trust me," I say.

Dick grins at me. "You're one tough cookie," he says, chomping his chocolate chip cookie in half.

I'm surprised when he pushes the other cookie in my direction.

"I gave you the bigger one," he says, and then my hit man actually winks at me.

"Thanks."

Chapter 59

Deepak calls me on my cell phone. I've skipped three tennis lessons so he's probably afraid that I've dropped the class.

"I'm concerned, Miss Maddy. Very concerned. I think maybe Deepak was too hard on you?" he asks, in his pleasant singsong voice.

"Not at all, Deepak. You're a fantastic tennis pro—the best," I assure him.

"Then why did I lose my two very good students?" he asks.

I pause a moment. This means Nick didn't show up at tennis, either. And I'm a little surprised. I thought he'd at least show up to see if I showed up. But I guess he doesn't want to see me after all.

"I can't speak for Nick," I say. "But I'm starting a new job so I was wondering if I could switch to your Saturday morning class?"

"Sure, sure, Miss Maddy. No problem at all," Deepak says. "I very much look forward to seeing you again. And seeing your most excellent skills on the court. By the way, do you know where I can reach Mr. Nicholas?"

"Don't you have his phone number?"

"I thought so, yes. But then I check my records, Miss Maddy.

Mr. Nicholas left me no contact information. No address. No phone number. Just his name."

"Nicholas Montana?"

"Nicholas Nolt-Tee," Deepak says, and his voice is utterly earnest.

Hmm. Maybe I should've told Deepak my name was Catherine Zeta Jones.

"So Nick is a ghost, huh?" I ask.

"No ghost. He is a real live man," Deepak says. He pauses for a moment and then says, "I thought maybe the two of you were romantic together."

"Why is that?"

"The way he looked at you . . . when you were not looking," Deepak replies.

"I barely know the guy," I say. "But don't worry. I'm sure he'll show up in class."

"I don't know. Maybe he leave town. Go on vacation. Who can say? Only God knows these things," Deepak says.

"Yeah. Only God knows," I say.

Chapter 60

Every good thing must come to an end, as they say. So, in the spirit of closure, I have my last meeting with Dick.

We decide to meet at Starbucks again because why mess with a good thing?

I'm wearing my usual street clothes. I figure since Nick dropped the tennis class, he's probably also started getting his daily caffeine fix from another coffee shop.

As I swing open the door, I see Dick sitting at our usual table. He's here to collect his payment. And I'm certainly not going to leave a former hit man in the lurch.

"So we're finished," he says, as I reach the table.

I scoot out my chair and plop down. "I guess that about covers it," I say.

"I brought you a little present," Dick says. He slides a clipboard across the table. On it is Carlton's signature. Scrolled big and bold across the page. An exaggerated movie star signature.

"How did he look when he opened the envelope?" I ask. I don't want to ask because it sounds catty, but I do.

"Captain Hook turned white as a ghost," Dick says, grinning with his shiny, white capped teeth. "I've never seen a man's face go the color of bleach before. Even when I've stuck my Marlon Brando into some dude's mouth and threatened to blow out his asshole, I still haven't seen a face go that white," Dick says, chuckling.

I smile and say, "Nice job."

Dick says, "You pistol-whipped that mother with a business card. I can't believe it." He shakes his head, and for a split second, I feel him looking upon me with admiration. I take this as my cue.

"Look Dick, about the money I owe you. Giganto is giving me a pretty decent salary so I was hoping . . . maybe I could give you some cash now and some after I get my first few paychecks. You know where I work, and I promise to pay you in full very soon. And with five percent interest . . ." I say, because I'm nervous. Do hit men usually accept payment plans?

"Please," Dick says, holding his hand up in a stop signal. "I don't expect no payment, Jane. I've learned more from you than I did with my old crew."

He smiles. "Hey, that rhymes," he says.

"Well, at least let me do something nice for you," I say.

Dick puffs his cheeks out and does the Marlon Brando underbite. He goes into his Don Corleone voice, "Some day, and that day may never come, I'll call upon you to do a service for me," he says, in his perfect Godfather voice.

I laugh. "You really should be an actor," I say. "But seriously, what can I do for you? This is quid pro quo, remember."

"Send me some other female clients," Dick says. "So I can get my new business off the ground."

"Your new business?"

"Muscle work ain't what it used to be," Dick says, tapping his forehead. "You've taught me to use my ticker, instead. So, I'm only accepting female clients now. To perform nonviolent services."

Dick smiles broadly and shoots me a wink. "I hear it's a killer."

I look at Dick a moment. "Hey, I never thought I'd say this, but I hope you keep in touch."

"You too," Dick says, even though we both know it'll never happen. Our worlds were never meant to collide. People from two different worlds don't usually hang out after the fact.

Dick sticks out his hand in a formal gesture and says, "Nice meeting you."

"The pleasure was all mine," I say, slipping my palm into his broad hand. I was expecting his skin to be rough, but it's as soft as a satin pillow.

"You've got soft hands," I say.

"Soft hands, hard heart," he chuckles.

"Oh come on, Dick. Don't give me that tough guy routine. I know you better than that."

Dick grins and stands from his chair. He tucks his thumbs underneath the lapels of his leather jacket and starts to glide toward the door. I watch as he suddenly spins on his heel and glances back at me for one last time.

"Oh, and Jane?"

"Yeah?"

"My name isn't really Dick."

I look at him and smile.

Chapter 61

I leave Starbucks and skip down the street. For the first time in months, I feel free. Breezy. And light as a bird. I even hum a little tune.

At the corner, I bend down and retie the laces on my tennis shoes. It's a gorgeous day in Austin, Texas. The sun is shining and a cool breeze is sweeping in from the hill country. The mountain laurels are in full bloom so the air smells of lavender.

Suddenly I hear a car and the sound of screeching tires. I look up and see a black Lincoln on the street in front of me. It jerks to a stop. Two men in suits jump out.

"DEA! You're under arrest! Hands on your head!" one of them shouts. I think, but I can't be sure because as I jerk my head up to see where the noise is coming from, the sun hits me squarely in the eye.

I stand up, slowly. With my hands in the air. I'm so still, I can't feel myself breathing. For some reason, I think my heart has stopped.

My pupils adjust to the sunlight, and I see more clearly now. One of the men standing in front of me, conveniently, is Nick. And he isn't smiling.

He flashes his fed credentials and a badge. "I'm agent Nicholas Montana, with the DEA," he says, crisply. He nods toward the other gentlemen. "This is my partner, Agent Sanchez. We're going to need to take you in for questioning," he says, and then adds, "Right now, Madeline."

So that's that. We're back to formal names again. No more Maddy. In the blink of an eye, we're back to Madeline.

"DEA?" I ask, my voice cracking.

"Drug Enforcement Agency," Agent Sanchez pipes up.

"I know what DEA stands for, but why am I being taken in for questioning?"

"Conspiring with your brother, Mr. Ronald Piatro, a known drug trafficker, and with Florence "Dickie" Ferguson, a known drug hit man."

"Florence "Dickie" Ferguson?"

Nick points up the street. I turn and see Dick being dragged out of Starbucks. His hands cuffed behind his back. He's shouting something out about being a "Legitimate Business Man!" He glances down the street and spots me.

I've still got my hands up in the air, as if I'm being arrested, thank God.

"I'm a legitimate bid-ness man!" Dick shouts again, sounding ridiculous.

"Yeah, that's Florence Ferguson," Nick says, motioning toward Dick.

"Now I know why he never gave me his real name," I say.

Nick says, "What?"

"Never mind," I say.

Agent Sanchez informs me: "You have the right for an attorney to be present during questioning."

"Save it," I say, sharply. And I see the hint of a smile streak across Nick's lips.

Agent Sanchez pulls out a pair of handcuffs and Nick says, "Those won't be necessary, Antonio."

Nick takes me gently by the arm and leads me to the sedan. I notice that he shields my head when he slides me into the backseat.

Instead of getting scared and shaky, I suddenly become myself again. In the blink of an eye, it's as if my body has regained all of the strength that had been sapped away that last year with Carlton.

I feel strong. Bold. Outspoken. Like I always used to feel.

"You know, you guys are really making fools of yourselves," I say. "This is a huge mistake."

Agent Sanchez starts counting out a list on his fingers. "Number one, criminal solicitation. Number two, murder-for-hire. Number three, conspiracy to commit murder. Do I need to go on?" he asks.

I notice Agent Sanchez is a short, squat, machine of a guy. He's wearing a gunstrap underneath his jacket, and I can tell, because the bulge is clearly visible.

"There was never any murder-for-hire. Besides a little Robin Hood theft job of a bicycle and a wristwatch, it was all fairly innocent," I inform him.

Nick turns around in the front seat and I see that he's looking at me with regretful eyes. As if he wishes it weren't really me sitting in the back seat.

"He's dead, Madeline. It's over," he says, quietly.

The words sink in slowly.

He's dead, Madeline. It's over . . .

Chapter 62

He's dead, Madeline.

Carlton! No!

My body goes cold. And my mind whirls in circles. Carlton is dead. And I, Madeline Piatro, killed him. It wasn't an intentional murder, but I did hire Florence or Dickie or whatever his name is. I did show him Carlton's photograph. And I'm responsible for whatever happened next.

"H-h-how?" I ask, and my voice is hoarse. Cracking.

"Multiple gunshot wounds," Nick replies. He's staring at me from the front passenger seat, while Agent Sanchez drives us toward some federal building, or maybe a police station.

I feel sick, suddenly. My stomach jumps into my throat. I start gagging a little, and making gurgling noises like I'm going to puke.

Nick swings around to Agent Sanchez and says, "Pull over."

The sedan screeches over to the curb, and I watch as Nick jumps out and runs inside a convenience store. He returns a minute later with a bottle of Ginger Ale.

"Drink," he says, handing me the cold bottle from the front seat.

I take a small sip and wait for my churning stomach to settle down.

"Better?" Nick asks.

I consider the question. How can I feel better knowing that my ex-fiancé is dead? And that I, essentially, had him killed?

Thoughts go whizzing through my head. I consider how this happened in the first place. Me—stubborn, ridiculous, scorned, damaged little me—going to my brother to ask him for a name of a bruiser. Someone in the business of breaking ribs. And then I hire a guy I barely know—to do these little projects for me. And—just like in the movies—things turn violent. Maybe Dick is a psychopath. Or maybe Carlton pissed him off and Dick decided to shoot him. Even if Dick took matters into his own hands, I'm still to blame. It was me—all me.

I drop my head into my hands and let the tears come. I literally sob. A loud, heaving type of sob.

I think of my brother saying to me, *"What would Jesus do?"*

And Heather advising me to *"Let it go, Maddy."*

And then, I think of Carlton. My sobbing grows louder as a world of regret and shame comes crashing down on me. After the break-up, I was filled with so much loathing toward him. So much angst.

But, now—Now that he's dead—All I feel is a tremendous and unflinching sorrow.

Carlton. Dead!

Oh, God!

I wipe wet snot from my nose and look through my blustery tears at Nick.

"This is the second time in my life that someone I was very close to died tragically!" I whimper.

Nick stares off into the distance.

"I'm sorry about the loss of your parents, Madeline," he says, finally, taking a deep breath. "But what did you expect would happen this time? You hired a professional hit man for chris-sakes!"

I nod and hiccup. More sobbing. I start saying, "Oh God! Oh God!" And I can't stop.

We pull into the back of an official bureaucratic-looking build-ing that I didn't even know existed. It's gray and imposing, with small square windows. I'm suddenly frightened and my body shivers uncontrollably.

Nick steps out of the car, opens the back door, takes my arm, and leads me gently out of the car.

Agent Sanchez pushes a buzzer on the building, flashes his credentials to a camera, and the three of us walk inside.

I consider calling Michael. That would be the smart thing to do. The calculated thing. But should I really hide behind the cloak of a lawyer at this point? When it's my fault to begin with?

I think of the words engraved in the clock tower at the University of Texas. My Alma Mater.

And the Truth Shall Set You Free.

I gulp down some air, steady my shaking hands, and decide to accept my fate. Telling the truth—and the whole truth—is my only option.

Nick leads me into a plain-looking interrogation room. I was expecting a two-way mirror, like you see in the movies. But there's just a small round table and a few chairs.

Agent Sanchez informs me that the conversation is being re-corded.

We sit down and Nick and Agent Sanchez look at me a mo-ment, as if waiting for me to start. I notice that both agents rest their arms flat on the table. Not crossed over their chests. They're trying to assume a relaxed, physical stance, as if to encourage the criminal to start talking.

I don't say a word.

The minutes tick by, and then Nick says, "Look, Madeline. I know your brother put you up to this. That you were just the middleman in the whole deal. The go-between. Because, obviously, Ronnie Piatro can't be seen in public meeting with Florence "Dickie" Ferguson. And he didn't want to leave a record of phone calls or e-mails that could be traced. So he enlisted you—his older sister—to do his dirty work for him. What I don't understand is— why you agreed to it?"

I look at Nick and, in the firmest voice I can muster, say, "My brother had absolutely NOTHING to do with this. It was ALL ME."

"No use trying to protect him, now," Agent Sanchez says. He raps his fist loudly on the table, and the noise makes me jump in my seat.

"Ronnie Piatro may not have been the triggerman himself," Agent Sanchez says, "but what he did is get you involved in conspiracy to commit murder. You'll both be charged as accomplices."

I look into Nick's eyes, and he watches me, carefully, as a tear rolls down my cheek.

"This can't be right," I whisper.

"If you testify against your brother, we'll work out a deal," Agent Sanchez says.

"Hey, take it easy," Nick says to Agent Sanchez.

I guess they're giving me the good cop/ bad cop routine.

"Your brother is *going down*," Agent Sanchez says, his eyes narrowing to little slits.

"Ronnie is innocent! He's a drug rehab counselor! He had no motive!" I nearly shout.

Both of the agents digest this information, and then Nick says, "We disagree. He had a very big motive. And it's called 'money.' Pure and simple."

I think of the twenty-thousand-dollar donation I made to Ronnie's anonymous "Just Say Yes!" to Sobriety fund.

"As if my brother would commit murder for twenty thousand dollars," I say, hanging my head.

I can't believe I got Ronnie mixed up with this. If I were my brother, I'd never forgive me. No matter how Christian he is.

"Twenty thousand dollars?" Nick asks. "Try again, Madeline."

"Please listen to me! You've got it all wrong!" I say, in a pleading voice. "How can I convince you that it was all my idea . . ."

Chapter 63

Nick passes a large manila envelope across the table.

I stare down at it. "What is this?"

"Photographs," he says. "Of the crime scene."

I finger the envelope and my body goes cold. Photographs of Carlton. Dead. With multiple gunshot wounds.

"Wh-wh-where did it happen?" I ask.

"In his car," Nick says.

I think of Carlton inside his black BMW. Shot to death. I can't bear to look at the photographs.

Agent Sanchez grabs the envelope, opens it impatiently, and sends the photos flying across the table.

I look up at the spackled ceiling. At the brown watermark stain creeping out from the air conditioning vent. This will be my fate from now on. Miserable jailhouse conditions. The smell of mold and stale, recirculated air. And I deserve every minute of it.

I grip the table with my hands and steady myself for what comes next.

The first photograph is blurry. I pick it up. It's the inside of a car, and what looks like blood stains over the seats.

The second picture is more graphic. It's of the top of a man's head. Slouched over the steering wheel. There's blood everywhere in the car, all over the upholstery.

My heart is suddenly pounding in my chest and I can barely breathe.

I pick up the third photograph and gasp.

The dead man is in clear view now. He's the same size and build as Carlton, and even has the same movie star quality hair. But, he's definitely *not* Carlton Connors.

"I don't understand," I say, in a meek voice. "Is this some kind of trick?"

Agent Sanchez says, "This is the drug lord, Teddy Santino. Better known as Snoop. That's the name he goes by on the streets. Snoop Santino. This is the man who you hired Florence 'Dick' Ferguson to kill. The man your brother wanted dead."

I sit for a moment in total silence. Taking it all in.

"S-so. Carlton isn't dead?"

Nick leans across the table and stares into my eyes. "Who's Carlton?" he asks.

Chapter 64

Michael bursts into the interrogation room, jabs his finger into my chest and says, "Never talk to the feds without your lawyer present."

He's wearing a suit and tie and carrying his briefcase. He sets it on the floor and takes an empty chair next to me.

"How did you know I was here?" I ask.

"A little birdie called me—your brother. They've got him in another interrogation room down the hall," Michael says.

He looks from Nick to Agent Sanchez, and then at Nick again. "This is a case of misunderstandin' and you guys know it. My clients, Ronnie Piatro and Madeline Piatro had nothing to do with the murder of Snoop Santino. Zero. Zip. You fellows are grabbin' at straws."

Nick looks at Michael and says, "The weapon used at the crime scene matches the gun that Florence 'Dickie' Ferguson carries."

"I've spoken to Mr. Ferguson, and he's also retained me as his attorney." Michael pulls a sheet of paper from his briefcase and passes it to Nick. Here's my contract with Mr. Ferguson's signature on the bottom," he says.

Nick looks down at the Retainer Agreement and says, "Continue."

"Mr. Ferguson is retired from his old business. He's had no contact with Snoop Santino for several months. He thinks he knows who killed Snoop Santino, though, and he's willing to talk, in exchange for full immunity."

"So you're telling us that Maddy was meeting with Florence Ferguson for reasons other than the murder of Snoop Santino?" Nick asks, and I notice his voice sounds almost hopeful. He also called me Maddy.

Michael looks at me, pointedly, and crosses his arms over his chest.

"I think Ms. Piatro can best explain her reasons for meeting with Mr. Ferguson," he says, and then adds, "at Starbucks coffee of all places."

Nick, Agent Sanchez, and Michael all turn in their chairs and stare at me.

I take a deep breath. "It started back in grad school . . ." I begin. "At one of these cocktail mixers for young professionals . . ."

Chapter 65

An hour later, I'm in a large holding cell with my brother and Florence "Dickie" Ferguson. There's another guy in there with us. Ronnie tells me that he's probably an undercover agent posing as a busted criminal. I can smell the guy's cologne. The same shit Carlton used to wear.

Terrific.

It doesn't smell like a romantic log cabin in the woods. It smells like a damn forest fire.

"What kind of cologne are you wearing?" I ask the undercover guy.

"It's called 'Audacity'," he says.

Perfect, I think.

My brother glances around the jail cell. Apparently, he knows his way around the place.

"Have I told you lately, Maddy, how much I love the DEA?" Ronnie says, in a sarcastic tone.

I chew on my lip because what can I say? I'm the reason he's here.

"I'm really pissed off at you, Sister," Ronnie says. But he doesn't have to say it. I can see it in his eyes. He's back to his old eyes again. The angry eyes I used to see all the time when he was doing drugs. Funny how my brother forgets the whole "Jesus forgiveness" thing when the shit hits the fan.

"What happened to turning the other cheek?" I ask. I'm not trying to rile him up; I'm just making a point.

I'm surprised when my brother says, staring down at his feet. "You're absolutely right, Maddy. We should pray." He bows his head and makes the Sign of the Cross.

"Wow, you really do practice what you preach."

"I'd be a hypocrite if I didn't."

He mumbles a few words, a silent prayer under his breath. I know he's asking God to forgive me and so on and so forth.

"You wanna tell me what's going on with our favorite SS guard?" Florence "Dickie" Ferguson asks, pointing to the undercover guy joining us in the cell.

"Don't worry. I think Michael will be springing us soon," I say, and I actually use the phrase "springing us."

Florence "Dickie" Ferguson glances at his watch and sighs.

"Wherever Florence goes, the shit storm follows," he says, to no one in particular.

He turns to me and says, "I'm glad I retired from all that dirty business, Jane. Or else I'd be doing hard time. I've got you to thank for that."

"Uh. You're welcome, Dick," I say. It's odd for me to start calling him Florence, so I'm still calling him Dick. I think he likes it, because he smiles his big white smile.

Heather and Michael suddenly appear in front of the jail cell bars.

"My white knight has appeared," Florence says. He stares Heather up and down. "And he's brought a Princess with him. So, who might this be?"

"That's my wife, and she's off limits," Michael says, in a strong voice. And I guess he's kind of kidding, and kind of not. Michael can be a tough nut, sometimes.

A guard appears and lets us all out of the cell. I notice that the undercover guy steps out, too. Well, well.

Heather rushes up to me and gives me a little hug.

"Why didn't you tell me!" she squeals.

"I'm sorry," I say.

We exchange meaningful looks. Goodness. What would I do without my dear, sweet friend?

Michael says, "Heather's cookin' up a storm so you guys are welcome to come over for dinner, tonight."

Ronnie says, "Free food. You're on."

Florence shuffles his boot-clad foot along the floor. "Does that include me?"

Michael claps the former hit man on the shoulder. "Sure does, buddy. You're a new client, ain't ya?"

I watch Florence break out into a huge grin. He turns toward Heather and introduces himself with a formal handshake.

"Is this joker really your husband?" he asks, thumbing his finger toward Michael.

"My one and only," Heather says, kissing Michael on the cheek.

"Let me know if you ever have problems with him," Florence says.

"Why?" Heather asks.

"I'm an expert in nonviolent retribution," he says, winking at me. "I specialize in female revenge therapy."

"May come in handy," Heather replies.

Michael says, "Hey now. Be nice to your lawyer."

We start walking toward the door. I take Michael to the side and ask him if there are going to be any further ramifications with the Carlton issue. Particularly the stolen bike and stolen wristwatch.

"I wouldn't worry about it," Michael says. "The Feds don't dick around with nickel-and-dime stuff."

"It wasn't exactly nickels and dimes," I say.

"You gave the money to Ronnie's rehab program, didn't you?" Michael asks.

"Don't tell Ronnie. He'll be crushed."

Michael bolts around and grips me by the shoulders. "Okay, Maddy. But promise me you're finished with this."

I hold up three fingers and say, "Boy Scouts Honor."

Michael says, "That's not the way you do it, but it's close enough."

We reach the parking lot and amble toward Michael's car. Ronnie lights up a cigarette first thing. And Heather says, "You know those things will kill you."

Florence "Dickie" Ferguson chuckles out loud and says, "Among other things."

I hear someone calling out my name, "Maddy, wait!"

Turning, I see it's Nick. Racing across the parking lot. We all stop walking. Michael mutters under his breath. "Great. Now what?"

Nick Montana jogs over to us and I notice he's out of breath. Our eyes meet and the electric sparks are back. We could light up a stadium over here.

"May I speak to you a moment?" he asks. "In private."

Michael says, "Not without her lawyer."

"Hold on," Nick says, sticking his hand up in the air. "It's not about that."

I wave my hands to shoo away my friends, and my brother, who is eyeing me, suspiciously.

"It's alright. Go ahead, you guys. I'll catch up," I say.

Nick waits for everyone to get out of earshot.

"I want you to know that I felt there was something between us," he says, finally.

I look into his eyes, this stranger, and part of me wants to walk away. But I don't.

"I understand," I say. "You were just doing your job."

Nick stares down at the pavement. When he looks back at me, his eyes are burning a vivid blue. "I've been investigating a drug operation led by Snoop Santino. Florence Ferguson was Snoop Santino's main hit guy, so I followed him all the time. Imagine my surprise when I saw you meet up with him at that coffee shop. And then to find out who your brother was. Talk about a smoking gun."

"Clever tactic, Nick. To join my tennis club and then take me out to dinner and make me think I was out on an actual date."

I shake my head. "Silly, silly me. You must've been shocked when I kissed you out of the blue."

"I have to admit, it's the first time I've been kissed by someone I was investigating."

"I'm glad I made history," I say.

Nick grabs my arm in that rock hard grip of his, but this time, instead of scaring me, it sends shivers running through me.

"Wait. Let's not end things like this. The night we went out—and at tennis—I felt . . ." he trails off.

"I don't know anything about you," I say.

Nick pulls me toward him and stares down into my eyes. "I told you my last name was Montana. I've never told a suspect my real last name," he says.

"I'm flattered."

Nick drops my arm. "How do you feel about giving this a second chance?" he asks. "Making it real this time."

I glance over my shoulder and see Heather and Ronnie staring at me from across the parking lot.

They're both giving me the thumbs-up sign.

I take a deep breath and think, *what the heck*?

"We're all going over to Michael and Heather's house for dinner, if you'd care to join us."

He looks at me and hesitates. "Are you sure? I mean, I'd love to. But I don't want to intrude."

"Leap first, look later," I say.

Nick grins and reaches for my hand, lacing his fingers through mine. I don't know what it is, but I feel great all of a sudden. The best I've felt in a very long time.

"Shall we?" he asks.

I nod. "Yes."

As we turn toward the car, Michael, Heather, Ronnie, and Florence "Dickie" Ferguson begin to clap.

~ Epilogue

The Financial Daily Times

Breaking News . . .

Managing Director Madeline Piatro, of Giganto Foods, has just been named President and CEO in a surprise unanimous vote by the Giganto Board of Directors.

Ms. Piatro, who was married earlier this year, is the first female President and CEO in the Company's 35-year history. At 41 years old, she now joins the ranks as one of the youngest CEOs on Wall Street. And is making history as the first CEO to be pregnant while taking over the reins of a Fortune 500 Company.

It is rumored that Ms. Piatro announced her pregnancy to the Giganto Board of Directors in June, but despite the news, they voted to install her as CEO two months later in August.

Ms. Piatro began her career as an executive consultant with Henry Wrona Public Relations and Marketing, a boutique firm headquartered in Austin, Texas. She later moved on to become Vice President of Organics 4 Kids where it is rumored she developed the business plan for the company and then left under hostile circumstances.

Within a few months, Ms. Piatro became a rising star at Giganto as Vice President of the Organic Children's Division. The Financial Daily News reported that Ms. Piatro was "The Person to Watch," and Investor's Magazine named her in its prominent list of "The Top Ten Executives of the Year."

According to the latest Annual Report to Shareholders, Ms. Piatro has transformed the Organic Foods division into Giganto's most profitable unit, causing the stock price to rise a hefty 30 percent.

When asked whether the recent bankruptcy announcement by CEO Carlton Connors, of Organics 4 Kids, had anything to do with Giganto's enormously profitable performance, Ms. Piatro replied, "The failure of Organics 4 Kids was not due to direct competition from Giganto, but rather from a company that had lost its direction and turned away from its founding principles."

In a rare speech given at the Worldwide Organic Food Conference in San Francisco, California, where she accepted an award for her charitable contributions, Ms. Piatro was magnanimous in her words . . .

She first thanked the employees and staff of Giganto for their hard work and dedication, along with her husband, and her brother, Ronald Piatro, who Chairs the nonprofit drug rehab program: "The Miracle Teens."

"Companies are only as vibrant as the people who run them," Ms. Piatro said.

When teased by a reporter about whether Ms. Piatro would assume her husband's last name, she laughed and responded, simply, "My husband has never told me his last name."

Ms. Piatro's husband is rumored to work undercover for the FBI.

A+

AUTHOR INSIGHTS, EXTRAS, & MORE...

FROM
JO BARRETT
AND
AVON A

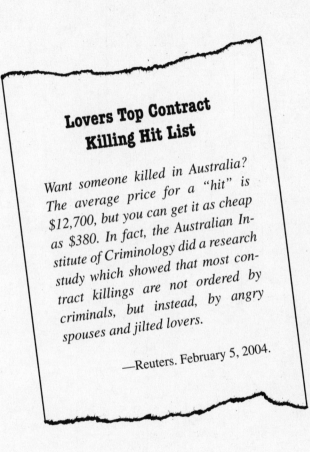

Lovers Top Contract Killing Hit List

Want someone killed in Australia? The average price for a "hit" is $12,700, but you can get it as cheap as $380. In fact, the Australian Institute of Criminology did a research study which showed that most contract killings are not ordered by criminals, but instead, by angry spouses and jilted lovers.

—Reuters. February 5, 2004.

Questions for Hitmen from the Author:

Hey, does the price for a "hit" include tax and tip?

Speaking of tips, does anyone know the tipping etiquette for a hit man? Do I tip him like my waiter? My hairstylist? Or like the skycap at the airport?

Uh . . . American Express?

What if my hit man is actually a woman? What happens then? Do I refer to her as a *hit person*? *Hit human?* Or possibly, *Hit Chick?*

Do hit men ever watch movies about hit men? And if so, which do you think is their favorite?

1.	*Grosse Point Blank*	John Cusack
2.	*Mr. and Mrs. Smith*	Brad Pitt, Angelina Jolie
3.	*Collateral*	Tom Cruise
4.	*The Matador*	Pierce Brosnan
5.	*Kill Bill, Volume 1*	Uma Thurman
6.	*Assassins*	Antonio Banderas, Sylvester Stallone
7.	*The Whole Nine Yards*	Bruce Willis
8.	*Pulp Fiction*	Samuel L. Jackson, John Travolta
9.	*Prizzi's Honor*	Jack Nicholson, Kathleen Turner
10.	*Contract Killer*	Jet Li

A+ AUTHOR INSIGHTS, EXTRAS, & MORE...

Are there any really hot, sexy hit men in real life? And if so, are they on Match.com? I mean, there must be one or two out there, right? They don't call it "muscle-for-hire" for nothing, right?

Official **Message from the Author Delivered at Gunpoint from Her Editor!**

For the record, I do not advocate *hiring a hit man* to avenge an ex-lover. I also don't recommend *baking poison brownies* and tasting them yourself. In fact, none of the retribution tools mentioned in this novel—*cyanide, arsenic, or carbon monoxide*—are worth trifling with.

However, I do believe some break-up stories leave open the possibility for a little good, clean fun. All's fair in love and war, right? And besides, whoever said there was anything wrong with "getting back" at Mr. Right?

I live in Texas and have many "normal" girlfriends. But even these girls have a little Alex Forrest in them. Come to think of it, every woman I know has a little "Alex Forrest" in her.

Do you remember Alex Forrest?

She was the character played by Glenn Close in *Fatal Attraction.*

Now, I know some of you reading this are probably saying to yourself: "Oh no! Not me. I am *certainly no* Alex Forrest."

Ah, but I respectfully disagree. Although many of us would never stoop to psychotic acts of revenge such as boiling pet rabbits, there have been countless women in history who have personified the age-old phrase, "Hell Hath No Fury Like A Woman Scorned."

(P.S. While many people attribute this quote to William Shakespeare, it actually comes from a play called *The Mourning Bride* written in 1697 by William Congreve. The complete quote is:

"Heaven has no rage like love to hatred turned/ Nor hell a fury like a woman scorned.")

But let's get back to Alex Forrest, shall we?

After I finished writing this novel, I decided to interview a smattering of women across the country to find out exactly whether my Alex Forrest theory is true. That is, does the average "normal" woman have a penchant for avenging an ex? And if so, what is the craziest/over-the-top "Revenging-The-Ex" story you've ever heard?

I began my intensive research by picking up the phone. It was a Saturday morning. I had just eaten *tres leches* for breakfast. (P.S. *Tres leches* is a delicious Mexican dessert. But even Mexicans don't eat it for breakfast.)

Anyway, I called several friends of mine, who in turn, called their friends. Remember. This was on Saturday.

By Sunday, I was fielding phone calls like a 911 Operator.

Upon hearing the news that some author in Texas was collecting "Best-Your-Ex" stories, my cell phone buzzed like crazy.

Here are some of those stories.

Ladies, you know who you are . . .

"I lost fifteen pounds and started sleeping with his room-mate who was in Med School and was totally hot, hot."
—Washington, D.C.

"He had a baseball that he caught in a World Series Game. He always bragged about how he had snatched it away from everyone else. Well, guess what? It's mine now."
—Houston, TX

"I called his ex-wife and some of the other women he had dated and we all got together for coffee and compared notes. Turns out we weren't quite the monsters he'd made us out to be.

We recorded the entire thing on video cam and sent him the DVD."

—Newport Beach, CA

"I went to a local Bait & Tackle Shop, bought some bait, and ended up sewing it between his curtains. Later, he told his friends that his apartment reeked of fish, and he couldn't figure out why.

I know it sounds gross, but I always hated those curtains. His mother bought them."

—South Florida

"When my fiancé told me he was "having second thoughts," I left a framed 8x10 photo on his bedside table. It was a picture of me bending over in the nude. The perfect ass shot. I intended the photo to be funny—a shot of me 'mooning' him. My fiancé told me he thought it was the sexiest thing I'd done in a long time.

That's what had been missing in our relationship, he said. (A little zing.)

We ended up getting married. My husband still keeps the photo inside his desk at work."

—Austin, Texas

For more "Revenge-The-Ex" stories, or to add your own, please visit www.JoBarrettBooks.com

Photo by Ashley Garmon

JO BARRETT's previous novel, *The Men's Guide to the Women's Bathroom*, was published in five countries and optioned by CBS/Paramount Pictures. She is a frequent guest on television and radio shows nationwide.

Ms. Barrett was born in Japan, grew up in Texas, and graduated from the University of Texas, Austin, and Georgetown Law Center in Washington, D.C.

She is a former Capitol Hill staffer for Congressman Collin Peterson, and member of the Texas State Bar.

Currently, she divides her time between Texas and the two coasts.

For more information about the author, please go to: JoBarrettBooks.com.